THE SPIRIT OF WANT

THE SPIRIT OF WANT

by

William H. Coles

Published September, 2016

Story in Literary Fiction
Salt Lake City, Utah 84101

www.storyinliteraryfiction.com
facebook.com/storyinliteraryfiction

Cover art and illustrations by Betty Harper

ISBN: 978-0-9976729-7-8 (softcover)
ISBN: 978-0-9976729-8-5 (hardcover)
ISBN: 978-0-9976729-9-2 (ebook)

PART ONE

CHAPTER 1

Luke
1984

Luke Osbourne drove two and a half hours north of Atlanta to the lake facility of the Atlanta Club to arrive after seven. Inside the clubhouse ballroom, more than two hundred guests, mostly couples, gathered in daisy-cluster conversation groups or sat at small round tables munching buffet-style dinner food served by waiters in white jackets and tuxedo pants. A layer of cigarette smoke hovered over the crowd dimming the lights of the two giant, wedding-cake-tiered, crystal chandeliers. The mood was buoyant. Wine and cocktail glasses were raised high in congratulatory toasts as sweat beaded on the brows of men in tuxedos, and the women—many in off-the-shoulder, full-length gowns—clandestinely dabbed hankies and tissues to their underarms. These were the donors who had helped make the new Eye Institute possible, and A.J. MacMiel had made it happen by wooing donors and securing public and private grants. He climbed onto the bandstand. He grabbed a microphone; the orchestra stopped with a drum roll. With a voice more exhausted than exuberant, he thanked the crowd for attending and for their generous giving. The bar would remain open until midnight.

Thank you, thank you.

At first, Luke chatted with MD colleagues he knew, then moved on to other stray singles or abandoned significant others. He had neither the social status nor the money to be considered for membership at the club. He tried to appear confident and justified in attending, although he didn't really know why A.J. had invited him. After an hour, A.J.'s wife, Agnes, sought him out and took his hand with more enthusiasm than was warranted by their few brief meetings over the years. "Come," she said. "I want you to meet my two babies."

He'd met her daughters, Lucy and Elizabeth, more than a few times before. Now they were standing together near the band, and neither seemed to recognize him when he was introduced. Agnes immediately excused herself to work the crowd.

Lucy, a light-bronze-skinned, dark-eyed, stunningly beautiful woman of thirty-four or thirty-five stared at the singer on the bandstand without a word. She was a lawyer, famous for little tolerance for inferior intelligence. Engrossed in the music, she walked away.

"Impressive," Luke murmured to Elizabeth, gazing at the revelers in the ballroom.

"I'm proud of what my father's done," she said. She shared none of the stunning characteristics of her sister. But she was not unattractive. Her delicate features and sharp blue eyes complemented her fair, blemish-free skin. But her slightly overweight figure, with sturdy legs and thick ankles had no resemblance to Lucy's slim beauty.

"Were you involved in the institute?" she continued.

"Not directly," he said. She seemed thoroughly bored, which, given the circumstances of conversation with someone she couldn't remember, he decided was forgivable, if not understandable.

"Are you a donor?" she asked.

"I work with your father."

"Oh." She thought for a few seconds. "Haven't we met before?"

"A few times," he said.

Lucy returned, nibbling a bacon-wrapped scallop on a stick, and stared. "Who are you?" she asked.

"Mother just told you," Elizabeth said. "Luke Osborne, isn't it? He's in daddy's department."

"The pleasure is mine," he said, nodding slightly to Lucy and offering his hand, which she ignored.

Lucy would not look at Elizabeth. "You're an eye surgeon?" she asked Luke with a touch of disdain.

"Retina."

"You don't like lawyers, do you? No surgeon likes lawyers."

"Don't start," Elizabeth said.

"I'm not starting," Lucy said. "I stated a fact with which the doctor cannot disagree. Isn't that right, doctor?"

Luke said nothing.

Lucy, her neck veins pulsing, looked at Elizabeth for many seconds now.

"Do you do malpractice?" Luke finally asked Lucy.

"She's a defense lawyer," Elizabeth said.

"I'm not an ambulance chaser, if that's what you're implying," Lucy said, glaring at Elizabeth but talking to Luke.

"I don't think that's what he meant," said Elizabeth.

"That's what he thinks," Lucy said.

"You can't know what he thinks," Elizabeth said.

"I worry about malpractice," Luke said. "There are a lot of unnecessary suits."

"A lot of unnecessary harm done," Lucy said.

Lucy turned to see the singer again, who had started another song. "It's not just the mistakes that piss me off, it's the cover-ups."

Luke did not agree to oversimplification and partial truth, but he kept quiet.

Elizabeth touched Luke's arm, her face faintly flushed, and side-glanced at her sister. "Enjoyed seeing you," she said.

He expressed pleasure at seeing her, unable to suppress his sarcasm.

She leaned toward his ear. "Sorry," she whispered so Lucy wouldn't hear.

Elizabeth disappeared into the crowd. Lucy gave him a sardonic smile.

"We've been having a spat," she said. "She thinks I'm rude to the rich folk." She paused, smiling ruefully. "We fight all the time. Since we were kids." Her voice had softened a bit.

"May I bring you a drink from the bar?" Luke asked.

Lucy held up her full martini glass. "I get my own drinks," she said, without a smile now. She turned and walked away with a little wobble in her gait. "Enjoy yourself," she said over her shoulder.

He was relieved she was gone but he missed looking at her. Her beauty was the only pleasant memory about her. One glance could up the heartbeat of a dead man.

The crowd got louder. With drinks flowing, the intense chatter was punctuated with cries of mostly false delight, and occasionally angry outbursts, so that comfortable conversation became almost impossible. Luke wanted to leave. He walked up to A.J.

"Congratulations. A great party," Luke said.

A.J. laughed and leaned over to whisper, "It's all bullshit, Luke. You know it. I know it. They've given a fraction of what they should."

That seemed a little ungrateful; these people were big donors, some had given more than a million dollars. Luke thought power had warped A.J.'s judgment over the years.

"I've got to get back. Surgery in the morning," Luke said.

A.J. slapped him on the back. "I'll walk with you to the car. I can't hear in here," he said loudly. "Did you valet?"

Luke had parked in the lot near the golf course. Outside, they walked side by side.

"I'd like to propose you for director of clinical research in the new building. There will be other candidates, of course, and the board will have final approval, but you're my man. What do you think?"

Luke closed his eyes briefly and took a long breath. "I don't know, A.J. I appreciate your thinking about me. But I'm a surgeon more than a research administrator, and I'm not sure it's what I want to do at this stage of my career."

"It would put a rocket in your ass, my friend. Boost you to the sky. It's an opportunity that won't come 'round again."

The night shadows of mature pines that bordered the lot obscured the cars. They slowed their pace.

"Damn it!" Luke said, pointing to his sedan.

"You can't drive it," A.J. said. Luke's sedan and two other cars were stripped. Tires, wheels, bumpers, mirrors, radio. The trunk lids were up, the trunks empty. "Done by pros," A.J. said.

"Isn't there some security?"

"They've increased patrols. They had a theft a couple weeks ago. The bastards come from the county road across the golf course. Big money in parts."

"I've got to get a ride," Luke said. "There must be people going back tonight."

A.J. nodded. "Lucy's going back tonight."

"I thought you all were staying over at your place for the weekend."

"We are. Until Tuesday. But not Lucy. She doesn't like it here."

The manager agreed to call the police and arrange towing, and Luke walked out the front of the club a few minutes later. The valet sat in a chair near one of the two columns that supported the portico jutting out from the main building over the drive. Two couples stood talking in the hot, humid night air.

"Dr. Osborne?" the valet asked.

Luke nodded. The valet waved in the direction of a red Porsche. The lights flashed and the car moved forward. Luke opened the passenger door.

"Lucy?" He bent down so he could see.

"Get in," she said. Even in half-silhouette her profile was exquisite—a straight, well-proportioned nose, high cheekbones, and a graceful curve to her chin.

He fastened his seat belt. The interior air was humid with the sweet smell of alcohol mixed with flowery, freshly applied perfume and mint-flavored mouthwash. As she revved the engine, her foot slipped off the clutch. The car jerked and the engine stalled.

"You okay?" he asked.

"I'm not drunk," she said testily, "if that's what you're implying."

She started the car and drove cautiously down the curved access road that skirted the edge of the golf course on one side and the lake on the other. She eased through the stop sign at the T-junction with the county road. When she turned the wheel right, she pressed too hard on the accelerator and the car leapt forward. She was slow to compensate and the left tires went off the road. She braked to a stop.

"I'll drive," Luke said.

"Shut up," she said. She drove on, seemingly in control, but after half a mile stopped the car, got out, and walked gingerly heel-to-toe for a few feet then strode into the night, taking her keys with her. Luke sat barely moving for five minutes. She was still out of sight when he decided to walk back to the club and hire someone to take him into town. He was about fifty yards on his way when she reappeared.

"I'm fine now," she yelled. He hesitated, wondering what was wise. A.J. was an important ally in the wars of academic medicine, and it was a risk to abandon his older daughter. Luke was sure A.J. was thinking of him as sort of a babysitter for the ride into town. He couldn't let him down. Luke walked back. As he got into the car, Lucy took two white tablets from her purse and washed them down with a swig from a half-empty bottle of Coke she extracted from under the seat.

"Feeling better?" Luke asked.

She cleared her head with a firm shake from side to side before inserting the key in the ignition after two unsuccessful jabs. Twenty minutes later, without speaking to Luke, she stopped at the access ramp to the interstate to mount a radar detector from the glove compartment on the windshield and then accelerated on the up-ramp headed for Atlanta. He gripped the door armrest as she merged into traffic, passing three cars on the right until the merging lane tapered to an end. She jerked the wheel to change lanes a few feet in front of a pickup and then jerked again forcing the car into the far-left fast lane. Luke's muscles tightened and he pressed his feet hard against the floor.

The moonless night left the countryside swept in darkness. He could make out shapes of houses and buildings, farms and fields, but no details. Then the car accelerated on the straightaway of the interstate. He leaned slightly left; the speedometer glowed a steady eighty-five.

"I've forgotten what Elizabeth does . . ." he said, to keep her thinking.

"She's a schoolteacher. Fourth grade. Ridiculous, really. No real money of her own. She lives off what daddy gives her." Her irritation coated her slow-minded words, but her tone was sharp and she seemed unwilling to talk about anything more.

The motor whined at higher intensity as she increased speed. She was still ten miles an hour over the limit.

The radar alarm went off. She braked and tucked in behind an eighteen-wheeler tanker.

"Bastards," she said.

"That thing works pretty well," Luke said of the radar detector, thankful it had slowed her down.

She didn't comment.

A few minutes later, the detector sputtered and stopped, and she left the protection of the big rig, quickly accelerating. In the side rearview mirror the truck's lights diminished like two fading stars at near light-warp speed.

"Where's your wife?" she asked, now in overdrive at fifteen above the limit. "Delores, isn't it?"

"Samantha," he said. "We're no longer married."

She still concentrated on the road. "Divorce?"

He paused. "She killed herself," he said.

The mention of Samantha brought guilt. He still thought he might have done more to prevent it. But he didn't really miss her. Toward the end, she was hard to be around—tense and confrontational, a hollow, angry person—and he'd never really known her before or understood her after she died.

Lucy slowed in a stretch where trees and foliage provided good hiding places for police, and settled into the monotony of driving the interstate, now darkened by growing cloud cover. Her head slowly nodded . . . the car drifted to the right. She jerked awake, adjusting to keep on the road. But a few minutes later, the car lurched as it left the paved road, the bottom scraping gravel and rocks, and she whipped the wheel left and brought the car back on the road.

"Stop," Luke said. "I want to drive."

"I'm fine!"

"You're not fine. You're falling asleep."

"Relax," she said. "I'm an excellent driver."

Impulsive, he thought. And not safe at any speed.

She was silent for a while. After many minutes, she said with a newly apologetic tone, "I hate those parties of A.J.'s. I drink when I'm unhappy."

"Why go?" he asked. She drove intently now, with a contemplative frown.

"He commanded us to be there," she said. "He likes the family at fundraisers. It makes him appear magnanimous and paternal."

"Isn't he?" he asked.

She thought for a while. "You know him. He thinks about himself."

Strange coming from her, the most self-centered by far in a covey of egotists.

She'd slowed down. "He doesn't like what I've become."

"Because you're a lawyer?"

"I don't think it's that." Although her driving was better, her speech was still fuzzy-edged.

A.J. must have been a bear of a father—authoritative, uncompromising, unreasonable. "He always seems proud of you," he said truthfully.

"He treats Elizabeth well. She's his own. She has his nose, those arched brows. She's not as smart as he is, but she thinks like he does."

There were no physical similarities between Elizabeth and Lucy. Lucy had cured-leather tan skin; dark, hard eyes; reddish-brown, shoulder-length hair. She was about five feet five, and her figure was thin and muscular, yet indisputably feminine, and her clothes were perfectly tailored, in contrast to Elizabeth, who was about the same height and wore altered, expensive designer clothes but was a little too chunky in spots, making it seem as if nothing exactly fit.

"I have five siblings," Luke said. "Each their own person."

"But you get along well?"

"I guess," he said. "Better than most . . . although I rarely hear from them anymore, except for my sister who's in grad school at Princeton . . . journalism."

"She's your favorite?"

"I feel protective of her. She's the youngest."

"I don't like Elizabeth most of the time," Lucy said. "I don't like to be around her."

He said nothing.

"Few know. And it's never discussed. But I'm the adopted one," Lucy said. "It's tiresome."

Adoption was new to him.

"I never do anything right," she added.

"They say that?"

"Of course not. It's how they act."

"They chose to adopt you, didn't they? They must have wanted you."

"I'm told father flew down twice to Puerto Rico to check me out. I was thirteen months old when they got me. My real name was Lucy Rivera. I think they probably adored me until Elizabeth came along two years later."

"You seem to have everything . . ."

"Except pride and respect." She'd sobered a little, but still the booze made her maudlin.

"I don't believe that," he said. "They seem proud of what you've done."

"They're racist. Oh, they don't hang people, but deep down in never-tell land they don't think colored folk can think or reason like whites. They still like looking down on those "pickaninies" that tap dance for coins in New Orleans, for Christ's sake. Mother says, 'They're ohhh, sooo cute.'"

"You're their daughter."

"Adopted daughter. Believe me, there's a difference. And I'm black."

"I thought you're Puerto Rican."

"My great grandfather on my mother's side was black. That's what A.J. said once to me."

"You're still Puerto Rican. Anyway, that doesn't make them dislike you."

"Bullshit to that. For years they talked about it. As if adopting me was a magnanimous gesture to the underprivileged—in mind and body."

She should quit drinking, Luke thought. Alcohol muddled her brain.

"Well, no one would know you're black," he said. "Stop worrying about it."

"That's a racist thing to say." Her tone was testy again. "Why would I worry about being black? I worry about parents who see me as inferior and embarrassing because they think I'm black."

"You know what I mean?"

"You meant I'm black but can pass for Puerto Rican. I don't like that. The world should see me as who I am."

"No offense," he said. She'd made this argument before.

She passed a car and pulled back into the right lane. After thirty minutes, her head seemed to clear a little more. She was speeding again. "I got a little crazy back there," she said, flashing a smile. "I didn't mean that stuff about family," she said, her voice softer. "Elizabeth is great in her own way."

She slowed as they approached the city. Ahead, under an exit sign, orange and white reflective cones glowed in the headlights.

"Is the exit closed?" she said.

"There's an arrow," Luke said.

She leaned forward, squinting. "I don't care about arrows. Can we get off?"

"No barriers I can see."

She turned right too late to cleanly clear the cones. Bang, bang, bang. The fourth cone caught on the undercarriage. She geared down, cut the wheel left, then right. The cone freed and the scraping stopped.

He turned to look out through the rear window. "There's a cone on the highway."

"You want me to back up against traffic for a cone?"

"It might be dangerous. Stop here. I can walk back and move it."

"'That's ridiculous," she said. "It's reflective. No one can miss it." She drove on.

Maneuvering in the high-end residential section on the outskirts of northwest Atlanta required new concentration. Two-lane roads snaked by heavily wooded lots with houses hidden in the landscaping, each home accessed by a private drive that could bridge a creek or a gulley, or mount a hill to circle in front of a majestic entrance. Many home fronts had columns two or three stories high.

The Porsche entered curves tight to the centerline as Lucy downshifted for control. Luke stared ahead into the dark. Police were rare on these side roads and she sped up at the height of a sharp curve, the car dangerously gravitating to the far side of the pavement. Only once did an oncoming car weakly illuminate the trees ahead . . . she geared down . . . and a few seconds later, as the Porsche crested the hill, she squinted in the glare of headlights. When the imageless dark took over again, with only the instrument panel glowing, they could see only a few car-lengths in the tight curves.

The Porsche descended a hill, curved right, and crossed a stone bridge. The road disappeared over a short, steep rise. The car rose as if on a ramp, giving a touch of weightlessness.

The eyes of a small animal reflected in the car lights, two bright holes in a dark background. The eyes disappeared when the headlights were directed away.

"Goddamn," she screamed. It was some breed of poodle. Then it was out of sight.

She braked. She cranked the wheel. The car skidded. Tires screeched on dry macadam . . . a definite thump, but no feeling. "What was that?" Luke said. The dog, maybe.

The car lurched to the left, off the road.

Lucy's head snapped forward and Luke braced his hands on the dashboard. The car went into a left-side-forward skid. She whipped the steering wheel left; the front wheels dipped into the roadside dirt.

The car rolled, going down, hitting a tree and turning one hundred and eighty degrees. The front lights went out as the chassis propelled backward and down. The rear end crunched with the scrape of metal and the cracking of glass.

"Are you all right?" Lucy asked. Luke couldn't see her in the dark.

Within seconds, the shapes of tree trunks emerged in the night. Lucy was half out of the car.

"Are you all right?" she asked again, her voice quivering. "Talk to me!"

Luke moaned from a sudden sharp pain in his leg.

She was out of the car now, leaning toward him. One rear taillight still glowed weakly and her face took on an extraterrestrial hue.

"Can you open the door?" she asked. A pine trunk blocked the door a few inches to his right. A jagged lower edge was all that was left of the window.

"I don't think so," Luke said hoarsely.

"You'll have to crawl over the gear box," she said. "Can you do that?"

He clutched the wheel, pulled himself over the stick shift headfirst, and crawled out of the car. Lucy pulled on his shirt to help.

"Can you walk?"

He didn't answer. Instead he rose slowly to stand and test his mobility.

She climbed on all fours up the side of a steep embankment. He followed, grasping saplings and tree limbs for support. At the top of the ravine, the centerline on the road was barely visible.

"We've got to find a house with a phone," she said over her shoulder.

He followed her, a searing pain shooting up his leg with each step as he limped along.

Luke caught up when Lucy stopped at the entrance to a private drive to wait for him.

"What's wrong with your leg?" she asked.

"Cut."

"We'll get help."

He followed her up the drive. The dark, pointed roof of an Elizabethan-style mansion cut a wedge into the barely illuminated, clouded night sky. Spotlights suddenly glared from the house and the top of the three-car garage. Lucy shielded her eyes with her hands.

"Stop," a voice said. No one was visible.

"We tripped something," she whispered. She turned toward the voice. "We had an accident," she called. "My friend is hurt."

Luke's head was swimming; his good leg shook uncontrollably.

A man in a robe, pajamas, and dress loafers approached. He held a double-barreled shotgun, the barrels at eye level.

"Let me see your hands," the man said.

"We're not thieves," Lucy said. She put her hands up high overhead.

"You," the man said to Luke. "Up!"

Luke was too weak to raise them much above the shoulders. "Higher." The man came closer and lowered his weapon. "My God," he said, staring.

Lucy turned to Luke. "You're covered in blood," she said, almost accusingly.

Luke lay down on the drive.

"I'll call an ambulance," the man said. Luke blacked out.

CHAPTER 2

Luke

A few days after Luke had been sutured and X-rayed and observed for twenty-four hours in a trauma holding-unit and still not able to return to work, the intercom bell from the condo security desk awakened him in the middle of the night. Lucy MacMiel, the concierge said, and her associate.

He told the concierge to send them up and slipped on his long white terry-cloth bathrobe, tying the sash loosely to avoid pain. The front gaped to show silk pajama bottoms and a bare chest taped from armpit to waist. The left leg of his pajamas bulged with the protective bandaging still required to prevent rebleeding.

The elevator to the top-floor apartment opened at the end of the hall. He moved to the front door peephole from habit. Lucy strode toward the apartment, distorted in the minute lens but still beautiful in her exotic way. He opened the door before she knocked. Lucy smiled apologetically and a tall older man with a gaunt look stood behind her in the hall.

"I thought your leg was cut," she said.

He shrugged. "It's the two cracked ribs that keep me awake."

"Peter Townsend," the man said from behind Lucy.

Luke didn't respond, still holding the door open and blocking their entrance. "What's up?"

"Thanks for seeing us," Townsend said.

"The tow truck driver found a body," Lucy said. Luke stared, not comprehending for a minute.

"It was on the same side of the road in a ditch. But not near the car."

"It had nothing to do with the accident," Townsend said.

"Could we talk?" Lucy asked.

Luke backed away from the door to let them in.

"Can we sit down somewhere?" she asked, motioning to Townsend and moving toward the living room.

Lucy sat with Townsend on a curved sofa. Luke eased painfully into an overstuffed armchair.

There was an awkward silence. Luke was fully awake now.

"It's gotten complicated," Lucy said. "The accident, I mean. The DA has hated me since law school . . ."

"They went to Yale together," Townsend interrupted.

"It's an opportunity to ruin me." She seemed almost breathless. "A woman's body was found near the accident, by the roadside. It was the widow of Judge Fogerty," she said loudly. "The family is crying for justice."

"And they don't even know how she died. They just say she was in excellent health," Townsend said.

"And we think the DA's investigation is to prove vehicular homicide."

"Even though the autopsy results haven't been completed. There's no evidence."

"The car's been impounded." Lucy breathed deeply and exhaled.

"And they've been to the club. Asking questions about the party." She uncrossed her legs and leaned forward. "They're trying to prove I was under the influence."

Townsend started to say something, but Lucy threw him a glare.

"What does this have to do with me?" Luke asked.

"We're sure the investigators will contact you tomorrow," Townsend said.

"It's this morning, now," Lucy said to Townsend. Then she turned to Luke. "We want to know what you'll remember. They'll ask you about everything that went on for the entire evening," she said.

"You don't think she was drunk, do you?" Townsend asked.

"I didn't examine her," Luke said. "I was there as a favor to her father."

"But you were a passenger. You wouldn't have gotten in a car voluntarily for a two-hour ride on an interstate with a drunk, would you?" Townsend asked.

Only for A.J., Luke thought.

"You didn't see a woman," Lucy stated. "We couldn't have hit that woman. We would have known."

"How would I know for sure?" Luke said. "We were in a skid. I felt jolts. The sounds for a few seconds were very loud."

"But if you hit a woman, you would know, wouldn't you?" Townsend said. "You were in the front seat of a small car. Not the back seat of a bus."

"I couldn't say," Luke said. "I can't prove a negative."

"Did you hear anything like a body?" she asked.

"I heard lots of things," Luke said.

"But nothing like hitting a human," Townsend said.

"I heard a thump as we left the road. I remember that. But I don't remember thinking we hit something. Even if I had thought about it, I would have thought of the dog."

"The dog was found unhurt," Lucy said, "dragging its leash a few hundred yards away."

"Could it have been a mound of dirt, a rock, a tree root?" Townsend asked Luke.

"It could have been any of those," Lucy said, before Luke could answer.

Lucy and Townsend looked to Luke, who lightly caressed the surgical tape around his rib cage.

"You finished?" Luke asked.

"We didn't have an agenda," Townsend said.

Luke winced. "It's late, counselor, too late to bullshit."

"We wanted to let you know about the investigation," Lucy said.

"You wanted to keep me from putting a noose around your neck," Luke said.

She paused. "That's untrue, and unethical." Her eyes, still veiled to revealing any real emotion, had a tint of pleading. "Will you?" she asked.

Luke looked at her intensely. "I'll tell what I remember. Nothing more. Nothing less."

"But you're sure we didn't hit that woman."

Luke sighed. "I don't know."

"Are you sure you weren't driving?" Townsend said with acrid sarcasm.

"That's not appropriate," Lucy said, glaring at Townsend.

Luke stood. "Time to go, counselors. You've been up too long without proper sleep."

"Peter didn't mean anything," she said.

"Peter meant that if I didn't say the right things, he'd involve me in any way he could. I don't like that."

"That's not what I meant," said Townsend.

"He's the best of criminal lawyers," Lucy said. "That's why I brought him. If the DA takes this to a grand jury, you'll be subpoenaed. Peter's the best."

Luke made no attempt to shake Townsend's hand as he pointed them toward the door. Lucy held out her hand and then thought better of it. She hugged Luke instead, giving him a peck of a kiss on the cheek. Luke closed the door and watched her through the peephole. He heard them talking as they waited for the elevator to arrive.

"That was stupid to say," Lucy said.

"Lower your voice."

"He can't hear," she said, but she did speak more softly.

"It'll make him cautious," Townsend replied.

"It just made him angry."

"Look, I know that woman died of blunt trauma. Like from an automobile. Not the heart. And I think they'll find evidence on the car. Blood. Pieces of clothing."

"Damn it, Peter. I thought you were my advocate."

"I think Winkler will go for manslaughter. I think your friend here will be his key witness."

"To a thump?"

"To driving while intoxicated. Leaving the scene of an accident."

"We didn't know about the woman."

"You crashed a sports car on a road. That's reckless driving. You didn't call the police. Even after you got to a phone."

"Don't articulate the obvious!"

"It was the wrecker that found the body. That's guilty behavior, especially for a lawyer."

"I called them to tow the car."

"The next morning."

"There was no reason to call the police."

"You screwed up. I'd get to know this guy real well, Lucy. There were injuries. I'd neutralize him as a witness. He'll have to go before a grand jury, if it comes to that."

"God. What a thought."

"Think about it. Use that legal brain to make it work."

The elevator dinged and the door opened.

The investigators questioned Luke the next day. Lucy called when Luke was finished.

"How did it go?" she asked.

"Fine, I think. I told them what I knew."

"Did it take long?"

"Two hours."

"It must have been grueling."

He didn't reply.

"Were they tough?"

"Professional. I thought reasonable. It wasn't an interrogation. Is it going to a grand jury?" he asked.

"I don't know. The evidence on the car was inconclusive."

"So my testimony is, like, live or die. Could you go to jail?"

"I don't think so."

"But it's possible?"

She paused. "I don't know."

A week later Lucy asked Luke if he wanted to go to dinner. This was a first try at neutralizing him, he thought. But he was widowed with only rare female companionship these days, and Lucy was a very attractive woman.

"Any day this week," she said.

Since the accident, images of Lucy came to Luke at odd times, and he had a dream where she was present, it seemed, but didn't have a clear role. The next morning she was all that stayed with him from the dream.

"It would be fun for me," she said.

He accepted.

She wore a dress above the knee, short sleeved, and with a V-neck that revealed a ruby pendant against the soft glow of her tan skin. He was charmed and pleased. She was pleasant and agreeable, a completely different person than the times he had met her before. She was lively, caring, speaking of her childhood with animated hand gestures. She spoke warmly about her family, as if all she had said before the accident about them had been forgotten. Elizabeth was a dear. A teddy bear of a sister. Lucy talked about her love of movies, and how she usually went alone to late-night shows after work to relax. She loved romances.

Over a linen-draped table for two, she stared intently, her face accented by warm shadows in the dim candlelight. Luke told her about his passive mother and domineering father, his Maine birth and Massachusetts upbringing, his five siblings and his vastly different feelings for each. She laughed sincerely at his humor.

He enjoyed the time. He found himself remembering almost every word of their conversation. He was convinced he had misjudged her purpose. She was so much more than she seemed on first meetings. So a week later, he called her and asked her to dinner. This time they talked about politics, pop culture, advancements in science. With a touch of concern at her unbroken attentiveness, and frankly wondering if she was still neutralizing him as a witness, he asked her, "Are you still worried about the DA?"

For an instant she was surprised and puzzled, as if unable to remember where he might have gotten such an idea. "I don't know," she said. Suddenly she turned cold and professional.

"Do you think about it?"

"Of course I think about it."

"Do you ever believe you hit that woman?"

She sipped from a glass of wine. "That's unlikely."

"But possible?"

"I think we'd know."

"Still no direct evidence?"

"We don't know. The DA is not forthcoming."

He looked away. "I worry about it," he said. "That something might have happened."

"My God, what is there for you to worry about?" She leaned forward intently. "It was an accident."

Drinking might make you responsible, he thought. But he said nothing.

"I reacted to that animal. And nothing I drank affected my responses—in any way." She hesitated. "My God. You know that, don't you?"

She'd been under the influence when they left the club. He was sure of that. But that was before they got to Atlanta.

"Well?"

"I don't know," he said.

"Even if there was contact, she was dead, or we'd have seen her with the dog."

"You're right," he said. "Forget it." But he wasn't sure, and he was concerned about what he would say of her intoxication if he were under oath. He was a doctor, after all, not inexperienced in judging someone's physical and mental competency.

After that they could not find topics to talk about, and the evening ended early by mutual consent.

Luke's doubt about Lucy festered over the next few days. Her denial of possible complicity worried him, and she didn't seem to have any concern for the dead woman, whether she had been involved or not. But there was nothing to do. Who would ever know if there was even a trace of blame for Lucy causing, or hastening, the poor woman's death?

Although he thought about her occasionally, he did not contact Lucy for weeks. He made sure she was out of his future, at least on a personal level, when her mother invited him to a lunch at their house followed by en masse attendance at the Tech-Georgia football game, which was in Atlanta that year. He didn't like luncheons or football and the thought of seeing Lucy made him pause, but he doubted Lucy would choose to be there, and he valued A.J.'s friendship and support. A day later he accepted.

CHAPTER 3

Luke

Lucy's mother's luncheon was a sit-down four-course lunch for nine guests seated at two tables, and catered by a local restaurant by four staff. Luke's place card was next to Elizabeth's, Lucy's sister, with Lucy in profile at the larger table a few feet away.

Elizabeth wore a tight-fitting print dress that exposed her full, round arms and suggested the curve of her breasts. She smiled frequently, at times inappropriately, and chatted nervously about trivia with an inoffensive gusto. Before the entrée was served, Elizabeth touched his hand to get his attention. "Are you worried about Lucy's grand jury?" she asked. "It's all we talk about now."

"I hope I'll never have to go."

"The DA thinks he will have enough evidence," Elizabeth said. "Vehicular manslaughter. Lucy's distraught."

Luke looked to Lucy, who seemed bored but not distraught. A servant placed the main course plate before Elizabeth. Luke waited to be served.

Elizabeth picked up her fork, pausing in midair. "It must be awkward, Luke. You were the only witness. What will you say if you're subpoenaed?"

"I'd tell only what I remember," he said. "But I can't make any judgments on whether alcohol influenced the accident."

"Do you think she hit that woman?"

"It was a surprise to me, Elizabeth. I don't really know." "The autopsy didn't conclusively determine a cause of death."

Luke had thought a lot about appearing before a grand jury. It would be almost impossible to deliver accurate testimony without swaying the jury in ways not suggested by the facts. Of course Lucy had been drinking, but there was no way to know if it affected her driving performance hours later. A blood alcohol was never drawn—it was too late the day after—and there would always be suspicion that Lucy's delay in reporting the accident was deliberate to avoid the test. The jury would take those facts and interpret them in the emotional cloud of a judge's healthy wife dying without clear cause. And they wouldn't like Lucy as a lawyer, whom they would see as privileged, and resent her success.

"We all know she had a lot to drink at the party," Elizabeth said. "She hates those parties. It's the only time I ever see her drink too much."

Luke swallowed a piece of dry chicken. "I don't think about it," he said. But he did. A lot.

"Surely you know if she was drunk," she said. "You're a doctor."

"I did not function that night as a doctor," he said.

Elizabeth frowned. "You got in the car for a two-and-a-half-hour ride. You must have thought about it. She was drinking when Mother introduced us to you."

"I'm not judgmental," he said.

Elizabeth abruptly turned to her lunch partner on the other side and asked about the weather.

In A.J.'s seasonal block of stadium seats, Lucy sat next to Luke.

She leaned close. "Mother thinks you're a perfect match for Elizabeth."

"What does Elizabeth think?"

"Don't look, but she's staring at you now. She's willing to be a perfect match for almost anyone."

Luke smiled. "I don't think that's true. She didn't seem very friendly to me."

"She's desperate for children, Luke. That's why she's teaching. It's a way to be with the kids. She certainly doesn't need to work. She's got money for life."

He decided not to answer. "The luncheon was fun," he said.

She laughed. "Don't bullshit a bullshitter."

He couldn't stay annoyed with her. He smiled.

She took his hand and he enjoyed the feel of her soft skin. The crowd stood and the opening kickoff sailed into the air.

He glanced at her beauty again. The air made her skin radiant. And as she sat close, he soon came to await the quick smile, warm and engaging, and her brown eyes, always in motion, as if searching for danger, maybe, or opportunity. She was so bright and so confident; he now believed she wasn't really afraid of anything. He knew she was ambitious, but that seemed an asset. And all his reservations about her submerged—her reasons for being with him, her quick temper, her bitterness about being adopted. In that instant, he knew he cared for her more than any woman he'd ever known.

He feigned interest as the game progressed, but he cared little for the sport or the teams. It was difficult to talk above the noise, and Lucy stayed somewhat subdued among the rabid fans, gazing around into the stands and rarely looking at the field.

After the half, Lucy's mother, Agnes, excused herself when she saw someone she knew in another section. She left, saying goodbye to her guests, just before the last quarter.

"She's going to the car," Lucy said. "They drink sherry straight from the bottle. It happens at every game I've ever attended."

Luke smiled.

Georgia was ahead thirty-eight to seven by the fourth quarter. He leaned over to Lucy. "Let's go," he said. "We could drive to Calloway. We still have time to enjoy the gardens."

"Really?" she asked.

He couldn't help but laugh. "On my honor."

She tightened her grip on his arm. "I'd like that," she said.

Amazing. She really did seem to want to go, and not just get out of the stadium. He was beyond being suspicious.

Outside the stadium they scuttled through the parking lot to the car, her hand in his.

Within weeks Luke was subpoenaed to appear before a grand jury. He hired a lawyer, but not Peter Townsend whom Lucy had recommended. The lawyer promised to help prepare and said he might be allowed to counsel him outside the courtroom during the hearing. No defense lawyers were allowed in the proceedings, however.

Luke was careful during the proceedings never to offer an opinion about things he could not know. He admitted to seeing Lucy drinking but was careful not to conclude she was under the influence at the time of the accident. He emphasized that if a woman had been hit, dead or alive, the possibility never occurred to him until he was told days after the accident. But the testimony must have seemed guarded. Surely the jury thought his agenda was to protect Lucy, that he was unwilling to state the obvious. And he felt bad for Lucy that he might have contributed to their decision.

She was indicted and charged with vehicular manslaughter.

CHAPTER 4

Luke

Six months later, Luke stood beside Lucy before a justice of the peace. Only her trusted legal assistant, Carrie Malroy, attended. Family would have wanted a church wedding with social prominence, and Lucy was determined never to allow family to take charge of her wedding, or for that matter anything in her life. And neither she nor Luke wanted to delay. Luke's parents were too infirm to travel, and most of his siblings had no time to exit their lives, however temporarily. The only one who could wouldn't for a second marriage. So the other required witnesses were strangers.

They honeymooned in St. Thomas, Virgin Islands. Every morning Lucy would wake and say "I love you," and Luke would tell her how lucky he was to have her as his best friend. Then she worked in the room, telephoning her office and clients. Before noon she bookmarked her required reading for later in the day, and they would stroll on the beach, boat around the island, or play tennis on the hotel's courts. Luke thought she was a miracle. In comparison to Samantha, she was vibrant and interesting. Of course she was seriously driven to succeed, but he continued to find that stimulating in ways he could not explain. And during their time on the island, Luke never considered that she had any reason for marrying him other than just caring. She did care. He would always believe that. When Peter Townsend called to give news that the DA had decided to drop the charges of manslaughter, the relieved smile on Lucy's face was a welcome sight. He held her as tears of relief streamed down her face.

On the beach on the fourth day, a bikini-clad Lucy lay full-length in an extended folding chair flattened almost horizontal. Luke read a book sitting in a chair next to her, his head down, his legs crossed.

Lucy's eyes were closed but she wasn't asleep. A wizened old black man close to five feet high, barefoot and wearing shorts, a T-shirt, and a backward baseball cap, approached them.

"You new marrieds?" he asked.

"Get lost," she said, keeping her eyes closed.

Luke sat up and put both feet on the sand. A towel slipped and revealed where a nine-inch scar was still healing, red and thick, on his thigh.

"A gift for the bride," the black man said.

"Go away. I'm not a bride."

"You too young for bride," he said, grinning.

"You've got nothing I'd want," Lucy said. She screwed the top back on a sunscreen tube.

"Why you speak so mean?" the man said.

"Look," she said, "we've come a long way to be alone."

"Where you come from?"

"The hotel," she said.

"No, in the States," the man said.

"Ohio. Akron, Ohio," she said.

"My wife and me go to States once. Florida." He smiled. He had crooked teeth and an incisor missing.

Lucy looked away. "Pester someone else," she said.

"Here," the man said, digging into his shorts pocket and handing a small rectangular slip of purple paper to Luke. "You be happy, you two," the man said.

"What the hell is that?" she asked.

Luke stared at the slip. "Bluebeard's Restaurant. Buy one entrée, get one free as long as it's cheaper or equal in value."

"That's ridiculous," she said. "You buy two entrées, you pay the price of the more expensive."

"Don't be technical."

"It's a scam."

"Harmless," he said. "Just poorly worded."

"Get out," she said sharply to the man.

"Wait," Luke said. He reached for his wallet under a towel and took out a $10 bill, which he handed to the man.

"God bless," the man said, turning and shuffling away.

She waited until the man was out of hearing. "Don't ever deride me in front of others," she said, her eyes hard with anger.

"I wasn't deriding you," Luke said.

"Don't do it. Giving that trash money."

"He's poor," Luke said.

She turned away, bending down to pick up her towel and beach gear. "I'm going to shower."

"I'll come with you."

She looked at him. "I want to be alone, Luke."

"Don't, Luce."

She paused. "It's more than just that creep," she said.

"What, then?"

But she turned and left without speaking.

Luke sat back down. He turned pages but couldn't read and stayed alone on the beach for another two hours, uncertain about invading Lucy's privacy.

At seven the next morning they were showered and ready for breakfast before a morning on the beach when Carrie Malroy from Lucy's office called. Lucy was cheerful, without a hint of irritation. Luke sat on the bed while Lucy stood near the nightstand holding the phone, listening intently. She hung up. The memory of their argument on the beach lurked in both of their minds, and neither was willing to mention it for fear of anger returning.

"I've got to go back," she said.

He stood. "Tomorrow?"

"I've got to try for today."

She threw things into a single small suitcase, yanking clothes off hangers, laying out the gray business suit she wanted to wear back.

"What's going on?"

"A chance for lead defense."

She was pushing down on the suitcase lid, fumbling with the latch. "Some evangelist accused of rape," she added.

"Guilty?"

"Probably. But he still will need defense."

"Not pro bono?" he asked, miffed that work was coming before honeymoon.

"Not pro bono."

"Lucrative?" he asked.

She stopped packing. "Probably." Her lips were a tight line. "Is that all right with you?" she said. She must still be upset about yesterday. The poor guy on the beach. "It's an aggressive question," she said. "As if I'm some sleazeball shyster, or something."

"I didn't say that."

"Oh, yeah. That's how you sounded."

"I just don't know how you defend those you think are guilty."

"Everyone has a right to defense. We're trained to be objective."

"A sex offender, for Christ's sake," he said angrily.

"It's the way justice works," she said. "I serve the system."

"What about the victims?"

"They're represented."

He turned away.

"Don't be so self-righteous," she said. "You're no angel."

"There has to be a better way to make a living!" he said.

She slammed down the suitcase top. "I married a jerk."

He walked out onto the small balcony, closing the French doors behind him, and did not move to come back into the room until she had left.

CHAPTER 5

Lucy

The next day at six AM Lucy and one of her senior partners, Alan McCormick, waited at the county jail for the prisoner to be escorted into the holding room. Fifteen minutes later guards escorted in Hower Bain, chained hand and foot, and shoved him into a chair at a small table. Two guards were positioned outside the door.

"Who are you?" Bain asked, looking up at the standing lawyers, his dark eyes under heavy black eyebrows fixed on Lucy's face.

"Lucy MacMiel. Johnson, McCormick, Lippencott, and Furman."

"Alan McCormick," Alan said, standing slightly to Lucy's left and behind her.

"A woman?" Bain asked.

"A competent woman," McCormick said.

"Really?"

"The church has already paid the retainer," McCormick said.

"The church and I hired the firm. We've never heard of Ms. MacMiel."

"She's well known," McCormick said.

"By whom?"

"The legal community. The unjustly accused," McCormick said.

"This won't go to trial," Bain said.

"What makes you think that?" Lucy asked.

"It's not true."

"The fact that it was consensual?"

"Don't try to trap me, counselor. It never happened."

"Look," McCormick said. "If this goes to trial, you'll need a woman working the jury."

"I want Peabody, or whatever your guy's name is in San Francisco. I'll hire him."

"Panetta," Lucy said. "He's not taking cases. He's on chemo and radiation for some cancer."

"And he's not as good as Ms. MacMiel," McCormick said.

"That's bullshit," Bain said. "He's the best."

"They've got a video surveillance tape of you alone with the girl. Did you know that? It's been on television," Lucy said.

"There are probably many. Doesn't prove rape. Give me a break, lady."

"I'm Ms. MacMiel to you." Lucy glared at him.

"Ms. MacMiel."

"Don't ever forget it."

Bain remained impassive. "I'll defend myself."

"And the jury will take two hours to send you to prison for life."

"I'll take the public defender."

"You won't qualify," Lucy said.

"You're wasting time," McCormick said. "We need to get started."

"You, then, man," Bain said.

"Our entire firm will be behind you. But Lucy has a credibility men don't have, especially in underage sex trials."

Bain relaxed in his chair. He flashed a flirtatious smile. "Let's be practical," he said, looking at Lucy. "I don't want jealous jurors eyeing my lawyer like she doesn't deserve to be good looking."

Lucy recoiled at his sexism.

"The DA will load the jury with atheists, not jealous women," McCormick said.

Hower Bain stared at Lucy for many seconds. "If you're no good, I'll fire you."

"That is always your option," Lucy said, now hesitant about taking the case.

"Damn right. Just keep it in mind."

Lucy pulled out sheets of paper from a file. McCormick handed her an ink pen, which she handed to Bain, and she asked the guard to send in the notary

Lucy forgot to call Luke after the meeting with Bain. Their just-purchased six-thousand-square-foot penthouse was being re-floored and to avoid the mess, she went to the Four Seasons Hotel close to the courthouse. She showered and ordered soup and salad from room service.

She thought about Luke then, but still didn't call. She wasn't going back to St. Thomas yet. She'd use the case as an excuse. Of course she could go back if she wanted. But she didn't want to. She'd known it when she left. She'd have to lie about her dislike of the place. Pretend it was paradise. And she was tired of acting happy. Tired of pretending to have a good time. Why was marriage special, anyway? She'd have to face it soon, but with the Bain case and being freed up from the manslaughter worry, her life would be busy, and her career could again become what she wanted it to be. Of course she'd have to call Luke. But not tonight. She'd do it in the morning.

She called Luke the next morning. "I'm sorry, baby," she said. "Our first fight."

He said he missed her. "My fault," he said. "I didn't mean anything by it."

"It was the lawyer stuff, Luke."

"Pretend I never said it."

"I've got to stay to investigate this guy. The girl was underage."

"What does he say?"

"He's denied it to the press, of course. But he's an arrogant, powerful man who I think would lie if he thought the truth might damage his mission."

"Can you get back tomorrow?"

"He'll probably have a bail hearing coming up. I can't."

He paused longer than was necessary. "Not at all?"

"You know I love you," she said.

"You're not still angry about the guy on the beach?"

"Of course not, you silly. But it will be intense here for the next few weeks."

He paused again. "I miss you," he said. "I wish it wasn't this way," she said.

"I can pack and be at the airport within the hour. I'll get on standby."

"Call me when you get in," she said. "I probably won't be able to pick you up," she lied.

CHAPTER 6

Lucy

Lucy arrived at the Apostolic Church of Christ compound in north Georgia before nine. Hower Bain did not tell her why, but his second in command, Jason Campbell, was assigned to talk to her. She needed to interview church members about the charges. She needed to know who supported Bain and who didn't—and why.

She parked in a designated paved lot outside the gates. The church owned more than ten thousand acres of contiguous land, much of it mountainous. At least three thousand church members lived on the grounds in accommodations that had once been a summer Methodist retreat. Some of the old sleeping facilities, dining halls, and an auditorium were still used, but many new buildings, including a four-story administration complex and a church/auditorium that seated five thousand and served as the studio for a weekly Sunday cable telecast, dominated the area.

After identifying herself to the guard, she entered through electronically controlled swinging gates that blocked the two-lane road. A pleasant young black youth took her in a golf cart to administration, where Jason Campbell greeted her and took her to his second floor office with a floor-to-ceiling-view window that looked over the community to the mountains. People bustled between living quarters and work sites where crafts were made for sale. Musicians and singers practiced in two large, open-air concrete rectangular function areas covered with tiled, pointed roofs supported with painted wood pillars at the corners.

"Impressive," she said, nodding to the view. She noticed two large huts that Campbell told her processed food grown on the grounds.

"It's all Hower. He's brought so many to accept Jesus," Campbell said.

"Can you get in without accepting Jesus?"

"You must be committed to Christ to live here," Campbell said, "or be seeking redemption." He poured coffee from a thermos into a paper cup for Lucy. "Cream or sugar?"

"Neither," Lucy said, preferring sweetened fresh milk to cream. She accepted the cup and sipped. The coffee was weak and tasteless. She set it down on the edge of Campbell's metal desk.

He settled back in a chrome tilt-back office chair on rollers. He crossed his right ankle on his left knee and settled his arms on the leather armrests.

"Have you accepted Christ as your savior, Ms. MacMiel?"

How arrogant. "I won't be one of your converts," she said.

He smiled. "Hower warned me about you. But he said I was to talk to you openly about anything you asked. What do you want to know?"

"Did he have sex with a child?"

"I expected you to be professional. How would I know?"

"You won't say, you mean."

"I wouldn't comment on rumor, counselor."

"It's a key question, Mr. Campbell. You should comment. Your boss may well be indicted for statutory rape. At least, molestation. I'm not sure he can be salvaged. And without your and other of his friends' full cooperation, I'm sure he'll sink faster than the Titanic."

Campbell's smile had become fixed now, his capped, porcelain-white teeth showing.

"Do you think Reverend Bain is guilty?" Lucy asked.

"Of course not."

"Why are you so sure?"

"Hower Bain is a man of God, leader of the church."

"But is he guilty of what he has been accused?"

Campbell's smile was gone. "I resent your tone, counselor."

"My tone is the tone of courtroom defense. You need to get used to it."

"I must be frank. It's an enigma to me why Hower hired you."

"You want a man for the defense, I presume," she said.

"Not at all," he said, but she could tell he didn't like professional women. She could feel it.

"He hired me because I have an excellent reputation as a defense lawyer," Lucy said. "Hower Bain needs quality representation."

"He's innocent. I believe God's will will prevail."

"God's will may be directed through me. Had you thought of that?" Campbell's insincere smile returned.

"Do you know the accuser?" Lucy continued.

"Everyone knows her."

"The jury won't know her if this goes to trial. And I'll be the one to tell them about her. So I need to know what you think."

"She's a misguided young woman."

"By law, she's a child."

"But misguided."

"Really? In what way?"

"About Hower. It's fantasy."

"What about the Reverend is fantasy for her?"

Campbell uncrossed his legs and leaned forward. "I mean . . . any encounters were imagined."

"And how can you know that?"

"He told me. I know him well. He does not lie. It is against his core belief."

"Does Hower fear God, Mr. Campbell?"

"We all fear our maker."

She did not respond for many seconds. "Does God love you, Mr. Campbell?"

He shook his head. "Your hostility will never be effective, Ms. MacMiel," he said.

"And your evasion will convict your boss."

He glared at her for many seconds. Then he smiled again, his face transformed in an instant.

"I'm a fool. Of course you're right, Ms. MacMiel. I'm sorry." He interlocked his fingers and leaned forward with his hands on the desk. "Now where were we?"

"Does Bain fear God?"

"I think Hower fears no one. It is the essence of his success."

"As a man or a preacher?"

"Both . . ."

"Is he successful with women in his life?"

"That is not appropriate."

"He's being accused of penetrating a minor. How appropriate is that?"

"The Reverend Bain has no time for feminine relations."

"Do you know his wife?"

"I've seen her occasionally."

"And where is his wife? Here?"

"Oh, no. She is not of the faith. They separated years ago."

"What about his children?"

"Two. A boy and a girl."

"Does he see them often?"

"Rarely that I know. I think it's more lack of time than a lack of desire."

"And why did his wife leave him?"

"That, I must point out, is a question to ask her."

"I'm interested in your opinion."

Campbell sighed. "Incompatibility."

"Sexual incapability?"

"Don't be stupid. Who could know that? I believe it was her failure to accept Christ. She couldn't see the value of Hower's dedication to the Lord."

"Was it amiable?"

"I don't believe so."

"You don't 'believe' so?"

He frowned. "It was not amiable. They haven't spoken for years."

"Does he support her and the children?"

"I think so."

"Aren't you sure?"

He paused. "I do not know his financial arrangements with her."

"But you manage his business affairs."

"I do not manage his personal finances."

Lucy stood up and held her notebook in her hand, ready for notes. "Talking to you makes me agitated," she said. "I don't trust you." She thought for a moment. "It will not serve you well in court."

"I believe most people trust me implicitly. Especially those who know me well."

"What about the girl? How well do you know her?"

"I've known her for more than two years."

"Is she sexually active?"

"Absolutely not. She is one of us. She serves Christ. Sex before marriage is a sin."

"Mortal or venial?"

"I don't categorize sin, counselor."

"Do you see her every day?"

"Of course not."

"But she lives here on the compound?"

"There are very few converts I see every day. There are too many converts. And she is in school."

Lucy sat back down and leaned forward. "You have told me nothing of value, Mr. Campbell. Your lack of cooperation is not wise. For you. Or for Mr. Bain."

"I've been open with you, Miss MacMiel. I resent your accusations."

"I haven't really accused you yet, Mr. Campbell. But the day will come. And I suggest you decide to support your boss's defense openly and with enthusiasm."

He stood. "I assure you, I will do everything to protect Hower Bain."

"Stonewalling is not a good start."

He held out his hand that she reluctantly took. "It's been a pleasure meeting you," he said, but his tone said he didn't look forward to talking to her again.

That evening Lucy arranged to attend the weekly televised meeting of the Apostolic Church of Christ that had made Hower Bain famous. She was told to buy a ticket, although seating was open. Members of the church were, of course, allowed in for free. When she asked why the charge, she was informed there were anti-Christians eager to disrupt church services, and ticket purchases helped screen the audience. Lucy laughed. And it makes money, she observed. There was no reply. She bought a ticket.

She chose a seat in the tiered balcony that wrapped around almost three quarters of the auditorium. Portable wooden folding chairs were positioned on the cement flooring of each tier. Similar chairs were lined up in four major sections on the main floor, separated by aisles ten feet wide. All chairs faced a raised platform with stairs in the center and on each side. To platform-left loomed an oak pipe organ with a curved mirror so the organist could see the stage and the audience, and to the side, off the platform, nine musicians sat mixed in among speakers, instrument cases, and tangles of wiring. Six red-upholstered armchairs for dignitaries were lined up in front of metal bleachers where a fifty-member choir stood wearing red robes with white collars and gold trim on the sleeves and hems. The director of music, a woman, was at stage right dressed in a black robe. Technicians manning three permanent TV cameras positioned in the balcony and two mounted cameras placed on each side of the stage made their checks. There were at least three men with shoulder-mounted cameras being readied to one side. The glass-enclosed production booth between two of the exits at the back of the auditorium glowed with a fluorescent hue. Overhead metal braces crisscrossed the ceiling, supporting rows of floodlights that flickered as they were tested.

Well before air time, a heavyset black woman in stage makeup and a white off-the-shoulder sequined gown spoke to the crowd through a handheld cordless mike. "Hello out there, brothers and sisters. I'm Sister Margarite McCall. Welcome and thank you for coming to this glorious evening we have arranged for you." She urged people to sit. "And now I want to introduce you to your host for the evening. The Reverend Maynard M. Jackson." A tall, heavy black man in a tight-fitting tuxedo trotted awkwardly onto the stage, raising his mike to his mouth. "God bless. May God bless each and every one of you." His voice was commanding, and people were hurrying to sit down.

The woman outlined basic protocols for the audience and introduced a teleprompter that would aid in directing crowd responses. The Reverend then announced the hymns that would be sung during the program. Attendants passed out sheets printed with the words. Three times he had the audience stand to sing, as they would during the show. He led the choir, and the audience slowly joined in. Within minutes, the audience was spellbound as the Sister and the Reverend continued to involve them. At the corner of the stage, a thin young man in jeans and a T-shirt held up cards marking the time remaining before show time.

The on-air portion of the show picked up without pause from the warmup session. Hymns were sung, and both Sister and the Reverend read from the Gospels. Little Margo, an eleven-year-old boy dressed in a tailored white suit, dark-blue shirt, white tie, and an American flag pin the size of a credit card on his lapel, delivered the first sermon. He was thin with a high, prepubescent voice. His long curly hair was tied into a ponytail. His teeth were white and flashed in the lights when he smiled. He urged the crowd to accept Jesus. He told parables, quoted scripture, related personal anecdotes of his conversion to the Kingdom of God. He jumped, he knelt, he waved his arms, and he paced back and forth across the stage. He led the choir in a hymn and the audience joined in as his high voice was amplified to stand out above all others. He cried at the end with joy for the thousands who were with him tonight. The crowd cheered. The Reverend picked him up, hugged him, and asked for another round of applause. Little Margo left the stage running with interspersed leaps until he disappeared behind the curtain near the organ.

Hower Bain was introduced. He walked out from behind the crowd at the side of the stage in a gray business suit, white shirt, and red tie. He mounted the stage. Lucy felt the confidence in his stride. He accepted a microphone from Sister McCall and faced the audience. He paused for absolute silence. A baby cried. He looked with gentle, loving compassion toward the offender and waited, smiling as the mother quieted the child. The audience held its breath. He began. Cameras swept the worshipers' faces staring up at him, most too engaged to be aware they were the target of the lens.

Lucy did not take her eyes from her client. His voice was rich and forceful. She could not suppress the pleasure she felt in just hearing him. "Well, beloved. When I awoke this morning, I heard a woeful sound. I heard the screams of thousands of lost souls. Terrible sounds of pain and suffering. The souls of modern men and women departed from this life and seeking the divine. But it was too late. Too late. Too late for them ever to see the light that they chose not to follow. And I say to you, brothers and sisters, don't you be lost when the time cometh." He turned to rhythmic, often rhymed, challenges to the audience to believe, to accept, to surrender. He proffered taunts and questions that were answered with unified chants. He injected an interlude where he led the choir in song, his voice a beacon for the audience to follow.

Near the conclusion, attendants lined up the ill and infirm in lines at each side of the stage. With timed regularity, a sufferer was brought to him. "Heal!" he would yell, his hands on a skull or over a wounded heart. "Is it gone? Can you feel it? Receive the power of the Lord!" He blessed a cripple and threw each crutch to the floor while he supported the victim with a hand on the arm. "Praise, God. Walk. Walk as God intended." The victim stumbled forward and an attendant caught him. "The first steps," Bain called out. "And with faith in the Lord, these will be the first steps of millions. Praise God." Men, women, and children paraded by. He cured a young man of his homosexuality. "You must commit yourself to Christ," he said, and bear-hugged the man.

As he moved to conclusion, he called for all those who sought to accept Christ as their Lord and Savior. More than a hundred made their way up the wide aisles. As he converted each one, they were led to the side to stand together as testimony to the power of the Lord. He touched a teenage boy who was moaning on his knees, and the boy convulsed, jerking toward Bain. Bain grabbed him, expertly turning him over, holding his head back and to the side for unrestricted breathing, and an attendant wedged a cloth-wrapped tongue blade between the sufferer's teeth. As the convulsions stopped, Bain held him close, cradling his head while continuously praying into the microphone he still held. "Save this soul. Give him the strength to serve you, dear Lord." The boy was helped off by attendants and Bain regained the stage to join with dignitaries and friends and converts, arm in arm, swaying to a fast version of "Just a Closer Walk with Thee," as he closed the show.

Lucy sat mesmerized as the auditorium began to clear. Her quickened heart slowly returned to normal. She was surprised how she had been drawn into the excitement.

Her thoughts began to surface. The entire display was atrocious, of course, a detestable scam that surely damaged more than it helped. Yet the core power of the performance, the unity of so many frenzied levels of consciousness, was beyond her expectation, and she resented and admired it at the same time.

She slowly made her way from the balcony, feeling no urgency to hurry her exit. She began to see how Bain's personality could work for him . . . and against him. Jury selection, if it came to that, would be crucial. And she knew now that each juror would have a different feeling about Bain that would have little to do with faith in the Apostolic Church of Christ, or religion, for that matter, and reactions would be intensely emotional, drowning out objectivity in deliberations. She was among the last to leave the auditorium.

Thirty minutes later Lucy entered the guesthouse where she had been assigned a room. It was inexpensive—a single room that shared a bath with another room. These two rooms shared with another set of paired rooms a common area that had a sofa and overstuffed chairs, a TV, a small refrigerator under a sink, and a microwave on a counter to one side. Two women were sitting on the sofa holding cans of soda pop. A continuous rerun of the show just completed was playing on the closed-circuit TV. Lucy took a bottle of water from the refrigerator and approached. "May I join you?" she asked.

Neither woman responded. One, heavyset with a round face and dyed gray hair, wore a tight-fitting green pantsuit with a necklace of white, irregular cut-glass stones the size of large grapes. The other, slight and much shorter, wore a gray skirt and dark-blue blouse. Her gray hair was braided in a ponytail that went down to her waist. Lucy sat down. Little Margo was doing his act in rerun on the small screen.

"I can't stand it," Ponytail said, and she stood to turn off the TV and returned to her seat.

"I was watching that, sister," Green said. "I love Little Margo."

"You can see it over and over. All night."

Green twisted her weight awkwardly to stare at Ponytail. "What's wrong with you?"

"It's grotesque. It's simply a crime to rob that child of his youth."

"He's preaching the Gospel and he's good at it, too. Ain't none like him," Green said.

Ponytail clamped her jaw shut, the jaw muscles bulging firm and definite at the sides of her face.

"I take it you're not a convert," Lucy said to Ponytail.

"It's a form of child abuse," Ponytail said.

Green took a deep breath. "He love doin' it or he wouldn't be good at it."

Ponytail put her arms on her knees and put her head in her hands.

"Why'd you come, anyway?" Green said. "No need making yourself so upset over nothing."

"It's not nothing."

"Well, it ain't Christian to be beatifying against something you don't know nothing about at all."

"I don't want to talk about it."

Green leaned back on the sofa and closed her eyes. Lucy relaxed and Ponytail didn't move. After a couple minutes, Green leaned forward and touched Ponytail briefly on the back.

"You know, I'm sorry 'bout what I said, honey. It weren't Christian of me. The real good is your coming to praise God."

Ponytail sat up. She spoke softly, her anger dissipated. "I came to see my daughter. She sings in the choir."

"Praise, God. She took Christ?"

"She and her father."

"And why not you, sister?"

Ponytail sighed and paused. "I'm divorced. He has custody. I'm not allowed to see my daughter. And I'm Jewish."

"He has a restraining order on you?" Lucy asked, surprised at the possibility.

"For the time being."

"Oh, I'm so sorry for you," Green said, distressed. "And that's your only one?"

Ponytail nodded.

"That's so sad."

They sat, each lost in her thoughts, as Lucy studied their faces, trying to detect their emotions. Finally she said to Ponytail, "Do you know the Reverend Bain?"

"Ain't he wonderful?" Green answered.

"He was real good to my Cindee," Ponytail said to Lucy, deliberately ignoring Green.

"How so?" Lucy asked.

"He gave her purpose. Talked to her many times. I was there sometimes with my husband, too."

"Why do you like him?" Lucy asked Green.

Green laughed. "He's good looking."

"It's not just that," Ponytail said. "I think he really cares."

"Your daughter. Was she always comfortable with the sessions?" Lucy asked.

"She was afraid at first."

"Of what?"

"Baring her soul, I think. But over time, she opened up and he was able to guide her."

"Ain't that wonderful," Green said.

"It was extraordinary," Ponytail said.

"But you don't like him using Little Margo?" Lucy asked.

"I don't think he's involved in making those decisions. It would be out of character. Besides, that boy is older than most of our adult children. He's just small for his age."

"Course the Reverend chose him," said Green. "The boy preach the word of God better than most real preachers."

"He probably did approve," Ponytail conceded. "Just not recruited."

Lucy excused herself and prepared for bed. She turned out the overhead light. The bed was a thin mattress on coiled springs. The sheets were old but clean. She lay on her back and stared at the ceiling. Through the closed plywood door she could hear the two women arguing.

CHAPTER 7

Luke

Luke and Lucy rode alone in an elevator in the Peachtree North Building on their way to sign purchase papers for their new penthouse. Lucy turned to Luke before the door opened and said softly, almost apologetically, "Luke, I'm pregnant."

He had not even suspected. They'd been married for months, but he had often not seen her for days at a time. She had been swamped with the Bain defense and three other pending cases, often sleeping in her office on a pullout sofa. Luke was on call at the hospital often, too. And when they were home together, it was always at night, usually late, and one of them was asleep when the other arrived home.

The door started to close. "That's wonderful. When did you find out?" he asked.

She waved a hand between the doors. "Last week." The doors opened.

"Why didn't you tell me?" he asked. They stepped out. She said nothing.

"You don't sound happy about it," he said, as they walked toward the lawyer's conference room.

"I don't want to talk about it now. I just thought you should know." He felt anger rise, as it did often now when they were together and talked about almost any subject. "You don't want to talk about our child?"

She paused in front of the door. "Don't treat me like a slave, Luke. I'm not alive to meet your every expectation."

"It's our baby, Luce. It's a new life. Why wouldn't I want to talk about it?" He held her arm as she reached for the doorknob.

"Don't touch me," she said.

"How do you feel?"

"I feel just fine, Luke. I feel just fine. Now drop it."

She opened the door and went in, waving to the receptionist as she headed for the conference room. After introductions to the seller and legal staff, they signed what was needed. Lucy frowned with excess concentration; Luke barely listened to the lawyer's explanations and disclosures.

In the elevator on the way down, they stood side by side looking at the closed steel doors.

"I don't understand, Luce."

"What is it you don't understand?" she said, not looking at him.

"We ought to be celebrating."

The doors opened. They walked into the noisy lobby crowded with patrons.

"I don't want a child," she said loudly. A woman passing looked at her briefly. "I don't have time for children," she almost whispered. "I'm going to get rid of it."

"No!" Luke said reflexively. He grabbed her arm, forcing her to stop. "I will not allow it."

She twisted in his grip. "Let go of me." He released her. "It is not your decision," she said.

"It's my child, too."

She made a hissing sound.

"We need to talk," he said.

"Not now."

"When?"

"Later."

"Tonight?" he asked.

"I don't know if I'll be home tonight."

"This is important to me. I won't have you aborting my child." "It's my child, Luke."

"I have a say."

"I'll make the decision. Call me tomorrow," she said. She walked out the door. He tried to follow, but she turned around. "Don't Luke, I'm not in the mood."

Luke called and drove directly to Lucy's mother's house. A.J. wasn't home, but Elizabeth, who still lived with her parents, joined her mother Agnes and Luke around the table for four that was in the patio off the kitchen. Agnes had prepared coffee, which she and Luke drank, and Elizabeth had Diet Coke.

"I can't believe it," Agnes said about the pregnancy. "We've dreamed about it. But to have it happen?"

"When will it come?" Elizabeth asked.

"I don't know," Luke said. "She told me this morning on the way to the signing."

"Surely she must have an idea. Babies take nine months. It's routine."

"She wasn't herself," he said.

Agnes spoke after a long pause. "We haven't seen her in so long. Only once since you've been married."

"I've called her to go out twice," Elizabeth said, "but she doesn't have time."

"She doesn't want the baby. She wants to get rid of it," he said.

Agnes closed her eyes.

"She can't do that," Elizabeth said. "That's taking an innocent life." She was squeezing interlocked fingers until her skin blanched.

Luke leaned forward and touched Agnes's hand. "Is there something you could do? Talk to her?"

Agnes lowered her head. "She doesn't listen to us anymore. She won't let us be her parents." She looked at Luke accusingly. "You married without us even knowing."

He searched for the right words. "She was afraid you would want a big wedding. She didn't want that."

Elizabeth turned to Luke. "She's rarely considerate about anything when it comes to family," she said.

"It's been difficult for her," Agnes said to Elizabeth. Then she turned to Luke. "She's always arguing with A.J."

"You've given her everything," Elizabeth said to Agnes. "She won't listen."

"She doesn't feel a part of the family," Luke said.

Agnes sighed. "After all we've done."

"She's never been appreciated," Elizabeth added.

"It's more complicated than that," Luke said. "And I know she respects all of you."

Agnes frowned in disagreement. "She doesn't even tolerate us anymore."

"Is there something you could say to her?" he asked. "About the baby?"

"She wouldn't listen."

"I can't let her do this," he said.

Elizabeth shifted in her chair, her clear blue eyes looked out the picture window. She yearned for children of her own. She would never understand destroying a child.

"You need to call her," Elizabeth said to her mother.

"I wouldn't know what to say," Agnes replied. She seemed confused. She would always want grandchildren. But raising Lucy had exhausted her. She had no rage about anything anymore, and it was rage she desperately needed, or something intense, to relieve the helplessness she felt now.

"What about A.J.?" Luke asked.

Agnes responded quickly, as if offended by the idea. "He would make it worse. She would go against anything he says."

"But you'll tell him," he said.

"Of course I'll tell him," she said with irritation. "And he'll try to call her. But she won't talk to him. Trust me."

"She thinks he doesn't respect her," he said.

"How could she think that?" Agnes said.

"If A.J. could just listen with a little compassion," Luke said.

"He's rarely been a comfort for any of us," Elizabeth said.

"I'm afraid that's all we can do," Agnes said.

"It's not enough," Luke said, angry with their conceits.

The next day A.J. called Lucy and talked to her. He asked her to consider the importance of taking the life of their grandchild. Lucy said she, and her child, were not of their blood. She was adopted. A.J. said that his years of caring about her and loving her did make it a blood relationship. Lucy turned silent, suspicious of his words. Why did most women so crave the pleasures of children? Such cravings had never reached her. My God, she had too much to do, too much to achieve.

"Will you think about it?" A.J. asked.

She hung up, disturbed at the revelations of affection she had never expected.

CHAPTER 8

Elizabeth

Elizabeth MacMiel fretted to herself the night her father said he talked to Lucy. He said that Lucy gave no clue as to what she might or might not do about the pregnancy. The delicate light from the moonlit sky filtered in through the two bedroom windows that looked out over the lawn of her parents' house.

She stared in a state of sleepless agitation at the dark-shadowed, frosted light globe on the ceiling, intent on the shadowy speck of a dead fly on the inside that had gravitated to the bottom. Lucy was adopted, but she was family. This fetus was a part of the family, and to act as if it was her decision alone was exactly what Elizabeth had grown to dislike about Lucy over the years. Lucy was, in almost everything she did, self-centered and inconsiderate. Besides, it was a moral issue. This wasn't rape or incest; this child was conceived in marriage. And Elizabeth had no tolerance for abortion of convenience. She loved children. She'd chosen to devote herself to the formative years of third and fourth graders. It had never been a job for her; she didn't need money to live. Outside the classroom, she had decided to reach out to all children, privileged or not, through stories. She wrote fresh and unique tales with morals and lessons for life, and made them interesting. After failing to find illustrators who could visually create what she wanted to support her work, she learned to paint. Her illustrations were never frightening, always realistic—she deplored the illustrations drawn with gaudy images and cute creatures to sell books mainly to the parents. Her five books—published under a pseudonym—had sold well, and she had just won an international award for her first.

It was past midnight. She could not just let the possibility of aborting float along like a dandelion seed in the wind. She would talk to Lucy. Convince her. It would not be easy. But she would never forgive herself if she didn't at least try.

The next day was Saturday. Elizabeth went to the gym where she knew Lucy would be working out. Lucy could not avoid her there, as she would if she tried to make an appointment. She found Lucy on a treadmill and convinced her to leave the exercise room. The locker room had people in it but the basketball court was empty except for a lone player shooting baskets at one end. Elizabeth suggested they sit on the first row of the wooden bleachers.

"What's up?" Lucy asked. She was breathing hard and light perspiration glistened on her skin. Elizabeth noted her beauty with a touch of envy . . . as she always had.

"It's about the baby," Elizabeth said.

"Off limits, Elizabeth. I mean it."

"It's about family."

Lucy tensed, and stared at her.

"It's important to mother especially," Elizabeth continued. "It's her first grandchild."

"Find a man, Elizabeth. Have your family. Give them grandchildren."

Elizabeth stared at the turn-around jump shot the player had just released, watched the arc; but the ball was six inches short of the rim. She looked at Lucy. "That's not a solution," she said.

"You'll never find a man sitting on your ass at home. Get out. Enjoy yourself," Lucy said.

The player repeated the same shot and missed again. "Must you personalize your irritation?" Elizabeth asked.

"What, pray tell, does that mean, Elizabeth? 'Personalize my irritation.'"

"My failure to find a man is not the reason you should let this baby come to term. If you don't want a child, let others care for it. This is the age of a career woman with a surrogate mother."

"I don't know what I'll do," Lucy said.

"Luke must be devastated," Elizabeth said.

"Believe me. Luke orbits in his own spaceship."

The player was trying foul shots. He hadn't made one yet.

"Just please consider all of us."

Lucy looked to the wall clock behind her. "This is my baby, my problem, my future," she said.

"Just consider us."

"I've never really been a MacMiel. But I'll consider your concerns." She paused. "My heart is not in it, Elizabeth. And when I decide, it will be for my own reasons, not because you came here today, or because mother wants to send out pictures of her grandchild at Christmas."

Elizabeth had made no progress with Lucy. But she had tried. She worried for Luke. Lucy seemed unaware of the value of Luke's love for her.

God, how she disliked Lucy at times.

CHAPTER 9

Luke

Months later, Lucy delivered a baby girl. Luke waited with Agnes and Elizabeth in the hospital family room and all cheered at the news. Lucy seemed proud and pleased. She named her daughter Jennifer, after her mother in Puerto Rico.

Lucy spent one night in hospital. Her blood pressure had been high from preeclampsia, and she had been heavily sedated. Jennifer weighed less than three pounds and spent three weeks in a neonatal intensive care unit.

At home, Lucy's exhaustion never allowed restful sleep. Luke helped as best he could. Her body ached and she hated lying still but couldn't muster the energy to move. She was either hot or cold and always aware of her discomfort. Luke tried to keep family away. Lucy told her mother she wanted to be alone, but then Lucy was irritated after her mother left by her mother's "lack of attention."

Lucy slept in a separate bedroom, and although she went to see Jennifer every day at the hospital, she did not leave the condo for anything else. Agnes, and sometimes Elizabeth, brought her food and ran errands. As the time came to bring Jennifer home, Agnes suggested Jennifer and Lucy come live with them for a while. Plenty of room. Luke said no without asking Lucy. Lucy would never agree. So Agnes spent weeks carefully investigating a live-in nanny to take care of Jennifer—a Mrs. Crowder, widowed and sixty-two, with only a high school education, but the experience of raising five of her own children. She would stay in one of the guest bedrooms next to where Jennifer would be, able to keep a constant watch.

　

Luke filled his block surgical time at the hospital early in the month and needed to operate routine cases as emergencies any time he could get priority on the schedule. His visits to Lucy became infrequent.

When Mrs. Crowder arrived, Lucy felt better. She slept regularly and well. But Mrs. Crowder was a constant presence that invaded Lucy's world. And Lucy couldn't wait to escape. Soon she was back at work, her days interrupted only by regular workout sessions to regain her body tone and lose the few pounds she had gained during the pregnancy.

CHAPTER 10

Lucy

Hower Bain was indicted. Lucy and the firm filed a number of unsuccessful motions. The DA was determined to convict—he didn't like Hower Bain any more than he liked Lucy MacMiel, and he saw political advantage in prosecuting a well-known celebrity.

"Is he guilty?" Alan McCormick, the senior partner, asked Lucy.

She gave him an impatient glance. "What difference does it make?"

They were standing by the coffeepot in the empty employees' lounge.

"It makes a difference in how you'll frame the trial. But it will also change your effectiveness. It's hard to be enthusiastic when you know he's guilty."

"It's complex, Alan. Most of his followers believe he cannot be guilty. The girl is fifteen, but she looks twenty. I don't think there's a man alive who would even come close to thinking about her age, much less guessing correctly. So if it happened, it might have been accidental."

"Any updates from the investigators?"

"They've confirmed she wasn't a virgin. One guy might be willing to testify, if he has immunity. He's only seventeen."

"You'd need that. You'll never get the girl to admit that on the stand."

"I hate that the press has tried the case already."

"From what I've heard, they think Bain's guilty."

"With the exception of a rare right-wing conservative paper," Lucy said.

"Do you like him any better?"

Lucy shifted her weight from left foot to right as she answered. "I never disliked him."

McCormick laughed. "The few times I've seen you together, you were at each other's throats."

Sometimes she liked Hower Bain better than she liked Alan McCormick. She didn't like McCormick talking down to her. And she didn't like his always-present, barely disguised sexism. In Lucy's opinion, he had always seen her as a token addition to the firm—no woman would ever be a partner—and he dismissed her intellect as inconsequential.

Lucy told Hower Bain to never give an interview to the press. She insisted. Hours later he allowed a five-minute interview with a local TV reporter while he was standing in front of the courthouse. He denied all. He took the stance of a victim. He was arrogant and unlikeable. And he hurt his image.

Lucy called him immediately. "Don't ever do that again," she said.

"You're not my mother."

"You've compromised your defense. Even the judge warned you not to use the media."

"I told the truth."

"You explained. You were unlikeable."

"Not to my followers."

"To those who might make up the jury. I guarantee you, there will be few if any followers on that jury."

"I'll defend myself at every opportunity."

"Not publicly. And not on TV."

"That's not how it's going to be, counselor. I'll do what I think is right."

"Then find yourself another lawyer."

"With pleasure."

She hung up.

Two hours later, Jason Campbell, Bain's lieutenant, called. "Hower's sorry, Ms. MacMiel. He did not speak appropriately."

"True. And I'm happy to be off his case."

"He wants you back."

"Way too many risks for my career, Mr. Campbell. I don't think he'll do well with this no matter what he thinks about what God's will is doing for him." She hung up without saying goodbye.

She cleaned her desk of Bain's case files and took the day off. Later that evening Alan McCormick called from the firm.

"You can't quit," he said.

"I can and I will."

"We need this case. And you're the best to handle it."

"You or anyone else can 'handle' it," she said.

"You are the only chance for a win. It's high-profile, Lucy."

"He's a loser."

"You've already started to paint him as a saint. His popularity will make that credible. A man of God. And you've nailed the girl for what she is."

"She's a child, Alan."

"But she's a sexually active child long before the alleged incident."

"Her life is screwed up enough as it is."

"You'll just be pointing out reality. That she's unreliable. We can't trust what she says about anything. And there are no witnesses. Are there?"

"Of course not."

"Can you be sure?"

"Not totally. But we'll never get full disclosure. Would you if you were the DA?"

McCormick didn't answer.

"I don't like Bain," Lucy said.

"How many defendants have you liked?"

"He's misogynistic and arrogant."

"Never allow him to testify."

"I don't even want him on TV."

"He's promised to obey, Lucy."

"He'll never obey. Me, or anyone."

"I've got to insist. We need this case. We need to win."

Lucy remained silent. She didn't like to be pressed by senior partners. It reminded her of her junior status as a woman lawyer.

"Can I call him?" McCormick asked.

She paused. "I'm not happy."

McCormick laughed. "You're the best," he said.

CHAPTER 11

Luke
1987

Mrs. Crowder had the weekend off to be with her sister in Valdosta. Luke came in from the garage, back from Saturday morning rounds. Lucy sat on a stool and fed strained peaches to Jennifer with a solid sterling spoon Agnes had given her. Jennifer pushed it out of her mouth with her tongue and it ran down her chin and plopped on the messy high chair tray. Lucy swore under her breath and wiped Jennifer's mouth with a paper towel.

"Late breakfast?" Luke asked.

She didn't answer. She was trying to force another spoonful at Jennifer, who started to cry.

He put his briefcase by the central island. "How's it going?"

"Don't ask."

"That bad."

"She won't eat."

"Maybe she's not hungry."

"She's ornery."

"I wonder where she got that from?" he said, laughing.

Lucy threw a wad of paper towels onto the floor and stood up. "I don't have to take this crap."

"I meant me," he said. "Not you." And he moved by the high chair to take Lucy in his arms.

But she shoved him away. "I'm not good at this, Luke. I need someone to help when Mrs. Crowder isn't here."

He reached under the sink for a rag that he wet under the faucet.

"Clean her up and put her in the crib. I'll clean up here and put on a pot of coffee."

Lucy lifted Jennifer from the chair and, holding her stiff-armed so Jennifer's legs were dangling, took her into the bathroom to clean her up.

Luke wiped down the high chair, cleaned the counter and floor, and brewed coffee. He called to Lucy to meet him in the living room when the coffee was ready and she was there in seconds, taking the overstuffed chair opposite where he was sitting.

"How were rounds?" she asked.

"So-so. They presented another case I don't think should have been operated."

"It's worse, isn't it? The quest for gold."

"It may be me behind the times. This case had a cataract removed with vision in both eyes better than your mother's, who leads a useful and contented life, at least as far as her vision is concerned."

"Are there quotas?"

"Not openly. But there are bonuses paid on volume of surgery and office visits."

"Conflict of interest."

"And this case has a blinding complication in an eye with relatively good vision to start. I don't feel good about it."

"What does A.J. think?"

"He doesn't think about it, that I know of."

"The other docs?"

"Most are upset."

"How can this happen at an academic level?"

"It's changed at lot, Luce. Especially for the anterior-segment cataract surgeons. When A.J. presents the monthly financial report at faculty meetings, income is far more important than science for him. He's proud that gross billings are in the millions. Even in the clinical research report, it's not the search for knowledge, but for something we can patent."

"And of course you can't talk to him about it."

"He gets angry."

She nodded. "Tell me about it."

Jennifer cried. He started to stand but Lucy was already on her feet. "I'll check," she said.

She was back in minutes. "She's fine." He had refreshed her cup. She settled back down.

"You are a good mother, Luce. You shouldn't be thinking anything else."

"I'm not, Luke. I get angry. I resent what I have to do."

"You love to be around her."

She paused. "Not always. Sometimes I don't want her around."

He smiled gently. "We all feel like that occasionally."

"I'm not sure. And it's not what normal mothers feel. I can't imagine Elizabeth ever wanting to be away from a child. She would be a perfect mother. Always making the right decisions. Always feeling love and pride. I don't have it. And I don't know how to get it."

"You made the right decision about bringing her into the world."

"I don't know."

"She's a happy child, Luce, full of potential."

"She's not happy. She's being brought up by a stranger. When I spend time with her, it's all scolding and correcting. That's not happiness."

"That's necessity. That's parenting. And she's growing and learning. She smiles and laughs."

"Not often with me."

"All the time with you."

Lucy closed her eyes and remained silent.

"I'll be sure to have someone here to help when Mrs. Crowder's away," Luke finally said.

"With the Bain trial coming up, I'll have less time at home."

"But when you can't be here, I'll get it arranged."

Lucy took her cup to the kitchen and Luke stayed in his chair, his arms on the armrest, his head back, his eyes closed for more than ten minutes.

CHAPTER 12

Lucy

Hower Bain began to ignore Lucy, diverting all her calls to staff who often couldn't answer the questions the investigators uncovered and the press evoked. And he refused to come to Atlanta for conferences. She sent legal assistants for a while. The drive to the church compound was four and a half hours one way. But as the defense developed, she had more need to question him.

She and Alan McCormick had deposed the accuser. The girl was a natural. She had the ability to look and sound vulnerable and victimized. She seemed unable to deviate from the truth. Almost nothing seemed contrived. She said she had gone to many one-on-one conferences with Reverend Bain. Most had been with her mother but a few other times when her mother was at work as a waitress, her mother's boyfriend dropped her off.

She said Howie was helping her find Christ as her savior. That she had sinned. She'd made love to boys and Howie had helped her find redemption and the strength to be good again. With Howie's help she believed God had forgiven her.

Lucy had carefully prepared her questions about the rape. The girl said she was talking about her mother to Howie, telling him how her mother thought so low of her and when it happened, she was not so upset. It was . . . like slow motion. Howie put his hand on her knee. She was sitting on a sofa in his office conference room; he was sitting in an armchair that he had pulled up beside her. She didn't stop talking. He asked her more questions about her mother. She was sure about this. He moved his hand under her dress. She felt his caress—movement, she actually said. She stopped talking and looked at him. "He was looking at me and his eyes did not move away. His hand slipped up my leg, near my privates. I had panties on, I'm sure I did. No, sometimes when I was in a hurry I might not wear panties. Well, he touched me. Yes. I did say something. 'Don't,' I said. He took his hand away and got up out of the chair and kneeled beside me. He told me how beautiful I was. Like an angel, he said. I think I giggled, I was so nervous. But he touched my lips with his finger. Then he kissed me all over, never on the lips, really, just all over. He took my hand and put it on his pants so I could feel him. It was warm even through the cloth. And then he took me. No. I was too afraid. I didn't know what might happen if I yelled. No, I don't think he would have beat me or anything. It hurt me down there at first but I didn't scream. The panties? He took them off. He pulled them down over my legs. Yes, my dress was still on, wadded up around my waist. I don't remember where the panties went."

Alan McCormick took over the questioning.

"He said he loved me. He would always love me. He walked me through the office where the secretaries sit. He always did that after a session. Yes, I told my mother right away when I got home. She said I had been violated and she called a friend who gave her the name of a lawyer. Well, the police came. I didn't have the panties. I don't know where they are. I must have left them in the office. I was too afraid to think about it when I left."

Lucy and Alan McCormick sat in the room used for depositions after the accuser and the DA and his staff had left, and the court recorder and video man had packed up. They were alone.

"It never happened," Lucy said. "In his office? With staff outside the door?"

McCormick nodded. "Doesn't seem likely."

"It's her fantasy."

"She may believe that fantasy happened. It gives her a lot of credibility in the presentation."

"I think I can easily find discrepancies the next time she tells it."

"Maybe."

"You think she's that smart?"

"I think she's imaginative and clever, and more misguided by her wants than evil. I think she'll be consistent and a great witness. They'll put her on the stand if they can." He stood. "I'd get to Bain. See how he reacts to the story. And I'd interview the secretaries and the staff and see what they remember."

"I'm doing that," Lucy said curtly.

"I know you are. We'd better arrange to subpoena the mother for a deposition. I'd like to know her story."

Lucy had already started the arrangements and resented McCormick's paternalistic tone.

"And I'd get the police report," he said.

"Don't treat me like an assistant. The report is incomplete and of little help to either side." He was acting like the lead on this case. She began to believe the only reason he didn't take it himself was that he knew it wasn't winnable.

McCormick shrugged before he pushed back the chair to leave the room. She went directly to make arrangements to again visit the compound of the Apostolic Church of Christ.

CHAPTER 13

Luke

Luke worked in his office late on Thursday. Eileen Turner, a fellow faculty member and Director of Fellowship training, a five-foot-six woman with a masculine physique kept in peak condition, short dark hair, and prominent facial features dominated by clear blue eyes, opened the door to his office and directed in Sandra Perez, one of the fellows, without asking Luke's permission. This was Eileen's way. Luke said nothing about her rudeness because of their long-standing friendship.

Eileen pointed for Sandra to sit down in a straight-backed chair and remained standing in front of Luke, glaring.

"What's the crisis?" he asked.

"Sandra's got bad news."

Sandra sat rigid, her face a tense mask.

"You know I don't have anything to do with the fellows," he said to Eileen.

"This is not about fellows."

"Get to the point, Eileen."

"Sandra got an official notice from human resources. She's been dismissed from the program."

Sandra looked away. She seemed about to cry. Luke came from behind the desk and pulled up a chair; he motioned for Eileen to sit, too.

"What happened?" he asked Sandra.

"I don't know," she said.

"I called human services," Eileen said. "It came without warning, and without reason. They said their action was protected by confidentiality, and that they had told Sandra everything that was required for dismissal of a fellow, which is a different status than the staff. Well, they told her nothing."

"That's unfair," he said.

"We didn't come for the obvious," Eileen said. "Of course it's unfair."

"You must have some idea," he said to Sandra.

"I really don't, Dr. Osborne. I've always done my best. I've never made major errors. Patients seem to like me."

"Her faculty evaluations are almost perfect," Eileen said.

He stared at Eileen, waiting for the exception.

Eileen frowned. "Except for Modesto Sanchez's last one a few weeks ago. Everything poor. For the last two years he's been here, he has always given her excellent ratings."

"What's the point?" he asked.

"There's no reason for it. Sandra is an excellent doc, she's worked hard, placed in the ninetieth percentile on her OKAP exams." Eileen took a deep breath. "And she's a single parent with two young children."

"What do you want me to do?" he asked Eileen.

"Make it right. She should be allowed to finish, and recommended for whatever she wants to do."

"I'm not the chair."

"Go to A.J., then. He can make a difference."

"You'd do it better."

"I was told to make an appointment. Next appointment is next month."

"Grab him in the hall."

"He won't listen. You're Chief of Service, and respected. Help out. Delays will keep her from finishing on time even if she's reinstated."

He was moved by Sandra's distress and the unfairness of what they'd described. It was a reasonable request. "Okay," he said. "I'll see what I can do."

Luke went to confront Modesto Sanchez in the doctors' dressing room on the surgery floor. He was waiting for a patient to be placed in an OR room.

"Luke, my man," he said. "I got a case."

He was a small man, dark in complexion with guarded dark eyes. He was hyperactive, and Luke felt uncomfortable around him.

"It's about Sandra Perez," Luke said. "She's been dismissed from the program."

Modesto's gaze didn't falter, as if he were concentrating on not looking away.

"Nothing to do with me," Modesto said.

"You are the only one that gave her a bad evaluation. And you've probably had less contact with her than most of us."

"Hey, Luke. I call 'em like I see 'em, man. It's part of the job."

"That's all?"

"What more is there?" Modesto left for the OR.

Luke went to A.J.'s office within the hour. A.J. was in conference, but promised to come to Luke as soon as he was finished. Three hours later, well past seven-thirty, A.J. showed up. He sat in the same chair Sandra Perez had occupied.

"How's my grandchild?" A.J. asked.

"Doing great. Talking up a storm," Luke laughed. "Nothing we can understand."

"You're great parents," A.J. said. "What's on the agenda?"

"Sandra Perez, A.J. What's with her?"

"Lawyer advice. Let her go."

"She's a good fellow. It seems unfair."

"She's not that good," A.J. said.

"She's been an exemplary fellow. I wish we had more like her."

"She had terrible evaluations."

"Only one, A.J. And by Modesto, who didn't even know her well."

"I don't get involved with fellows, Luke. You know that. It's valuable time wasted."

"You could reverse the decision with a phone call."

"I won't override staff. That's bad management. And there are circumstances that cannot be discussed."

"Sandra should be told why she's being dismissed."

"That's Eileen's problem. Ask her. She should handle it."

"She doesn't know the reason!"

A.J. stared over Luke's head for a second. "What's it to you?" he asked.

"It's wrong, A.J. It needs to be reversed."

A.J. shook his head. "I'd stay out of it, Luke. She's a fellow in training who can find training elsewhere. We'll help her do that, if she wants it."

"There's nothing good available this late in the year."

"Next year, then."

"It isn't fair."

"How can you be so sure?"

"I helped train her," Luke said.

A.J. stood. "It's a bad trait, Luke, this gallantry. Sometimes it's no good to be a knight in shining armor," he said as he left.

Luke called Lucy at work. He told her about Sandra's firing. "Don't you have someone who specializes in labor grievances?" he asked.

"Of course. And he's dealt with the university before. I'll call you back."

An hour later she called. "The labor guy says there's a reason she was fired and she's not telling you. She must suspect something. He'll be glad to consider being involved, but he wants more details and a $10,000 retainer."

"I was hoping for a little free direction on how to proceed."

"Find out the details. That's good advice, Luke. And that's free."

"I think A.J. knew about Sandra's reasons and he wouldn't say. He refused to reinstate her when I asked."

Lucy paused. "A cover-up? Something serious?"

"I doubt that. I think your lawyer friend is right. Sandra probably did something that A.J. doesn't want to reveal for her sake, but he had to discipline her."

"He may not be involved at all. Your department is a bureaucratic nightmare."

"I've got to be careful, especially if I've climbed out on a limb for a fellow who should have been dismissed."

"Seems prudent. Check sexual harassment issues and gender discrimination. Two of the most common reasons for female doctors' dismissals."

"I can't believe that."

"It's damn common," Lucy said.

Luke went back to Modesto Sanchez. Modesto was about to leave his office for the garage. He had on shorts and a T-shirt. He played squash three times a week.

"Got a tournament," he said, and started out the door.

Luke grabbed his shirtsleeve to stop him. "This won't take long."

Modesto shrugged.

"It looks like there will be legal involvement in the Sandra dismissal. No one will say what went down. And that always raises suspicion of sexual harassment."

"Bullshit," Modesto said. But there were glints of worry in his eyes.

"You didn't do anything that might provoke charges, did you?"

"She say that?"

"No."

"Of course I didn't. And I don't like your asking."

"Why write a poor evaluation on a doc who never had a poor evaluation before, and who rarely had duties on the cornea service?"

He took a deep breath. "Look, Luke. I'm no ass chaser. I got a family. I was told that she was a bad fellow and to write a bad evaluation. I assumed she wasn't any good. I didn't even know about her other evaluations."

"Almost all perfect."

"Well, I made a mistake."

"Correct it, then."

"I don't know that I can. I tried when asked. I said I was uncomfortable writing the bad report on a doctor I worked with only ten or twelve times."

"Why did you?"

"It was mentioned that I was up for promotion in two months."

"A threat?"

"Indirectly. But clear enough."

"Who was it?"

"I can't say."

"I'll find out, Modesto. Probably within a few hours."

"It's my career, man."

"It's Sandra's career. You don't want to be a part of the legal battle that might come up. The suspicions. The innuendo."

"A.J., my friend."

"He told you to do it?"

"He told me word for word what to put on the forms." Modesto turned to leave.

"I may ask you to tell someone else," Luke said.

"Not me, Luke. This is the last I'll ever speak about it. I'm not suicidal, man."

"You'll deny it?" Luke asked.

"Yes."

And Modesto hurried away.

Luke called home and told Mrs. Crowder to not keep Jennifer up and that he'd be home late. He had Eileen Turner find Sandra Perez and bring her to his office. They sat in chairs around his desk.

"Look, Sandra. This is not right. I called for legal advice. They said you must have some suspicion as to why you were released. That you were very probably holding back information."

The look on Eileen's face said that Sandra had not been forthright. "She's afraid," Eileen said. "She needs recommendations and contacts to find a position that would allow her to finish training. My God. You know how hard those are to find."

"It would be harder than being reinstated here," Luke agreed.

"Which is not likely," Eileen said.

"The only way to get reinstated is to have Dr. MacMiel cancel the dismissal," Sandra said. "I don't think anyone else can do it."

"That's the problem," Eileen said. "It's MacMiel."

Luke stared at them both. "I need more," he said. "Tell me."

Eileen glanced at Sandra, who looked at Luke and took a deep breath.

"There's a rumor that a malpractice suit is imminent," Eileen said.

"About what? I hear such rumors once a week."

"It has to do with Sandra not telling you," Eileen said. "Sandra thought if there was not a chance of reinstatement, it was best to get out as soon as she could."

Sandra raised her hand to speak. "It was a complicated case," she said. "I was operating with Dr. MacMiel. I had worked up this patient of his. Knew the patient well. It was Dr. MacMiel's big surgery day.

Thursday. He had thirteen cases, seven of them transplants. On those days, we worked two rooms; his patients were prepared and prepped in one room while an operation was completed in the other. It was the only way to do that many cases. Frequently I or one of the other fellows working with Dr. MacMiel would finish a case while he went to start the case in the next room.

"This day we were working three rooms, with a resident helping. Dr. MacMiel and I were near the end of a case. A patient, Eustace Jones, had already been rolled into another room. He was ready for block, prep, and drape. 'Finish up, Sandra,' Dr. MacMiel said. 'Yes, sir,' I said. He told the resident to take care of Eustace Jones. It was an unusual request to a resident, but this resident was senior and had had experience. The resident left. Dr. MacMiel went to a telephone in the hall with an outside line. I could hear him. I'm sure the anesthetist could, too. The circulator was not present. He was talking to his stockbroker. The call lasted maybe eight or nine minutes. He left without coming back into where I was finishing the case . . . I was having some difficulty with a running suture that I needed to replace. When he went to Eustace Jones, the patient was blocked and draped with the scope in place. The resident had already inserted the speculum and prepared the eye. Dr. MacMiel did the trephine and sent the corneal button to pathology. The transplant tissue was prepared and already on the eye. He had started the sutures by the time I finished in the other room and had rescrubbed.

"I knew the patient well, and knew when I sat down at the scope this was the wrong eye. I whispered it to Dr. MacMiel. He stopped operating but still held the needle holder and forceps motionless in the field under the scope. After a few seconds he said, 'Eustace?' to me, as if he'd remembered something about the patient. 'Eustace Jones,' I confirmed. 'Bilateral Fuchs' dystrophy with decompensation after bilateral cataract removal?' he asked. 'Yes,' I said, 'but with known macular degeneration in his eye with poor visual potential?' I nodded.

"Dr. MacMiel still held the instrument under the scope and he still peered into the oculars as I did on the assistant's side. His grip was without the slightest tremor, even under the magnification. 'Both eyes were to be done,' he said. But that wasn't true. Only the eye with potential vision was scheduled. 'I decided to do this one first,' he said, 'to see what vision could be recovered.' We finished the case. 'Correct the chart and anesthesia-preop records,' he said. 'OS to OD. Date it and initial it,' he said. 'I don't feel comfortable doing that,' I said. He glared at me. 'I didn't hear that,' he said. I hesitated and knew this was wrong for the patient. To go through two operations for a mistake. 'No.' I said, 'I won't do it.' He swore but didn't argue. He changed the records. He instructed me to start the next case while he went down to the family. I heard later he told the family he had, in the patient's best interest, decided to operate on the right eye to recover as much vision as possible before doing the left eye. That he was concerned with the pressure fluctuations in the good eye and the effect it might have on surgery. There were pressure changes, of course, but nothing that an iridotomy and medications couldn't have controlled. The family trusted him. He was a famous, experienced surgeon."

"And smooth talking," said Eileen.

"And nothing happened?" Luke asked.

"Two weeks later he operated the other eye. I was not allowed on the case. He did it with Andrew."

"That seems a short time between eyes for transplants."

"Even cataracts," said Eileen.

"We are taught the established time between transplants is six months, minimum," Sandra continued. "But Dr. MacMiel convinced the family it was best. I was there when he told them he was aiming to have one eye for near vision and the other for far."

"That was impossible," said Eileen.

"He made it seem more than likely. And that he wanted to get Eustace rehabilitated as soon as possible, especially at his age," Sandra said. "Both eyes rejected the grafts. I was no longer allowed to see the patient. But the first eye without good vision potential was quieted with the usual treatments. The better eye failed completely. Dr. MacMiel re-grafted while the eye was still inflamed. The patient had no functional vision and required full-time assistance. He could no longer watch TV— his football games mainly—or read even with a magnifying glass. He had difficulty learning to feed himself. The family took him out of Dr. MacMiel's care. A few weeks later the patient died from a heart attack. He'd had heart disease from hypertension."

"A poor operative risk?" Eileen asked.

"In my opinion," Sandra said. "All this happened over a few months. I heard a suit was filed last week."

"And A.J. wanted you out of the city," Eileen said.

"I was really the only one who saw the scenario and was close to him. Anesthesia won't have a tight memory of what happened or know the details. The resident is in Haiti on a surgical rotation. Rumor again has it he will not return before he graduates. He has a fellowship in L.A."

"Don't you see?" Eileen said to Luke, "they're already making discovery impossible."

"I'm the only one who realized there was an error," Sandra said. "MacMiel will insist his plan was in place. The resident knew, but I think he was thankful that Dr. MacMiel could handle the whole thing so efficiently."

"Although unethical," Eileen said. "I tried to find the chart. It's disappeared from medical records."

"I have a copy of the original chart of my care of the patient," Sandra said.

"I'd put it in a vault," Luke said.

"I'll help with that," Eileen said. "She needs legal counsel."

"The one lawyer my wife approached wants a $10,000 retainer."

"I don't have it," Sandra said.

"Maybe there's some way I can use part of the residents' fund," Eileen said.

Luke hesitated. The residents' fund was for education, not legal fees. Besides, although he believed all of what Sandra said, he wasn't sure if her perceptions about A.J.'s actions might be tainted a little by the emotions at the time. Medical ethics were never clear cut. Certainly A.J. had a different, if not reasonable, explanation for his actions in the OR. "He's my father-in-law," Luke said to Eileen. "I can't do anything more."

"What can we do, then?" Eileen asked. "Go to the dean?"

"I don't know, Eileen," Luke said, exasperated.

"Talk to A.J. now that you know the truth."

"One version of what happened."

"It is the truth," Sandra said.

"Don't spin things, Luke. It's not right," Eileen said loudly.

That hurt Luke. If he believed Sandra, he should help her until he had reason not to believe, father-in-law or not.

"I'll see what I can do," Luke said.

CHAPTER 14

Lucy

Lucy continued to resent traveling to the compound to talk to Bain. She didn't think Bain would demand it of McCormick, a male lawyer with stature. It was sexism, she was convinced, and it irritated her. And Bain treated her as an inferior. She'd often thought Bain had hired her because he could control her more easily than he could a man. She was sure of that now. The paradox was that she needed information to succeed, and to get valuable information she had to pretend, at least for the time being, she was a lawyer that she was not, a lawyer willing to bend to the will of her client, and not take control of the legal process. And she hadn't wanted to ask McCormick to step in and make Bain act like a respectful client. It would be her own defeat. So she was traveling again to talk to Bain about the deposition. But this would be the last time. She would make that clear.

She arrived a day before her meeting with Bain. She started, as soon as she had been assigned a room in the guest quarters, to talk to as many people as she could, not just to discover Bain, but also to see the thinking of those in the compound. Near the gymnasium was a Quonset hut. A placard on an easel anchored with stones at the feet and taped above for stability read: "Evolution and Creationism: Why Compromise?" Twenty or so people sat in folding chairs facing a young man with a cleric's collar who sat on a rectangular table, his feet dangling, his hands gripping the edges of the table, and leaning forward in a casual pose. He stopped talking when Lucy entered. "Welcome," he said. "Take a seat." He pointed to a chair in the front row.

She felt his eyes on her as she walked to the front. She sat, crossing her legs, her hands in her lap.

"The lawyer, isn't it?" he asked.

Lucy nodded, not sure whether she wanted to be here now, but deciding it was not in her best interest to leave.

"We're here to discuss evolution. Darwinism." He pronounced it "Dar-wine." For a bonding effect with his audience, Lucy was sure. "What do you believe?" he asked, looking at Lucy. "Are we from monkeys? Is that our folks?"

Lucy remained silent.

An older man behind her spoke. "That's not a fair question, Reverend."

"Quite the contrary," the Reverend said. "We know why the lawyer's here. If she expects us to be open with her, she should be open with us. Her beliefs are important. And I frankly have heard that she seems to think herself a little better than most of us."

By strong will, Lucy didn't move a muscle.

"You don't have anything to say?" the Reverend asked her.

Lucy stared at him, maintaining her control and denying him any clue as to her thoughts. She was interested that he was trying to demean her, and she wanted to find out if it was personal because of her or her profession, or whether he was acting out of loyalty and respect toward her client, Hower Bain.

"Cat got your tongue?" he said.

A woman at the side stood. "This is not Christian, Reverend Canby. The lawyer is a guest and should be treated with respect."

The Reverend smiled and waited before he responded. "Of course you are right, Mrs. Hardwick." He looked at Lucy. "My apologies. I hope you take no offense. No offense was intended, I assure you."

He seemed surprised when Lucy stood after a few seconds, looked at him briefly, and turned to face the audience. She glanced over the intent audience, all eyes on her. She saw no evidence of hostility on most of the faces. Some were unreadable.

"Hello," she said. "I am Lucy MacMiel, and as the Reverend mentioned, I am a lawyer. And if there is anyone who doesn't know, I represent Hower Bain." She turned briefly to the Reverend, "And you are right, sir. My opinions as counsel to Hower Bain are important, and you have every right to be curious. Your love and respect for the Reverend

Bain gives you that right." Her gaze swept over the audience again. "And, I am interested in this question of evolution. What do each of you believe? Why is it important to you? You have considered these issues. Frankly, it would help me form my own opinions. I would appreciate your views."

"We believe God created man. And not from monkeys," the Reverend said.

The man who had spoken previously stood. He dressed plainly in a plaid shirt and coveralls. His intelligent blue eyes and angular face held dignity.

"How one interprets evolution is not important for most of us, Miss MacMiel," he said. "Each of us must accept the wisdom of God and Christ as our savior, and evolution will always be a theory for interpretation by science and the preachers."

"Heretic," someone called out. The man sat down.

"It's about the children. They 'shudn't' be 'teached' wrong," a woman said from the back. Other people called out their views. "God's will can work through the theory of evolutionism," a woman to the side said.

"That would take away God's hand in the creation," a man said.

"Not at all. God's hand is in everything we do and experience. And it could very well be in parts of evolution," the woman said.

"So you believe we came from apes?" a woman's voice called out.

"I believe it's possible," the man answered, "But it doesn't lessen my belief in God, or in Jesus as my Savior."

"The work of the devil," someone from the rear yelled.

A short man in a suit and tie stood to Lucy's right. "I'm the church's representative to the International Council of Churches. Most of us believe in the new doctrine that evolution is an unproven theory, and should be taught in the schools only as a theory next to truths of creationism, as the Bible tells us so clearly." He sat down. There were scattered claps in the audience.

Another woman stood. "It ain't right teaching 'eve-vo-lu-shun' to chil'ren. It just ain't right."

The Reverend got down from the table and walked to within a few steps of Lucy. He stared at her.

Lucy continued to look to the audience. "Thank you," she said.

"Thank you for your candor." But she saw the pockets of ignorance mixed with fear that what is taught might not be true. It was bizarre, really, these beliefs that even seventy-five years ago were rejected by mainstream America and then were driven back into rural America where, in isolation, they could live mostly unthreatened by reality. And Bain commanded respect from these isolated, stagnant minds. This was why he was in the wilderness of the north Georgia mountains.

"It's our faith," the Reverend said. "It's our faith that lets us agree to disagree."

"Praise God," someone said.

"But I'd be interested, Miss MacMiel, in what you really think."

Lucy stepped forward to address the audience. "I don't pretend to know the answers to the questions you've posed. I do know much of the science, and it is theory, a theory that has a great deal of evidence. But I do not know how God's will does or does not relate to evolution. I will not presume to know that answer."

"Do you believe in God?" the Reverend said. "That's your problem. You don't have the faith."

"I admire your faith, Reverend. It is a special gift to have faith as strong as yours." She looked to the audience to include them.

"Will you accept God? Will you take Jesus as your Savior?" he asked.

A few "Amens" filled the silence.

Lucy smiled and took the Reverend's hand in both of hers. She pumped it slowly. "I owe you a lot, Reverend. Of course I'll consider. And to you, my thanks, for bringing it to the forefront of my life. I will have important decisions to make." She let go of his hand and moved to regain her seat.

The Reverend threw up his hands. "Praise God," he said. He rocked back and forth. Lucy watched. "Praise, God. Let us pray," he said.

She lowered her head slightly but did not take her eyes from him as he led the followers in the Lord's Prayer.

CHAPTER 15

Lucy

Lucy dressed for a day at the office even though at the compound all the leaders and followers were casual. But Bain was not in his office at the time he had agreed to meet with her. She found him at the exercise room, a small space off the basketball court. He was in a session with a personal trainer, a woman in her mid-fifties, fit and attractive. He apologized but insisted he finish his training session, and joined her a few minutes later outside at a weathered picnic table, one of two at either side of the entrance. He motioned for her to sit on the seat planks and sat opposite.

"I'm tired of being kept waiting," she said.

"Apologies. I simply forgot. As I get older, I get more intense about health."

She stared. "These are serious charges against you. It's about time you took them seriously."

"I take them very seriously," he said.

She relaxed a little. "My job would be a lot easier if you acted like this all meant something to you."

He smiled. "You're right," he said. "I'll do better."

She leaned forward slightly. "I finished a deposition on your accuser. Alan and I were impressed with her demeanor. She'll make many people believers."

"Do you think I'm guilty, counselor?"

"I'm a lawyer, and a defender. What I think is not relevant."

"Guilt or innocence has to affect the quality of your defense."

"Exactly why I don't make judgments."

He laughed. "Don't even suggest that you and your paternalistic partner haven't discussed my presumed guilt."

She shrugged. "Do you know what the girl says you did?"

"Made love to her."

"That's all? No details?"

He shook his head.

"She or her mother never confronted you?"

"Neither said anything. It was a surprise," he said.

"Off the record here. I may not be judging guilt or innocence, but I damn sure am intent on determining whether you lie."

"They did not confront me. Do you believe that?"

Lucy paused, passing an unspoken judgment on his honesty. She did believe him, at least about this.

"You never touched her in suggestive ways?" she asked. "Never had sex with her?"

"I do not seek nor would I enjoy sex with underage girls."

"But you enjoy sex with older women other than your wife."

"My adult sex life is not important."

"Really? You think the prosecutor won't bring up your infidelities in court? He's not an idiot."

"Making love to my wife was always, from the first, something you need to know nothing about."

"I assume it was unpleasant, then."

"Do not draw conclusions."

"But you haven't contacted her for years."

"I was happy to be rid of her."

"Because she would not accept Christ as her savior in the ways that would satisfy you."

"Ridiculous."

"Was that the reason? Answer me directly. You'll be required to in court."

"It had nothing to do with her faith."

"Was it the sex, then? Not satisfying? Too infrequent?"

"It's more complex than that. I'm not sure, looking back, I ever knew my own reasons well. And I've suppressed a lot, forgotten the rest."

"Why not reconcile? For the children."

"I get angry when I think about her."

"After ten years?"

"There were things about her I can't forgive."

"You're a Christian. Forgiveness is what you preach."

"But between you and me, Ms. MacMiel, forgiveness cannot always be willed."

"It should not be a problem for a God-fearing, above-average, self-reliant preacher of the Gospel."

"She makes me angry. Memories of her make me angry. Untruths she said about me irritate me. What she's done to our children infuriates me. They hate me. I pray for forgiveness. But it doesn't come on the emotional level."

"How do you feel about this girl who's accused you? Can you forgive her?"

"Not necessary, counselor. I don't blame her. And she is not evil."

"So how do you explain her accusations?"

"I helped her. She's told me that many times. I think she would have been dead or on the streets now as a drug-ridden prostitute. I helped her see a better way. I think she appreciated that, and she saw me as the father figure she barely had in her early life, and I think she confused gratitude with desire."

"But why accuse you of something you say didn't happen?"

"I don't know. My guess is her mother led her into the claim. The girl is really good and kind in many ways. I think her mother saw the opportunity for attention, and financial gain."

"We'll never prove that."

"I'd look for previous behavior. I'd be surprised if she hasn't tried this before."

"The girl?"

"I would think the mother."

A secretary from his office ran up. "You have a phone call."

"Take a message."

"It's central. They're holding."

"Excuse me, counselor," he said. He followed the secretary back to the office.

Lucy stood and leaned against the picnic table, her arms crossed. He did not return after half an hour. He was too busy to see her when she went to his office. Angry with what she felt was another slight from Bain, she returned to Atlanta.

CHAPTER 16

Luke

Luke rarely saw Lucy at home for meals, and they almost never ate together any more. Mrs. Crowder had become familiar as family, and now took permanent care of Jennifer. Luke found Lucy affectionate when they were home together alone. She talked about her work; she was close to jury selection in the Hower Bain trial.

Lucy had become awkward around Jennifer, seemingly afraid to compete with Jennifer's open affection for Mrs. Crowder. Lucy fed Jennifer infrequently and rarely bathed her.

As Jenifer began to walk and feed herself, Lucy let her spend weekends with Agnes and Elizabeth, which gave Mrs. Crowder a break, too. Elizabeth had a separate garage apartment with five rooms behind the family house, and Jennifer spent nights with her. It left time for Lucy and Luke to spend alone together.

One night when Jennifer was away, they were both in bed and awake.

"I miss Jennifer when she's gone," Luke said.

"Do you wish you had children with Samantha?" Lucy asked.

"I don't know. There was so little love between us."

She reached and found his hand. "Is it still painful, thinking about Samantha?"

Not painful. But it was not pleasant. The pleasing details of dating and getting married had long ago been pushed from his memory by the anger and distrust that had become constant between Samantha and him.

"Did you love her?" Lucy asked before he spoke.

He hesitated. She'd never asked about Samantha before. Why now?

"It was an attraction at first," he said, "and a need for what I thought was love that kept me with her. Life was hard for her. She spent every waking moment trying to convince the world she was a person she was not. Why do you ask?"

"Did she love you?"

"She was incapable of loving, I think. She thought she could, but she was too insecure to think about others in loving ways."

"Love is strange," she said softly.

She seemed to be searching for some understanding that he couldn't fathom. He forced any doubt about her reasons from his mind and enjoyed her rare moment of affection.

CHAPTER 17

Luke

A few weeks later, Luke and Lucy were having breakfast together. She ate bran flakes standing at the counter, and he had eggs sitting at the table. It was a Saturday, and he asked her about the Reverend Bain trial, which was taking up all of her professional time now.

"He's an asshole, Luke. But I don't think he did it. Depositions are still going. And the girl has an active sexual history we can document."

"Will that soften the underage thing?"

"I doubt it. We'll prove he didn't do it. Not that it was a mistake, or that he did it, but it was just one of many opportunities presented to him that he never acted on."

Mrs. Crowder brought Jennifer in and strapped her in a high chair, and then left to change linens on the crib.

Lucy poured a few Cheerios onto the high chair tray. Jennifer started picking them up one by one and getting them to her mouth.

Lucy lowered her voice. "I don't like Mrs. Crowder's attitude."

This was a first for Luke. "Seems pleasant to me," he said.

"She's too lenient."

"How can you say that? We're never around when Jennifer's awake."

"The woman is whining, Luke. 'I don't want you to do that.' Didn't you hear it? It's not good."

He didn't remember, and he said so.

"I think we should get rid of her."

"Who would we get?"

"We'll find someone. Can't be that hard."

"I think Jennifer likes her, Luce. They seem happy together."

"You don't know that any more than I do."

"I see them here together on weekends when you're away."

She paused for a moment as her anger mounted. "Don't start, Luke."

He'd touched a nerve again. "More coffee?" he asked.

"I can't help being away."

"Agreed," he said.

"You were being critical, Luke."

He stood up and poured a cup of coffee for himself, his back to both of them. "That's not true," he said.

"You were."

"I was not," he said, still not looking at her.

Lucy stood up. "You feed Jennifer. I'm going to the office."

"For the day?"

She said nothing.

"It's Saturday."

She walked toward the bedroom. He listened to the shower and the sounds of her getting clothes from the walk-in closet. She left without saying goodbye.

She spent Saturday and Sunday away from home, and Luke didn't see her until Monday night. She was exhausted but surprisingly loving to Jennifer, and oddly pleasant to Mrs. Crowder, as if she'd forgotten about her being whiny. And she didn't bring it up again.

CHAPTER 18

Elizabeth

Elizabeth went to Aunt Pattie's Porch for dinner with Clay Palmer, the forty-eight-year-old bachelor minister at the Presbyterian church. She immediately noticed he seemed quieter than usual. This was one of their favorite restaurants, and he was usually chatty to the extreme.

Clay greeted her on the restaurant steps and asked how her mother was.

"She's fine, Clay. She's worried about her granddaughter."

"I wish Lucy would bring little Jennifer to church on Sundays. It's never too young to start."

"Lucy has no use for religion."

"Does she denounce God?" He'd asked it before. Many times, actually.

"More apathy than rejection," Elizabeth said.

He touched her arm to direct her to their reserved table. The hostess hurried to lead them.

"Lucy's busy with her practice, and Luke has to spend most of his time at the hospital."

"Who takes care of the grandchild?"

"They've hired a live-in nanny, a widow with grown children." They were at the table and Clay held the chair for Elizabeth.

"Would you like the wine menu?" the hostess asked.

"Yes, of course," Elizabeth said. She looked for a frown on Clay's face. He abstained from alcohol. She didn't really care for most wines, but she didn't like Clay's repetitive rants against the evils of drink. She drank wine to provoke him a little on something she thought he took too seriously. If he realized she didn't agree with his platitudes, maybe they would be less frequently expressed. She ordered a Sauvignon Blanc and Clay ordered, emphatically, a cranberry juice without ice. She did not like the taste of cranberry juice.

Clay talked of his upcoming sermon as they had salads. He recycled most of his sermons, but he felt strongly now about war, and he had decided to write a sermon on the necessity of peace in the world. She listened to his argument that progressed slowly and she found her mind wandering. How self-centered Clay was, in a kind, almost insecure, way that was more boring than offensive. They went to church functions together, and were thought of as a couple by most of the parishioners, she was sure. They went to an occasional movie, and he invited her out to dinner every few weeks.

"I've come to believe war is a necessity," he said.

She tuned back in. That seemed a new thought for Clay. "For salvation?" she teased.

He did not see the humor. "For the advancement of society."

"For men," she said.

"Women, too. Look to history. Women have directed armies for their purposes."

Elizabeth put down her fork and wiped her mouth with her napkin. "Really. Who exactly are you referring to? Not Helen of Troy, I hope. She could hardly be considered a warmonger. She was a victim of men's desires."

"I wasn't thinking of her. More of Cleopatra."

"But the Romans attacked her, didn't they?"

"She led the response. That Mark Anthony joined her to fight the Romans shows the degree of power and respect she had as a politician and a warrior."

"What's your point?"

"That conflict is a part of human existence. Men and women. War just happens to relate to men because they historically were the political leaders for the most part. But there are war tendencies in humans, male and female, just at different levels."

"Aren't you a little uncomfortable with the religious wars of the Crusades? Those were hardly induced by women." She sipped her wine and picked up her fork again.

Clay sighed with exasperation. "I'm talking about conflict. Not just territorial battles and invasions. Conflict with the butcher over the price of a ham bone. Conflict with a neighbor over the height of a fence. Conflict with the car dealer who sold you a lemon."

Elizabeth shook her head. "I don't get how you want to bring individual conflict into a religious context for a sermon about the need for world peace. War is among groups. You're going to use individual conflict to explain the devastation of war among nations." She paused. "If you're going to preach about world peace and how religion will play the major role, you need to stay on topic."

She sipped more wine waiting for him to respond. How common this was between them on their night-out discussions. They disagreed about almost everything. He even questioned the strength of her faith at times. He suspected she didn't believe in God, or Jesus as her savior. Well, she hadn't ever been sure about God's existence. She went to church to be with her mother, with other people—people generally pleasant to be with. And to volunteer when she could. That was important. But she did not see her church-going as laying bricks for a pathway to heaven. That was the way Clay saw his faith, although he would deny it. He believed church a necessity for eternal presence. Frankly, she thought that infantile thinking, but would never say so.

"You're right," he said. "I need to find ways for the church and its teaching to prevent war before it starts, and intervene when it occurs."

He seemed deflated.

"Of course individual human conflict can help in exploring ways to prevent political, racial, religious wars," she said in conciliation. "I didn't mean that. But there is a big step between understanding the reasons for conflict and war and the actions needed to prevent war, some of which may have nothing to do with religion or religious institutions."

He smiled, "Religion is essential. You're wrong there. I need to focus the role of the church in world peace. Keep it objective. Find actions that will promote peace, do more than just speaking out from the safety of the sequestered pulpit."

Elizabeth laughed. "You sound like the church will go to war."

"That's not what I meant," he said with irritation. But he saw her smile. "You were teasing me again." He took her hand. "I like being with you," he said.

Elizabeth knew she should say something. But she felt, at this moment, that she could not honestly tell him she had enjoyed the last few minutes. His thoughts were tiny rocks on a barren plain, his emotions tepid, stagnant pools, his ambition a dead battery. She wondered again why she went out with him on these excursions. And she determined this was the last time. There was no other male in her life, but she would not let that make her resort to letting Clay take up her time. She could find other interests.

She moved her hand from under his and signaled the waitress. "Another glass of wine, please."

She thanked God he talked about sports, now. He loved the Yellow Jackets, and she barely listened, distracted by an idea for a character in another children's book, without need to respond.

As they lingered over coffee, guilt touched her. She shouldn't have been so critical. Clay was truly a good man, if not dynamic. And she had enjoyed many evenings with him. She smiled at him. "This has been so much fun," Elizabeth said. "Let's do it again soon. On me, next time."

He laughed. "Of course we'll do it. But these are my treats."

He walked her to her car after they finished. She unlocked the car and as she went to open the door, he took her hand away from the handle with both of his. "I've been trying to say it all evening," he said. She looked at him, puzzled. "I love you, Elizabeth. Will you marry me?" She could not speak. Her feelings for Clay were so far from marriage that she never anticipated a moment like this. She felt awkward, unprepared, frightened at the response that eluded her. She swallowed.

"I'm honored," she said.

Now he took both her hands in his, as if he wanted to hold her. "Say, yes. Please, say yes."

She could not embrace him. "I don't know what to say," she said. She took back her hands.

"Of course it's a surprise. I'm so clumsy, here in the parking lot. I should have told you earlier. And you don't have to say anything now. Just think about it."

She felt a panicky need to be away from him. "Clay. That's so sweet.

Of course I'll think about it." She opened the door and slid into the driver's seat.

"Call me?" he asked.

She hesitated before inserting the key in the ignition. "Sure." .

"Soon?"

She wanted to smile but couldn't. "Soon," she said, and powered up the engine.

"Thanks for the evening," he said.

She nodded and closed the door. She could see the disappointment on his face. He stood to one side as she backed out of the space. She was consumed with the thought of how poorly she had responded. She jolted over a speed bump. He had blindsided her, and she had not done well.

A few minutes after Elizabeth had arrived at her garage apartment, Agnes came to the door. Elizabeth had taken off her dress and put on a robe. She met Agnes at the door.

"Well?" her mother said.

"Well what?"

Her mother made a move to enter but Elizabeth didn't move, blocking her way.

"Did you accept?" her mother asked. "He asked me, you know. He told me tonight was the night."

"I don't want to talk about it now," Elizabeth said.

"You couldn't find a better husband."

"Please, Mother. Good night." She closed the door.

Elizabeth called Clay the next day and told him that she wasn't ready for marriage. She thanked him for his kindness in asking her. Her mother said she was making the mistake of her life. Elizabeth told her not to invite Clay to dinner, which she was sure was on her mother's mind.

CHAPTER 19

Luke

Sandra Perez was not reinstated. Eileen was able to find her a position where she could finish her training, and within two weeks Sandra had moved with her children to Oregon. School administration would not embrace the obvious unfairness of her treatment, and Sandra decided not to start a long fight for justice when the result might be months, or even years, away from advancing her career. Eileen and Luke loaned her moving expenses, which neither school would support, and Luke helped her load her belongings into a U-Haul trailer on her last Saturday in Atlanta.

For weeks Luke heard nothing more about the entire affair until he met A.J. in the hall one morning. A.J. insisted they meet.

"We can use my office," Luke said.

A.J. gave him a determined glare and shook his head, saying they should go separately and meet in five minutes on the third-floor parking level.

In the garage, they walked away from the elevators and up a ramp so that A.J. could see the entire floor and the elevators, too.

"I'm being investigated," he said. "I've been warned by my lawyers to suspect all types of eavesdropping."

"For what?"

"The surgery thing. Taylor Grimes is the lawyer. He got a copy of the patient's chart. No one knows where it came from."

"What difference does it make?"

"They're going to use it as proof it was the wrong eye. I made the decision to operate at the time, so of course the old chart would be different."

Luke still wasn't sure about all the details of the case. Most of the surgeons had not discussed what they knew about it, although many of the non-surgeons were thriving on rumor.

"Sandra's doing fine," Luke said.

A.J. shook his head. "She could have been the one to start the trouble. She's capable of leaking that chart."

Luke didn't think she was capable, but he didn't see any advantage to arguing.

A.J. swept his gaze 180 degrees, but didn't appear to see anything suspicious. "I need your help, Luke. The dean has appointed the hospital CEO to chair an investigative committee. It's part of the school's quality assurance response. You'll be on that committee."

"I don't want to be on a committee."

"You won't have a choice. They're requiring every full professor to serve."

"I'll claim conflict of interest. You're my father-in-law."

"It might work, but I need you there." A.J. stared intently. "I need to know what comes down in that committee."

That would be not only unethical, but wrong.

"It will help the lawyers map a strategy before it goes too far," A.J. continued.

"I'm uncomfortable," Luke said.

"Nothing illegal. I'm not asking you to do that. Just keep me informed."

"It'll probably come to nothing," Luke said.

"Don't believe that," A.J. said.

Luke said nothing more, determined to avoid serving by claiming conflict of interest.

"When you contact me from now on about anything," A.J. said, "be sure it's secure."

They left separately, A.J. moving slowly and peering around with paranoid glances as he left.

Luke made the argument to the hospital CEO appointed by the dean of the medical school that he would not be able to serve on a committee investigating his father-in-law. There could hardly be a more valid reason for not serving. The CEO said it was a fact-finding committee to make a report, not to pass judgment. "I'll tell you, Luke," he said, "All but one of the committee members made the same argument, some sort of conflict of interest. Can't accept it. And the job has to be done."

At the first committee meeting, assignments were made and resources allocated. Luke was to investigate A.J.'s interaction with referring physicians, which was in question because of his frequent caustic and demeaning replies to referring physicians about their patients. A non-surgeon neuro-ophthalmologist would investigate the wrong-eye case, determine as many facts as possible. The pathologist was to investigate a charge of excessive surgery. The plastics doc was to rule out any hint of racial discrimination in hiring practices or in patterns of patient care. They had three weeks until the next meeting, a meeting for progress reports. A final report would be ready for the dean in six weeks, no exceptions.

CHAPTER 20

Elizabeth

Lucy spent days at a time at the compound in north Georgia preparing the Bain defense. Mrs. Crowder had become ill. She was still staying with Jennifer, but unable to tend to her to Lucy or Luke's satisfaction. Mrs. Crowder had diabetes and heart disease, and one evening, when Luke had an emergency surgery and Lucy was five hours away in the mountains, Mrs. Crowder dialed 911 and collapsed. She was still unconscious as she was taken to the hospital. Luke asked Agnes to take care of Jennifer until he could get free. Agnes took Jennifer back to her house, and Elizabeth agreed to take care of her for the night. The next day Luke found a temporary replacement nanny and Lucy had returned to be sure Jennifer would be all right. Mrs. Crowder returned three days later, her diabetes under control. Lucy had to return to Bain's territory and left as soon as she was sure Mrs. Crowder could function adequately.

A few days later Agnes and Elizabeth had breakfast together.

"I know you liked having Jennifer here," Agnes said.

Elizabeth remained silent. She dreaded her mother's early morning philosophies and homilies. On most days, Elizabeth ate in the apartment alone.

"We should bring Jennifer here to stay. She can't be happy in that condo with a stranger taking care of her."

"Lucy wouldn't allow it."

Her mother had, long ago, ignored Lucy's needs and desires. She barely said more than a few words to her for months.

"She'll start talking in coherent sentences soon," Agnes said. "She needs family around. She needs someone brighter, healthier, and wiser than that old woman."

"That's hardly fair, Mother."

"It's Luke who would see the need. He's the one to convince."

Elizabeth had cared for Jennifer enough that she saw the harm of her learning around a declining woman. And Lucy was not paying Jennifer the attention she needed from a mother.

As Elizabeth continued to think about Jennifer, she knew she had to do something. She'd talk to Luke. But it would be delicate, and she needed to do it without Lucy around. She needed to wait until the right moment, when Luke would be receptive.

CHAPTER 21

Lucy

The Bain trial was short. Lucy met with McCormick within hours, as the appeal was being prepared.

"It had to do with that girl. She shouldn't have been allowed to take the stand," McCormick said.

"I wish I'd had a man for a judge," Lucy said.

McCormick didn't look from the newspaper headline story he was reading. "The press crucified him."

"They branded him the far right. But he's not political, at least in a public way."

"That's bullshit, Lucy. That church is political. And it's right wing."

"You don't know."

"Don't tell me they don't push candidates of the faith."

"Name one."

"I haven't kept up."

"Well, don't accuse him, then."

"What's with this? He's a client. Proven guilty. You're acting like you're sweet on the guy."

She flushed with anger. "That's sexist."

"Really?"

"I'm not 'sweet' on a client, and you know it. You wouldn't say that to a man."

"It's not just me, Lucy. Most in the firm have wondered why you spent so much time at the retreat. You handed off two other cases. All to work away from the office. Few could understand that."

"It was the only way. He's a difficult client."

"Are you sure you want to handle the appeal? There are some tough times coming along."

"What exactly is going on here? Are you speaking for the firm?"

McCormick took a deep breath and exhaled. "It's rumored you've been sleeping with the man," he said. "Bain's people have approached Avery Sheppard for the appeal. I doubt you'll even be in on it, and I'm pretty sure the firm will be off the case soon. We're sure Sheppard will base part of the appeal on the quality of the defense."

"The defense was perfect."

"Not if the lawyer had sex with the client."

"That's outrageous."

"And unethical."

"That's not what I meant."

"Nothing about the appeal will be outrageous. It's only outrageous to you."

Lucy slumped down in a chair away from McCormick. "Is it you or the firm?" she asked.

"Senior partners all agree."

"Is this a reprimand, Alan?"

McCormick shook his head from side to side. "You could be disbarred."

"I've done a lot for this firm."

"Every one of us knows that."

"There is no proof."

McCormick didn't respond. He placed the appeal papers on the desk and stood. "The facts will soon be public."

"Help me out here, Alan. We've been friends now for seven years." She watched his face for some sign of emotion, but he was impassive.

"There is a generous severance package. All the partners want the best for you."

"And what if nothing happens?"

He walked to the door.

"Tell me! If no charges are brought . . ."

"The damage is done, Lucy. No matter what happens. The firm's hand is forced. There is no alternative."

She drove directly to Bain's mountain retreat. It was after one in the morning when she went to his suite of rooms, set off from the main complex. Storm clouds covered the sky. She let herself in with her key through a back, partially concealed access. He was sitting in the dark in the living room. She sat on the sofa to the left of his wing chair.

She could not sense his mood, his face covered in shadows. As the silence continued, her anger mounted.

"You told them. How could you have done that?"

"You failed."

"I didn't fail. The jury found you guilty. That's not a failure. That's an expression of their belief as to your guilt or innocence. For all I know, they were right."

He spoke softly, a sharp contrast to her angry words. "You screwed up the defense . . . that girl should never have testified. And your argument was unconvincing, to say the least."

"I'm fired, Hower. The firm let me go. They think you've hired another lawyer for the appeal. I think you told them about us to make the appeal valid."

"I will never go to prison," he said.

"You took on another lawyer without talking to me."

"He's not hired yet that I know."

"But you want a new lawyer."

He paused. "Yes."

She stood, wanting to hit him.

The rain began, pelting the windows, drumming on the roof. She could not hear if he said anything. She was shocked at the violence she wanted to do. She forced herself to relax, still standing. He stood and walked into the bedroom. She followed. His lovemaking was wordless, ritualistic, mechanical, violent, and even during the pain, she wondered at her arousal and the ecstasy of his domination.

CHAPTER 22

Elizabeth

At eight o'clock, Elizabeth came home to her garage apartment after a signing for her new illustrated children's book. Her mother was sitting on a sofa in her living room. Elizabeth switched on the lights. Agnes's head was back, her eyes closed, her arms splayed, her feet straight out, and her body bent at the waist to fit the curve of the cushions.

"Mother!"

Agnes kept her eyes closed. "Don't shout."

Agnes's left cheek was purple, and a few drops of blood pooled in the pinna of her ear.

"What happened?"

"I am leaving your father."

Elizabeth had heard this many times before, usually after some boisterous fight over nothing of any importance she could discover.

"You're hurt."

"I can't hear."

Elizabeth went to the kitchen and wet a dishtowel. She wiped the blood from the ear and folded the towel and placed it on her mother's bruises. She sat down next to her and took her hand. She loved her mother in spite of her crankiness and smoldering exasperation . . . and her refusal to listen.

"Tell me, Mother. I need to know what to do." "It's nothing."

"Did Daddy do this to you?"

"I'm no longer married to your father. I'm filing for divorce."

"Does it hurt?" Elizabeth asked.

"I will not stay in the same house with him. Never again."

"Did you fall? You might have a concussion, a brain hemorrhage."

"I told him I was tired of his arrogance."

"I'm going to call an ambulance."

"No, no. If you must call, call Dr. Amherst."

Thirty minutes later Dr. Emery Amherst arrived. He examined Agnes, who was now groggy, her speech slowed.

"What happened?" he asked Elizabeth.

"I don't know."

He asked Agnes specific questions, but now she was unable to answer. He checked her pupils for a second time. He evoked reflexes with a hammer. He took her blood pressure. "She needs to go to Piedmont. I'll call an ambulance and wait here to go with her. I'll call the neurosurgeon. She may need surgery."

"Can I go with you?"

"I'll be sure you can," he said.

"I'll be right back," she said.

Elizabeth ran to the main house. She found A.J. in his study. He was sitting behind his desk reading a book, legs crossed. She stood before him.

"You hit, Mother," she said. "The doctor wants to know what happened."

"Please, Elizabeth."

"She's going to the hospital. She may need surgery."

"There is nothing I need to do."

"Did you hit her?"

"Do you really think I would ever hit your Mother? She fell." Elizabeth was breathless. "The way you treat us."

He closed his book deliberately. "Don't start Elizabeth. Your Mother brought it on herself."

"She didn't hit herself in the face. My God. She had blood coming out her ear!"

"I told you. She fell. Don't dramatize everything. It's an irritating trait."

"She's going to the hospital. She can barely speak!"

He looked at her impassively, controlling some deep anger she knew she would never fathom.

"I'm sure she'll be all right," he said.

"You should pray to God she'll be all right. I can never forgive you." She tensed. "What have you done?"

He didn't answer.

She gathered her thoughts, forcing herself to calm. She could do nothing to him. She wanted him to suffer as her mother had suffered. But he had no feelings. He could not be hurt. When she left he was reading his book at his desk, as if she had never been in his presence. She rejoined her mother and the doctor as the ambulance was backing into the drive.

Agnes was operated for a subdural hemorrhage. She was semiconscious for two days and then barely coherent for another three. Elizabeth stayed with her, leaving only to get fresh clothes, toiletries, and other essentials. She talked to her father but he claimed heavy workload as an excuse not to visit. Luke visited daily, which gave her comfort.

When her mother was home, they hired a full-time nursing service for twenty-four-hour care and surveillance. Her father's crass insensitivities to her mother enraged Elizabeth and forced her to bottle her emotions for a while. But finally, when her father was home early enough, working in his study, she went in to talk. She had no plan; she needed only to relieve her mounting anger with a father she could no longer like, much less love.

"I'm frightfully busy," he said to her as she walked into his study.

She closed the door. "I'm your daughter. I deserve a few moments of your time." She sat down in a chair, rigid, with space between her back and the upholstery. Her eyes remained fixed on him.

"Don't start, Elizabeth. You've been a whiner your entire life. It's not easy for me now. And I won't put up with your self-righteous judgment."

"You've lost all respect for your family . . ." she started. "But I'm wrong. You've never had respect for any of us."

He shook his head.

"You've treated mother horribly. And not just now. Always."

"You have no right to make any judgments about your mother and me."

"I've lived with your arrogance my entire life. That gives me the right to tell you the truth."

"As you see it!"

"And that's not valuable?"

He paused. "No, Elizabeth, it's not valuable."

"You almost killed Mother. That's one truth you have to deal with."

"Don't be stupid."

"I'm not stupid. You should be prosecuted."

"You're dull, Elizabeth. You think like a mechanical clock buried in quicksand. Like your mother."

"Mother has always given you everything she could. It's not been easy. And not because she's stupid."

"Don't be emotional. It's not becoming."

"Every waking moment Mother has been working to make your life better."

"Really? You truly think your mother is responsible for my success?"

"She's more than you deserve."

"She's obstinate, and irritating."

"And that's why you hit her?"

"Stop it. It wasn't like that!"

"What was it like? What exactly was it like?"

"Your mother can be unreasonable."

"You were fighting?"

He pounded the desk in a burst of anger. "She was screaming. It was none of her business."

"What were you doing, Father? Why was she screaming?"

He paused, trying to control his mounting anger. "She demanded support for Lucy."

"What support?"

"I've cut Lucy off. Closed her bank accounts. Dissolved her endowment. I've disinherited her."

Elizabeth moaned. "My God, Father, why?"

"She disgraced us."

"You've disgraced us."

"Don't you say that, Elizabeth. Don't you ever say that."

"You've ruined Lucy."

His face was flushed now, and Elizabeth backed away a little, pushing the chair back with her feet.

"I've given Lucy everything. And you, too. Don't be ridiculous."

"I am not being ridiculous!"

"She's better than you, Elizabeth. She's prettier, smarter. She's everything you should have been."

Elizabeth flinched at the accusation. She had always thought he had never really tolerated either of them, but she had always believed he thought more of Lucy's abilities than her own.

"Why abandon her now?"

"She's been disbarred, she's adulterous, she's disloyal to her family."

"She's adopted. By you."

"That's always hung up in your craw, hasn't it? Her adoption. That you were better than she. You're your mother, Elizabeth. You'll never equal up to Lucy."

Elizabeth considered. In truth, although she didn't like to think about it, equating Lucy to his real daughter had never set well with her. But what difference did it make? Stop thinking about it. He was only trying to hurt her.

"If you think so much of her," she said, "treat her as family now. We are not the same, but she does not deserve to be treated as evil."

"I warned her about that fraud of a preacher. She wouldn't listen."

"That's no reason to disinherit her, even if she's not your own. Treat her as family, for God's sake."

He stood up and leaned forward, his hands on the desk. He was trembling. "She is family!"

"Not real family." She immediately regretted letting him glimpse her feelings about Lucy's adoption.

"Stop arguing," he said.

"You've taken care of her as family." Now she felt the duty to defend Lucy.

"And you've always been jealous."

"That has nothing to do with it." Elizabeth shut her eyes and held her hands to her ears.

"She is my daughter," he said. "Do you get that?"

Elizabeth felt a void in her heart that might have sucked her in from the real world.

"That can't be true," she said.

"Oh, wouldn't you like that. She was born to a woman in Puerto Rico before you were conceived." He calmed somewhat and sank back in his chair.

"Does Mother know?"

"Mother knows nothing."

"And Lucy?"

He shook his head, no.

Elizabeth could find no more words. She needed to destroy him. But she couldn't do violence. And he was right; she was not smart enough to hurt him with words. There was nothing she could do. She stood without looking at him and went to the door.

"Elizabeth," she heard him say to her back, but she did not hesitate. She was sure he'd admonish her, tell her to never break confidences. She might not be able to bear that. He said no more that she heard and she did not return, although she knew he had moved to the door and was watching her.

PART TWO

CHAPTER 23

Lucy
1989

The plane landed in Ghana an hour late. In the terminal, Lucy saw "MacMiel" written in magic marker on a cardboard box lid held by a thin black man in a loose-fitting white T-shirt and knee-length khaki pants, his feet in tattered plastic sandals. She glanced around for Hower Bain, but he was not in the small crowd that was quickly dissipating at the door where she entered.

The back seat of the ten-year-old sedan had lost most of its padding, and Lucy felt the coiled springs when, within a few minutes, the car encountered rough roads, many unpaved. Stones and clods of dirt banged against the undercarriage. The smells from the oil leaking on hot motor parts nauseated her, and when she took deep breaths, the humid air seemed to stick in her lungs like paste.

She thought she could adjust, but she was no better after almost two hours. "How much longer?" she yelled to the driver. His face was pocked with scars and his hair was hacked at shoulder length, bushy and uneven. She thought he was maybe fifty but it was impossible to tell.

"You be sitting back and enjoying the ride," he said.

"How long?" Lucy said, leaning to the side to avoid having to yell to the back of his head.

He turned only partially. "It be hard to tell. Look like rain." The clouds were low and the color of gray mold on old bread.

"How long without rain?" she asked.

"Sometime road flood in valley."

She had expected Howie to meet her at the airport. He hadn't said that exactly, but his last letter had said how he missed her, how he dreamed of being with her again. My God, how she missed him. It was beyond reason. How could she be in love with a preacher, a philanderer, a stubborn, opinionated bully with deceitful charm? He was ruggedly handsome with gross features, loud at inappropriate times, and often untrustworthy. Why couldn't she just be without him, let her life go on?

And why was she traveling in the wilds of Africa to be with him? Well, he had seized her thoughts. Why didn't she miss her family more? It was sinful. She rarely thought of their dull existence, their chronically compromised lives. She wondered if watching Hower manipulate the crowds, shelter the weak, give hope to the hopeless, would thrill her the way it always had in the States. His lovemaking was rough and all about him, but she craved his passion and his desire for her. It was all touch and smell and sound for him and she loved it—sweaty, bruised, and sometimes bleeding. It was inexplicable when she thought about it like this. It made no sense. But she couldn't wait.

The car slowed and came to a stop. A goat bleated. She sat up and peered over the rusted hood of the car. A herd of maybe twenty blocked the road.

"Blow the horn," she said impatiently.

"Don't be doing good for goats. They stubborn."

Lucy got out of the car and walked up to a man with a stick in hand. The stick was crooked in places, but the full length went from the ground to two feet above his head.

"Can't you get them to move?" she asked. He smiled at her with no comprehension.

She waved her hands as if to shoo them away, but his expression did not change.

"Do you speak English?"

"No anglais," he said.

Lucy articulated slowly. "Move goat. Make goat go away." The driver had come out to look over the herd.

"No me," the stick man said.

"What?" Lucy said.

"They don't belong to him," the driver said.

"Can't he do something?"

"We wait. Not long, maybe. But they ain't liking to be pushed too much."

Rain began to fall. Large drops the size of pearls splattered on her face.

"You get in car," the driver said.

She closed the door. The wind from the storm blew the rain on her. She tried to crank the window up, but there was no handle.

"You be sliding over to that side," the driver said as he got in. From under his feet in the front, he handed her a thin sheet of wrinkled newspaper for protection.

"My God," Lucy said.

Twenty minutes later the rain stopped as if a spigot had been turned. The sun blazed onto the countryside. The goats seemed distracted but energized, their coats soaked to the skin. Haphazardly they dissipated as if they were dissolving into the countryside.

"We be going now soon," said the driver over his shoulder.

"Is it much longer?" she asked.

She thought he wouldn't answer but eventually he said, "It be about the same, I believe. About the same."

They arrived at the settlement at twilight.

"We be lucky tonight, yes? It no good drive in dark," he said.

"Really lucky," Lucy said. She was sure her driver was immune to sarcasm.

They had stopped in a cluster of shacks and a few one-story houses. "You be good to wait here," he said. He took out her bags and got back in the car.

"Where are you going?" Lucy asked.

He pointed to the east. "Go for petrol. Leave early with the light."

"Where should I go?"

"Someone be coming."

"Who? When?"

He smiled and nodded toward the houses. "You be having a nice stay now." He closed the door and drove off.

Someone was coming out of a shack away from the road near a

clump of trees. A man bent over, pushing a wheelbarrow. He came up to her and put the wheelbarrow down. He stared at her.

"Who are you?" she said.

He went to her bags without response and placed them in the wheelbarrow. He left in another direction than the one from which he'd come.

"Where is Reverend Bain?" she asked as he left.

He said something in his native tongue and then was out of hearing.

She walked down the single-lane dirt road toward a frame house with a flat roof, a door opening on the front with no door, and one half-open window on the side.

"Hello," she called through the door opening. The interior was black. "Hello."

"Yes," someone said behind her. She turned quickly. A small black woman glared at her, her features indistinct in the dimness of the night.

"I've come to visit the Reverend Bain."

"Yes. He come back later. You come." The woman turned and Lucy followed.

"Do you work for the reverend?" Lucy asked, walking alongside the woman and adjusting to her methodically slow pace.

"He need me."

"What do you do?"

"What he need me do."

"Do you cook?"

"Sometimes." The woman was in her forties, Lucy thought. She had not looked at her as they walked, and she kept three feet between them.

"Are you from here?"

"I am born in this place here. Long time."

They walked by many shacks and houses. They came to a wide one-room house with a dim light flickering.

"Do you have electricity?" Lucy asked.

"We do sometime for a generator. But is broke now, maybe two Sundays or more."

They came to a larger one-story clapboard building that had two windows on each side, dimly lit and flickering with yellow light, as if with an oil lamp or a few candles.

A light-skinned black woman met them at the door, holding a candle anchored with melted wax to a wooden holder with a stick handle. "Miss Lucy," the woman said in clear but accented English. "I am Collette. This is where you stay tonight." The woman who had brought her had disappeared.

Inside, guided by Collette's candle, she was taken to a single bed with a small mattress. Stacked haphazardly at the foot of the bed was her luggage.

"There is clean water in the bucket near the sink," Collette said. "I'll leave the candle for you."

"Is the Reverend Bain here?"

"He's not here. But you rest. He sure to come back soon." Collette placed the candle on the floor.

"Is there something to drink?" Lucy asked.

"I put drink near your bed." Collette leaned over and moved an open glass bottle half filled with orange soda near the candle. "We put you straight when morning come."

Lucy dipped water from the bucket and swished it though her teeth, unsure that she could find her toothbrush in her bags. She took off her dress and laid it folded on the luggage. Collette was already lying on her bed.

"That woman who met me. Who was she?"

"She called Manny."

"She was not friendly. Is that what I am to expect?"

"She not like everyone. But now too she does not feel good."

"She's sick?"

"It was child in her. She vomit sick and not sleep well. Child passed now."

How irritating. This was not what she had imagined. She felt alone because of the dark, and because everyone she had met so far had treated her as if they were completing an unpleasant task. Collette, too, although responsive, seemed guarded and definitely withdrawn.

Lucy lay down on the bed, blew out the candle, and stared at the ceiling. Collette's deep breathing was only a few feet away. When her eyes adapted, she could see Collette lying face-up on her bed with no pillow. The moon descended below the horizon and clouds moved to block the sky. In the new dark, the air still, the heat stifling, she heard the occasional faint noises of something alive, moving. She let the tears silently roll down her face onto the pillow. She could not be sure when she exactly closed her eyes to sleep, but it felt like hours.

She awoke. Something touched her arm. "Lucy," Hower Bain whispered. "Sweet Lucy."

She reached up and touched the face she could barely make out in the dark.

"Come," he said.

She sat up, her heart pounding. She felt for her dress. "Leave it," he said.

"My shoes."

He picked her up in his arms and carried her out into the night. She wrapped her arms around his neck, and kicked her bare feet in the air with delight. In a couple hundred yards he carried her over the threshold of a house with a small porch and a portico. Inside, he stripped off her slip and panties and backed her against a wall she couldn't see, and took her with all the passion only a long absence could amass. When he'd finished, her legs around him, her arms around his neck, she whispered, "I love you, Hower Bain," and laughed with pleasure. He took her to a large bed she could only feel in the dark, carrying her, never letting her feet touch the wood-planked floor.

Howie awoke at first light. He put on a robe. She watched him go to the screen door, open it, and pick up a clear glass of milk with a flat stone covering the top.

"You're a milk drinker now?" she said.

"Room service only for you," he said.

She sat up on the edge of the bed and grabbed for a sheet to cover herself.

"I forgot to order," she said.

He laughed. "We eat in the dining hall with all the staff," he said. "This milk is special. Manny brings it special for your coffee. I asked her."

She stood now, looking around to collect what clothes she had been in when he carried her from Collette's house last night.

He flipped a switch near the back door and a generator started behind the building. The windows had shades but no curtains. Beside the bed there was a straight-backed, unpainted wooden chair in front of a rectangular pine table, the surface marred with scratches and dents. There was a wooden bench next to a cabinet with a sink. He went to the cabinet and took out a small electric coffeepot and a bag of coffee.

He plugged in the pot, poured water with a ladle from a bucket beside the door, placed dark aromatic coffee into the filter, and adjusted the glass pot.

How wonderfully ridiculous. Nude, with only underwear on, in a shack, making coffee with the man she loved. She leaned back on the bed and gazed at the unshaven face, the dark eyes now mysterious, absorbed in staring at her. His lips full with a scar on the upper lip, slight but definite, from some injury long ago he hadn't yet told her about. She'd ask someday, but not now. There was so much she had to learn about him. She needed to know everything, every detail of the how a master of human beginnings created a lasting, wonderful image, strong, rugged, interesting—and hers. What was it about Hower Bain that made her want to surrender to him every conscious moment?

She smiled as he brought the coffee and milk to her and placed it on a bedside table made from a tree stump.

"We have our own cow. Three, actually. Milked daily," he said. "I know you like sugar, but I forgot to ask."

"I used to like sweetener," she said. "But I've given it up with the cancer scare in mice."

He brought up the chair from the table, sat down, and put his feet on the bed near her knees, cradled his coffee cup in his hands, and grinned. "Welcome to Africa."

"Thank you, oh King of the Christians."

He laughed. "A king without many subjects."

"I've seen Manny and Collette. And the driver."

"They work here. They belong, but they always let you know they have an exit strategy. Many live offsite in their villages. And they serve their own masters. It's the way in this country."

She sipped her coffee, bitter and strong, and added a little more milk.

"Is it only with foreigners?"

"Who can tell? They're hard to fathom. They believe in Christ but they believe in lots of other things—medicine men, elders. Respected men, almost always cruel, who easily grasp their attention and are always there for them."

"Don't you have real conversions?"

"They almost all convert. It's a matter of intensity and degree of commitment. The Americans who came with me are the real converts. The natives see conversion as a necessity, like a driver's license or a vaccination."

"You seem to have the respect of the natives."

He thought for a moment. "Yes. I think so. But there is always a level of distrust."

She reached out and touched him. "You sound discouraged."

"We're doing a lot. It's more giving them what Western culture can provide than changing their chances of ascent to an afterlife. We do give them new direction, I guess. And we do make their lives better."

"Morality?"

"I don't think so. They have their own roadmap for right and wrong. And they have their own recipe for justice, which I find a little bizarre."

"Harsh?"

"More emotional than based on evidence."

He lifted his coffee cup for the first time and tested the temperature. It was too hot and he settled it back down on his lap.

She leaned forward. "What's up for today?"

"Today is devoted to us. And tomorrow, too."

Manny burst in through the front door. She seemed to have been waiting outside. She stepped directly to Lucy, not looking at Howie.

"Finish, Miss?"

"Yes, Manny. And thank you. I'll keep the coffee cup."

Manny picked up the still half-full glass of milk and left.

"She that way all the time?"

"That was more talkative than I've noticed before," he said, smiling.

A boy of sixteen delivered Lucy's bags from Collette's shack to Hower's house in two trips. Hower put on shorts and a T-shirt and went to the dining hall to bring bowls of oatmeal with a slice of dark meat on top.

There was no place to store her things. She'd have to live out of the suitcases. While Howie was gone, she searched for toiletries and makeup. At first it was a feeling, some premonition that someone had gone through her belongings. Tops of bottles were looser than she usually tightened them down. A comb was oddly placed in a side pocket. She went through a second, larger suitcase with her clothes. Things had been refolded neatly, but there were clothes missing. She closed the suitcases, and mentioned it to Howie when he returned. Not to worry, he said. He was sure someone had taken her clothes to be washed and pressed. Four-star service, he said. But it seemed more than that. She realized it was silly to worry and determined to forget it.

CHAPTER 24

Lucy

On the third day, Howie went back to his ministry, which took him away from the mission settlement. Lucy insisted on having something to do, and he introduced her to Carla, who was from Ohio and had handled most of the administrative work at the compound in Georgia. Carla seemed pleased to have legal experience around.

But there was almost nothing to do. Lucy found herself reading anything that was available, which wasn't much, and almost nothing that wasn't with evangelical fervor or directly related to the Bible. Within the week she began to spend most of her time without Hower, in his room. She'd found decades-old volumes of the Encyclopedia Britannica with interesting antique illustrations from the last century and bizarre descriptions of obscure and extinct things and ideas.

On the fifth day, Howie returned after dark. Just before bed she told him she was feeling useless. He gave her a kiss. "Go with Collette. She needs help during the week."

"I'm not a nurse."

"She'll show you what to do. She's trained many others."

"Is she a doctor?"

"Oh, no. She worked at a hospital for a while when she was in school. But she knows all the doctors around and gets help when she needs it. She gets medicines from the government health clinic. We get some supplies from the States."

"I don't think I can do that," she said. But he offered no other solutions, and in two weeks, out of restless boredom, she did start going on excursions to villages and towns to administer to the sick. She learned injections, and after a few weeks with Collette, was able to administer routine vaccinations to an entire village. Her days were saturated with purpose for the first time since her arrival, and she became less restless.

One morning when Lucy and Collette were packing the Volvo to make a trip to a distant village, Manny ran up to them and babbled in the local dialect to Collette. Collette turned to Lucy. "Manny's child is delirious with fever. She has no one to bring her here. I'll have to go before we start," she said.

"I'll go with you," Lucy said. "What can I carry?"

They followed Manny, walking at a brisk pace as Manny ran ahead.

Manny lived alone with her daughter in a single-room hut at the edge of a cluster of shacks and lean-tos.

Her daughter lay on her back on a straw pallet with one knee drawn up. The other leg was straight, and swollen to double its normal size. A dirty sheet was wrapped around her shoulder, and in spite of her sweat-covered skin she was shivering.

"She is called Pearl," Collette said to Lucy. "Pearl," Collette said to the girl, "What happen?"

"She think spider bite her," Manny said.

"When?"

"She don't know."

Lucy watched as Collette's skilled hands exposed all of Pearl's body and then focused on the leg.

"See pus? Snake teeth," she said to Lucy.

Lucy could not distinguish anything definite in the inflammation. "Will she be all right?" she asked.

"Bring water," Collette said to Manny. She took a syringe from her bag and drew up antibiotic that she injected into the left buttock. When Manny brought water she crushed aspirin in a cup and added water. Holding Pearl's head, she placed the cup to her lips. Pearl resisted and swatted the cup, which fell to the ground. Collette ground more aspirin and filled the cup. She talked softly to Pearl, calming her, and soon, after a few swallows, had the medicine inside her.

"We will need to bring back fluids with sugar and juice. She will need IV, too. She will not be able to eat until tomorrow," Collette said to Manny. She helped Pearl drink more water. "She will need more medicine. She will need three cups of water an hour. And I will give you a cream to put on the bite. Can you do that?"

Manny was trembling. She nodded hesitantly.

"I must go on my rounds," Collette said to Manny.

"I'll come back with the fluids and be sure she gets the treatment," Lucy said. "I can do the IV. You go on."

Collette left to attend her appointed village, and Lucy returned to Pearl within the hour and gave dextrose and saline. She redressed the leg wound, which was smelly and gross, but she forced herself to stick with it. By midafternoon the fever broke. Later, near sunset, Collette brought Paul and the jeep to carry Pearl to the infirmary. There was not room for both Lucy and Manny in the jeep and, without speaking, Manny rode and Lucy walked back to the settlement alone.

Pearl was laid out on a metal cot on a two-inch-thick mattress near where Collette slept. Manny would sleep on the floor beside her.

When Pearl was able to walk and eager to return home, Lucy and Collette helped Pearl back to Manny's hut. They walked back. Lucy said, "Will she be back to normal?"

The sun was setting and there was a gentle breeze that stirred the dust on the rutted dirt road.

"It will take time. She lost the child."

Lucy looked at her friend. "She was pregnant?"

"It was very small. Short like banana. But she lost blood. She will be weak for long time. I give her iron. We must be sure she take it."

They walked for a while. "Who is the father?"

"She would not say."

"You must have some idea."

"Maybe the boy who deliver the bags."

"And how does Manny feel?"

"She was surprised. But very sad to not have grandchild."

Lucy continued in silence, sad for the likes of the Pearls and Mannys, whose lives were cursed with so few comforts and joys. She silently thanked God for her own blessings—and she thought of Jennifer.

Wondered what she was doing now.

She rarely heard from Luke and did not initiate contact with him. She had written Agnes and Elizabeth once but had not received any letters in return. She had only one picture of Jennifer, a snapshot now more than a year old. She would write Luke and ask for more pictures. And she would send a gift to Jennifer. Something African and colorful, something to make her even prettier.

CHAPTER 25

Luke

Luke found a package in the mail at the condo addressed to Jennifer. The date on the postmark indicated ten weeks in transit.

Jennifer was staying with Agnes and Elizabeth for a few days, and he took the package with him to the hospital, then went to the house to have dinner with Jennifer after work.

"Jennifer's got a package," he said to Agnes and Elizabeth as he walked into the kitchen through the back door from the drive. "It's from her mother."

Agnes came forward and took the package. "We'll put it up for her when she's older." She walked unsteadily into the family room, still recovering from her injuries.

Elizabeth strapped Jennifer into a child's chair and tore a grilled-cheese sandwich into small pieces. She put a child's plastic container of milk before Jennifer. Luke motioned to Elizabeth to come with him, and he followed Agnes into the family room.

"I think she should have it now," he said to Agnes. "It's her gift."

"It will only bring pain to her. A child whose mother has abandoned her does not need to be reminded she's alone."

Elizabeth joined them, standing so she could keep an eye on Jennifer in the kitchen.

"It's Jennifer's gift, Mother, let her have it," Elizabeth said. "Not from Lucy."

"It won't hurt," Luke said. He reached for the package but Agnes backed away.

"You can't do that, Mother," Elizabeth said.

"Lucy left her family to live with another man. She has no rights."

"Lucy is Jennifer's mother," Luke said. "She will always be. You can't hide the fact."

"How can you support her, Luke? After what she's done to you. It's embarrassing."

"Don't, Mother," Elizabeth said.

"Lucy has so much more than you know," Luke said.

"Not enough to love her child. Or her husband," Agnes said.

"She just wasn't prepared for motherhood," Luke said.

"In the name of God, Luke, she was blinded by her need for sex with another man. Blatant adultery without a trace of regret or remorse."

"Don't punish her now. She's reaching out to her daughter," Elizabeth said. "There is nothing wrong with that."

"Don't get involved," Agnes said to Elizabeth.

"It's none of your business, Agnes," Luke said.

"Jennifer's my grandchild."

"She's my daughter," Luke said.

Luke took the package from her. "We'll open it for her after dinner."

"Don't tell her who it's from."

"Of course I'll tell her."

Elizabeth carried the package into the kitchen. Agnes went elsewhere, her leather-soled shoes pounding the wooden steps to the second floor.

Luke ate with Jennifer and Elizabeth. After Elizabeth cleaned Jennifer, they settled in the family room, Jennifer between Elizabeth and Luke, and they opened Lucy's gift. It was a handmade sleeveless dress in greens and yellows. An exact fit. There was a note taped to a shoulder strap. "For Jennifer. Love. Mommy."

"She does think about her," Elizabeth said.

"She cares," Luke said. "Jennifer always needs to know that."

Elizabeth dressed Jennifer and Luke took a picture. They would send it to Lucy using the return address on the package.

CHAPTER 26

Lucy

Lucy kept busy for months helping Collette. Often she wouldn't see Hower for days.

"You enjoying the doctoring?" Hower asked Lucy as they were dressing one morning. She was sitting on the edge of the bed. Her eyes were circled with gray and her face was lined with fatigue.

"No. I'm tired of it," she said. "I don't like traveling. And I don't like spending the nights. I'm exhausted when I get back."

"Collette said you really had the skills. The patients love you."

"Not anymore."

"That bad?"

"It's miserable. And these people stare at me."

"You're beautiful."

She sulked. Maybe once she was beautiful. But now it was a lie. "No, I'm not," she said, "My skin is dry and peeling. My gums bleed. I think my teeth might fall out. I've lost weight."

He took her hands and looked down on her. "It's getting to you."

She took her hands away. "Don't say it like that. 'It's getting to you.'"

"It happens to all of us."

"To you?"

"Sometimes."

She'd rarely seen him down about anything. He was a steam engine on a downhill slope, always at full speed. She leaned back against a pillow while bringing her legs up onto the bed. "My health is gone. I've got no spirit left."

He handed her her usual cup of café au lait. "I've got to get you better."

"Really? How do you propose to do that?"

"Lie down," he said, pulling on his pants. "I'll get Collette."

"Collette?"

"You know what she can do. She's better than any doctor I've ever known. I need her opinion."

The screen door clattered as the long spring mounted to the top pulled it shut.

In five minutes Howie entered with Collette.

"What's wrong?" Collette said.

Without reason, Lucy began to cry.

"Leave us," Collette said to Hower. "Go start your day."

"You might need something," Hower said.

"First thing I need is you be gone."

Lucy lay with her eyes closed, still sobbing softly.

Collette slid a chair across the floor from a corner to the bedside. She sat silently for many minutes and Lucy felt the onset of blessed sleep. Collette must have waited for her to awake. Almost an hour later a hot breeze gushed through a window blowing loose papers to the floor from a table; they were the first thing she heard. She opened her eyes, disoriented for a moment.

"Do you know where you are?" Collette asked.

"Of course I know where I am," Lucy said sharply.

"Lie still," Collette said. "Open." She looked in Lucy's mouth. She took her pulse. She put her ear to Lucy's chest above her left breast. Then she listened to her stomach. Then she counted the sores and scabs on her skin.

"Do you want to talk?" Collette asked.

Lucy began crying again.

"Is it easy to cry?"

"I can't help it. I don't want to."

"You're not with child, are you?"

Lucy forced a laugh. "Never. Never again."

"Are you sure?"

"I've had a ligation."

Collette didn't understand the word.

"I had surgery so I would never have children."

"That too bad," Collette said,

"Sometimes I'm sorry. But most of the time I'm never really sure I should have had the child I had."

Collette stared at her with concern for a while. "You're very sick. I think you must come spend time with me in infirmary."

"Without Hower?"

"I need you close. I worry."

"I don't want to be without Hower."

Collette nodded slowly. "It is what you want." She poured water into a glass from a bucket. She held Lucy's head up. "Here, drink." Lucy swallowed with difficulty. "Rest. I'll come when I can," Collette said before she left.

Hower didn't return until after five. Lucy was still on the bed, her eyes closed, breathing in rapid, shallow intakes. He ran to Collette, who followed him back.

"She's dehydrated," Collette said, touching Lucy's skin.

"I am not," Lucy said, close to delirium.

"I must take care of her. Bring her to me," Collette said to Hower.

"My God, Collette. Why didn't you do it this morning?"

"She did not wish."

"She's not herself," he said. "Can't you see that?"

Collette covered Lucy with a sheet without speaking, and Hower carried her to the infirmary and put her in a bed a few feet from where Collette slept.

"Will she be all right?" he asked.

Collette frowned. "Ask your God," she said.

"He's your God, too."

"He does not speak to me. Only to you."

With constant care, Lucy improved. Collette took a blood sample that had to be dispatched by the routine courier to the city where her friend could send it away for analysis. She obtained the Reverend Bain's approval, since the cost was high, and for a nonmember. He was insistent it be sent immediately, at any cost, and dispatched Paul in the jeep to make the seven-hour round-trip drive. He scolded her for not doing it earlier.

"She could have died," he said to Collette. "Can you deny that?"

"No sir," she said. "Thank your God she get better. I think she be up and around in few days."

"Our God, Collette. He is our God!"

"I forget sometimes he is God for all," she said.

CHAPTER 27

Luke

Mrs. Crowder died a few months after Lucy left for Africa. Luke found a replacement who did not work out well, and although Agnes suggested Jennifer come live with her and Elizabeth, Luke refused. He did not want to be separated. But Agnes had anticipated Luke's response, and Elizabeth had already talked to him months before, insisting she would be better suited to help take care of Jennifer than anyone he could find. Together Agnes and Elizabeth persuaded him to move from the condo to Elizabeth's garage apartment, which they had already started to renovate. Elizabeth was already settled in the main house; Jennifer would have her own bedroom near Elizabeth's room. An impressive system of intercom monitoring was installed to assure Luke anyone could hear Jennifer from anywhere in the house and garage. Luke moved in and within a few weeks he sold the condo.

It was a perfect arrangement. Jennifer thrived under Elizabeth and Agnes's care. And Luke was never concerned for Jennifer's learning with Elizabeth around. Most of all, he got to see Jennifer often.

In August, Luke took Jennifer, Elizabeth, and Agnes to the beach for two weeks; they went to the family house on Boar Island off the coast, near Savannah. The house had been in Agnes's family for three generations, and had three floors, wraparound porches on two levels that faced the ocean, six bedrooms, and five bathrooms.

Luke had a private room on the second floor with a tester bed and three large windows set in a front bay. Agnes slept in a master bedroom in the south wing. Elizabeth and Jennifer stayed on the first floor in adjoining bedrooms.

When the weather was fine, they spent mornings on the beach and afternoons on trips to Savannah and Charleston. Jennifer, almost six, was old enough now to know her real mother wasn't around. Elizabeth insisted Jennifer call her auntie, but the word had become, for Jennifer, almost synonymous with Mommy. Elizabeth loved Jennifer as her own. She had a unique ability to direct and shape an independent, competent personality in Jennifer, without the timidity, sentimentality, and indecisiveness that would plague most surrogate mothers.

After mornings on the beach, Luke often played tennis with a neighbor in the afternoons. Days in the sun were exhausting, and he was always in bed and asleep by ten o'clock.

It was a Wednesday night. Agnes had gone to a hospital in Savannah to spend the night with a friend who was hospitalized with terminal cancer. Jennifer and Elizabeth had been in bed for hours. Luke awoke slowly well after midnight as if still in a dream. He felt a presence, a gentle, caressing warmth like a breeze on a summer night. He drifted into a complicated dream, a court case, a subpoena to testify, a decision to operate, indecision about the patient's best interest, a lawyer who seemed vaguely like his father. He was startled awake. The absence of a presence registered as he drifted back to sleep as if hypnotized, and with the pleasant feeling he wasn't alone in the world. He didn't think to reach out. When he awoke well after sunrise, he sat up and looked around. He was alone.

Two nights later, he was nudged awake by the movements of sheets and covers over him. He stared into the moonless dark. A faint tension held the room silent. Someone was beside him; he was not awake enough to sort out who it might be, unwilling to fracture his contentment by too much knowing. He quickly drifted into a deep sleep and awoke to an empty bed the next morning. As he came to the first floor for breakfast, he saw Elizabeth in her room, folding clothes. "Good morning," she said without looking at him.

The next time Elizabeth came to him in the middle of the night, he awoke immediately, filled with a vague apprehension. His heartbeat quickened and he was conscious of his breathing. The space between them was real in so many ways; they lay on their backs without moving.

He could smell her feminine attraction mixed with her resistance to what might happen. The comfort of his awareness became a longing; the spirit of desire lay between them. He knew now that he loved her, a love that cradled pristine respect, admiration, and beauty in the want.

Her breathing quickened. She slipped her legs over the edge of the bed and sat up to leave. Apprehension seized him. He didn't want her to go.

He reached out and found her upper arm. She stopped moving, and he gently held her. She was trembling. She sobbed. He slipped his arm around her waist and pulled her closer to him. He had never seen her nude but the sensations of touching in the semi-dark excited him with imagined images. She lay back down and turned toward him as he adjusted his arm to cradle her head. Her full length was against him. He kissed her forehead as she was crying; he felt her relax. Her trembling subsided. Together through the half-open window they listened to soft swells of the ocean, the light touch of the wind in the live oaks, the rhapsodic calls of the cicadas.

CHAPTER 28

Lucy

For weeks, Lucy rested under the care and attention of Collette in the infirmary. She could only drink nourishment at first but then the nausea subsided and she was able to eat soups and stews that Collette prepared. Then, by sheer will, she was able to sit for short periods and take walks for a few hundred yards. Hower visited daily when he was in the settlement. He usually came after dinner.

This evening the sun had set. He pulled up a chair close to Lucy's bedside. Collette had propped Lucy up on three pillows before she left to give them privacy.

"She's still taking good care of you?" he asked.

Lucy looked her affirmation. "She's a special human being."

"Who God sent to us."

Lucy smiled. "I never get the sense that she believes in God, much less that He sent her to me. Not that she disbelieves. I don't think she needs verification of God to live her life."

"Like you?"

She thought for a moment. "I can see how you could think that. I'm not sure anymore. I don't know that that's wrong, though."

He leaned forward and touched her hand. "Never wrong."

"But you preach the need for salvation."

"For many, God needs to be a palpable presence in their lives. But not for everyone."

"And not for you?"

He leaned back. After a while he spoke. "That God exists in the hearts and minds of millions of people is enough for me to believe He exists."

"But you're not sure?"

"I'm sure that He exists in the hearts and minds of humans," he said.

"But not that someday you might kneel before Him and kiss the back of His hand."

"Why is it necessary to think of blood and bones?"

She rolled on her side to look at him. "So what you preach so passionately from the Bible does not come from a God with a presence somewhere? That He's a myth?"

"What difference does it make, Lucy? If the Bible is real to many, then it exists. That's enough to make the teaching legitimate. And useful for us to direct our lives."

"The same with the Quran?"

"My heritage gives me more faith in the Bible. But I'm sure the same thoughts could be applied to Islam."

"So you don't believe the Bible comes from a higher source than humans."

"I believe the teachings of the Bible have collectively brought ideas that most, if not all, individuals are incapable of creating on their own."

She rolled onto her back, looking at the ceiling. "Does God intervene in our lives?"

Again he thought for a while. "I prayed for him to make you well. It seems to be working."

"That's not proof of intervention."

He smiled. "Who cares about proof if it's working."

"So you do have faith in someone or something that intervenes. Answers your prayers."

"I don't know, Lucy. I do pray. It is easy for people to believe someone is out there who cares enough to take care of them. And I want them to believe that. Their lives are easier and richer for the belief."

"Is it healthy for humanity to take mythical symbols and teachings and make them fact? They're confusing symbol and reality. God created earth in seven days is a fact for the fundamentalists."

"I don't see the harm."

"But is someone taking care of you, Hower Bain? Keeping an eye out for you?" she asked.

"I don't know. I really don't."

She sat up on the edge of the bed. "I'd like to take my walk. Do you have time?"

"Of course."

He helped her to stand and she put her arms around his neck and smiled. "I love you, Hower Bain."

"And I love you, sweet Lucy MacMiel." he said.

CHAPTER 29

Luke

By the end of their time at the beach, Luke had surrendered himself to Elizabeth. She came to him in the night as often as she could, even though both believed Agnes knew. They were pleased when Agnes said nothing, and, for the last few days at Boar Island, Agnes volunteered to take Jennifer places to give them time alone.

They played tennis. Elizabeth was quite accomplished, with accurate groundstrokes and a surprisingly wide variety of shots. She'd played competitive college tennis, and still played regularly. She always wore white on the courts, and she was quite attractive, her skin tanned and her light, untethered hair bleached by the sun. Her level of accomplishment was like everything else Luke was discovering about her: so much value, always there, but never flaunted. And he loved most the blue of her eyes, and her petite shy smile, always quick to appear and stay for a long time.

They walked hand in hand on the beach in the late afternoon. "How do you feel about Lucy?" she asked one day as the sun was half an hour above the horizon.

He didn't answer immediately. Would Lucy always be between them rather than behind them? He couldn't let that happen. Lucy had affected their lives too much already.

"I love you," he said.

"But you must think about her. What is that like?"

Her words had the tint of an inquisition. But it meant a lot to her, he could understand that.

"I think about her. But not very often. I don't miss her or long for her, if that's what you mean. Mostly I wonder what it is about her that makes everything go wrong. Why does she make those terrible decisions?"

"She's selfish," she said and paused, "but aren't we all?"

"Not you," he said truthfully. She laughed, her hair ruffled by the offshore breeze.

"I've never understood why we've never gotten along," she said. "I've tried to love her as a sister. But she's difficult. And I wanted to understand why you loved her." She shook her head. "Did you ever wonder how you would feel if you ever admitted you disliked her? I think about that, and it doesn't feel good."

He stared ahead at the shoreline. "I think I hated her when she first left," he said. "She made me want her so much for so long. That's mostly gone now. What bothers me most is that she doesn't seem to be a mother to Jennifer. I'm not sure I can forgive that."

"Do you think she still loves you, Luke?"

Elizabeth's presence beside him lent a comfort he'd never experienced with Lucy. He could never have talked like this with Lucy.

"She never loved me, really," he said. "Sometimes I believe she married me to make me an unpalatable witness for the prosecution. But that's hard to think about, so I like to believe she was attracted to me as much as she could be at the time."

"What do you think happened with Bain?"

"I think she needed him in some way we'll never understand."

They strolled in silence for a while.

"She was always so intense—and unhappy," he said.

"I've wondered about that facet of her," she said. "I rarely saw humor, only sarcasm and ridicule. She was always on edge."

"Agnes couldn't help but remind her she was adopted, don't you think? I know it hurt her. She told me about the family the night of the accident. She thought A.J. discriminated against her because she believed one of her great grandparents was black."

"I don't know about Father. But Mother was relentless."

"She is so beautiful and so smart," Luke said. "And yet I think she has zero confidence. I know she felt unloved by everyone."

"But you loved her. She never appreciated the value of that."

He didn't respond right away. He had loved her, and in some ways he never lost yearning for the happy times they'd had together, times when she seemed genuinely unguarded and calm with who she was. He might still carry a wisp of nostalgia for those times, but he didn't love her as she was today; he couldn't transfer his caring for what she was in the past to what she was now.

"She's a memory now," he smiled, "without feeling." She squeezed his hand and put her head on his shoulder. They turned and headed back toward the beach house.

"I will never understand why Father treated Lucy that way," she said.

He didn't understand.

"I've never told anyone, Luke. And when I found out I was finally able to love her in ways I'd withheld since our childhood. Father told me one night in an angry outburst . . . he fathered Lucy. She is my half-sister. I think it happened during one of those conventions that the doctors love to have in exotic places. He conquered a hotel maid, and he went back to her many times."

When he saw her eyes, he knew it was true. "No one else knows?" he asked.

"No. Not even Mother. But worse, Lucy has never known. It was cruel."

"To protect his reputation."

Their pace slowed a little and Elizabeth was standing close to him.

"And what might have happened if Lucy could have known she had real family, a sister, a father," Elizabeth said. "That she was loved enough to know how to love others."

"He ruined her life," he said, almost as a question.

"There is no doubt he crippled her. And there is nothing that can be done now."

"You've stayed silent."

"What could I do? If I told her, no matter what her reaction, it could not change her for the better. She'd just be flooded with strong feelings against all of us, feelings that she'd be dealing with for as long as she's alive."

An evening offshore breeze was picking up. Elizabeth leaned toward him as they walked so he could hear.

"I don't know how to feel about Daddy. He needs me with all this trouble at the hospital. But I'm afraid I can't give any more. I know I should, and it worries me."

They walked on in silence, and by the time they reached the path from the beach to the house, he knew his love for Elizabeth had become an inseparable part of him, never to be doubted, and it would continue to grow with time, never to go away. He thanked God for Elizabeth. He'd been blessed in ways few others are allowed in a lifetime.

CHAPTER 30

Lucy

Lucy continued to stay with Colette, who helped her every day and night. Lucy was still too weak to prepare food or travel to the dining hall for more than one meal a day. She was taking walks in the early morning and late evening to gain strength while avoiding the midday heat.

Late one evening she left for a walk on her own while Collette tended an infant with fever brought to her for care. The sun had set more than two hours before, but the sky glowed with a nearly full moon well above the horizon.

She met no one on the path. The few houses she passed were set well back. After a few hundred yards she came close to the administrative offices, three one-story Quonset hut–style buildings. There was one where her desk still sat, unused now for months. There were no lights, but she heard Hower's laugh. Her heart tightened as another laugh of a woman rippled through the darkness. She must turn and go back. But her suspicion deepened.

She walked slowly down the dirt path that led to the buildings. She could hear voices. The man's words were too fast to be distinguishable, but he made exuberant sounds filled with pleasure. And the woman made cooing sounds and laughed.

The windows were dark. She stopped twenty feet from where the sound was coming. Her imagination cluttered her mind with images of two mating humans, distorted in bizarre positions. No. She halted her thoughts. I'm wrong. And there was silence. No more voices. No movement. Of course there was no one there. She had imagined it all. She stood frozen for a second, cursing her suspicions. It was being away from him for so long. She'd been ill, in and out of reality. She waited and heard nothing more. She turned, walking silently so she could still listen, but there was only emptiness in the building behind her.

"Was the walk pleasant?" Collette asked when she returned.

"Do you know if Reverend Bain is here tonight?"

"Yes. I see him."

"When did he get back?"

"I saw him at the dining hall."

Lucy slipped out of her dress to lie down. Sleep did not come, even after Collette turned off the light and went to bed. The sound of Howie's laugh stayed with her, as real as if it had happened.

CHAPTER 31

Lucy

Lucy continued to improve, gaining weight, able to concentrate enough to read. She was asleep when Collette returned after dark from her monthly trip to the city. Collette shook her awake.

"Here." Collette removed medicine pills from a bottle. "This will be good for you." Lucy took the ladle with water from the bucket and swallowed the pills.

"What was that?" Lucy asked about the pills.

"The tests return," Collette said.

"What is wrong with me?"

"I asked doctor about you. He speak long. He said he see cases." Collette took other pills from another bottle. "You need these," she said.

"What are they?"

"Vitamins. Iron. Your blood thin. You do not clot good. And you no fight infections."

"What do I have?"

"The doctor look long at your blood and hear me tell of you troubles. He is thankful you getting better."

"What is it, Collette?"

"Something you eat. In food. A very little, or it kill you first time. But it no accidental now. No, no. Now you getting better living here with me. It no longer goes in and you get better. No way it be accident."

"You mean if I hadn't come to the infirmary, I'd be dead."

"The doctor, he say, 'Sure. She would have died.' Exact words."

"What was it?"

"Poison. He say in Ghana it probably something to kill rats."

"Rat poison?"

"We try hard now. Remember all you ate before you came to infirmary."

"I never ate rat poison."

"It bitter, doctor say. You eat strong foods?"

"I always ate cereal for breakfast. Sometimes oatmeal. Sometimes canned fruit. I ate fresh bread for lunch sometimes. Soups. Goat cheese."

"From what doctor say, you might know something different."

"I don't think I ever noticed any change in taste. In the evenings I ate the stew and the pasta at dinner."

"Those spicy?"

"You know, Collette. They are often spicy."

"That might be time for me to look."

Lucy was sitting up now. Collette sat on a stool.

"Why would someone want to poison me? Could it be meant for someone else?"

"I do not see it easy," Collette said. "Maybe."

"But many people do not like the whites," Lucy said.

"I think no one just kill you for white."

"I'm afraid, Collette."

"I check food. Look to cooks and servers."

"Can I help?"

"You still sick. I do it quick."

Lucy was still awake when Hower came to her at Collette's. He sat on the foot of the bed. "Collette told me," he said. "Poison. It must have been meant for someone else."

"It seems to have gotten to me every time."

"And you never tasted anything weird?"

"A lot of that food served at night in the dining hall tastes weird."

"Collette has found no one else sick like this."

It had to be put in the food. How else could it have been done?

"Collette would know if others are affected," Hower said. "She thinks now the person would have to do it while serving you. While you were watching. Did the same person serve you every time?"

"It was never consistent at the dining hall. There are usually two or three serving. The person closest to the food at the time of my arrival served me."

"And I was usually with you when I was here."

"It must have been small amounts so I wouldn't taste it, and it had to be consistent for weeks, if not months, to have its effect."

Collette returned. "I searched the kitchen," she said. "There are jugs of rat poison in each room. Hammond said they kill three or four a night—at least those are the ones they find."

"Obviously it wasn't accidental," said Hower. "The target was too specific."

"I'll get the cooks. We'll ask them."

One by one Collette brought the cooks. Each one was puzzled. None appeared guilty. Each employee searched for ways it might happen but came up with nothing not already considered.

"We'll have someone watch every night when you eat," Hower said.

"I'm not eating there anymore. You can't believe I could do that," Lucy said sharply.

"I'll prepare food," Collette said. "That way I know."

Hower stood. "I want you back home with me," he said to Lucy. He looked at Collette.

"It be soon, for sure," Collette said.

Two days later Lucy moved back with Hower, and twice a day Collette brought Lucy food she herself had prepared.

CHAPTER 32

Elizabeth

Elizabeth went to Luke in the garage apartment after midnight, slipping into his bed, placing the monitor to Jennifer's room on the bedside table.

"You awake?" she asked.

He kissed her. "I am now."

She fluffed up a pillow for her back and got in, pulling the covers over her and taking his hand.

"People are beginning to treat me strangely, Luke."

"Who?"

"People at school, mostly. Other teachers, parents."

He rolled over to see her better in the dark of the room. "What did they say?"

"It's nothing specific. It's how they look at me, as if I had some terrible disease and they don't know if it will kill them, or they have some caution, as if I'm not what I appear to be."

"Could be your imagination."

"I don't think so. I think it's the rumors about A.J. They're afraid to ask me about it. And they're not sure who I really am."

Luke rolled over on his back, put his hands behind his head on the pillow, and stared toward the ceiling. "It was in the paper again this morning," he said.

"Did you see the editorial? It called for investigation, prosecution, and major reform."

She had followed the papers closely. There were charges of racism surfacing. From the billing records, A.J. was quick to operate on poor blacks on Medicare. "What is going on?" she asked.

"The ad hoc professors committee will meet soon."

"He's not confided in me or mother. We don't know what to think."

"He'll need you."

"He's never needed any of us."

"I think he's always depended on you and Agnes. Since I've known him," he said.

"No, Luke. He's treated mother as an intellectual deficient and ignored her, as if she were an irritating chicken squawking in a barnyard. And he's always thought Lucy superior to me in every way. He's told me that at times when I've frustrated him."

Luke took her hand. "It's inexcusable."

"It's not been easy thinking he might be a crook," she said. "A surgeon without morality."

"But no one is all bad. He's done a lot of good. He's been a teacher, a healer, a fundraiser. He's created a center for patient care."

"If he did operate on the wrong eye and then cover it up by doing more surgery and blinding a man . . ."

"It will be hard to sort out."

"But the family knows. And someone in the department must know the truth."

Luke was silent. She listened to the soft whisper of his breathing. She loved him unconditionally. She would never believe he could do what her father was accused of. If he had, would her love protect her from ever accepting the truth and judging him in ways that might turn her love sour? She couldn't know. But she could not escape her feelings, that she didn't have paternal love for her father anymore—or respect. Worst of all, she knew that she believed him capable of all that he was accused of.

"Is he guilty?" she asked.

Luke hesitated. "I've come to believe he could have done it."

"Why? What about him made you believe that?"

"Maybe it's always been in the background. But he fired a good and competent fellow who knew about the case. It was unjust and he refused to make it right."

"You knew her?"

"I helped train her."

"Is she doing all right now?"

"I think so. But she was a few months from finishing. Leaving this program affected her career. I've never felt good about it."

She closed her eyes to the dark, her lids damp with tears. Luke sat up and put his arm around her.

"I don't know what to do," she said.

"You'll make the right choices," he said. "You always have."

She wasn't sure. Maybe the right choice was to speak out. Lucy spoke out. She acted as if she hated father. In many ways she and her father were too much alike to ever agree on anything. Lucy was lucky to be away at a time like this. She wasn't expected to do anything. She hadn't pretended to love him all these years. But I did, Elizabeth thought, and I can't remember if I ever did really love him. I just can't remember a time.

"What will you do, Luke?" she asked. "He'll expect you to back him."

"I don't know," he said.

"But it will come to that, won't it?"

He didn't answer, but she did not doubt he knew it was true. "You'll be asked to speak against what you believe. Maybe even lie," she said.

He held her tightly for a few seconds.

"I love you," she said. She could feel his heart beating.

CHAPTER 33

Luke

"You ready for this?" Luke asked Tim Roberts, chair of the committee investigating A.J. and CEO of the hospital, who was already sitting at the head of the rectangular oak table. There would be eight members attending today.

Tim laughed. "God, no. It's a fucking catch-22. If we find nothing, people will believe I didn't look hard enough. A cover up. If we find wrongdoing, it happened because I wasn't doing my job as CEO."

"No one can blame you."

"They can and they will. I've come close to resigning. Something blown up this big always takes down innocents."

"The newspapers have been relentless."

"They're focused on the medical legal aspects. That's the tasty stuff for them, and they can speculate for eternity."

The other six members arrived within a few minutes. Some had already given reports verbally at another meeting. Surgical volume. Visual results. Re-ops. Today sensitive information was bound to come out. There had been absolute secrecy outside the committee room. The administration demanded there be no discussions among the members, and it was pretty much adhered to.

Tim called the meeting to order. The ocular pathologist went first.

"I've reviewed all the MacMiel transplant slides. More than a thousand slides representing more than eight hundred cases. All MacMiel's. Eighteen percent were trauma, scars mostly, but also corneal blood staining. All had pathology confirming the clinical diagnosis. Another twenty-two percent were post-infectious and all the pathology matched the clinical findings. Almost all the rest were bullous keratopathy, Fuchs' endothelial dystrophy, and the like. In these cases, forty-three percent had no pathologic changes to confirm the diagnosis."

Tim as CEO didn't see the significance, and he spoke up. "Does this mean that these grafts were done without indication?"

The pathologist nodded. "I checked the charts. Visual acuities varied from multiple examinations, as would be expected. Some were photographed, but rarely with high-magnification slit lamp biomicroscopy. Besides, most of these conditions have fluid in the cornea, and it's hard to evaluate on path specimens for degree of fluid and its effects on vision. I checked corneal thickness measurements of all surgeons. When measurements were present, thickness seemed to correlate directly with poor vision. But there was a disturbing finding when I correlated those grafts removed by MacMiel that had no pathology with pre-op corneal thickness and visual acuity. In one hundred and eighty three, the corneal thickness was normal or within the errors consistent with measurement techniques and," he paused, "in fifty-eight cases, at least two visual acuity measurements in the last two months before surgery were better than 20/40."

"He was operating on normal eyes?"

"Functional eyes. There is always a surgeon's judgment, but no other corneal surgeon has these findings." He looked around the room. "And to make it worse, even though his rejection rate was only a few percentage points above colleagues, many of these patients did not have functional vision in the eye after the transplant."

"They were blind?" Tim asked.

"Legally 20/200 or worse."

The glaucoma specialist rose to speak. "The glaucoma statistics are not good. I found forty-two grafts followed in glaucoma clinic that were referred for decreased vision after transplant surgery. All had been treated for graft rejection with steroids."

"Steroids cause glaucoma?" Tim asked.

"In a certain percentage of patients, if used long enough."

"Steroids are routine," another of the corneal surgeons countered.

"I know, Jerry, but twelve of these patients had cupped out optic nerves and were blind or had only light perception. The glaucoma caused by the steroids was missed. Often the pressures were in the fifties." He looked to the corneal surgeon. "You don't miss those patients. Your post-ops aren't in our clinics."

Cornea said nothing.

"Many of A.J.'s patients are followed by the fellows," Luke said. "He may not have known."

"He may be your father-in-law, but he still has the responsibility for the patients he operates or supervises. This is malpractice."

Tim held up his hand for silence. "Strong words. How many of you would agree this is malpractice? Raise your hand."

All agreed.

"What about the indications?" Tim asked Cornea.

"It's tough. We try to help people. Advice for surgery is individual with each surgeon."

"He was building an empire on income from clinical practice," Neuro-op said. "Grossing three million a year."

"And taking home a third of it. I've reviewed the figures with Barry."

"It's worse," Pathology said. "I looked at gender, age, and race. I compared A.J.'s stats with others. Eighty percent of his cases were on blacks compared to forty-six percent for the other surgeons. All were Medicare, or self-pay. No indigents. Not so with the other surgeons."

"I've seen his caseload and payment stats," Tim said. "He operated on those who could pay full surgical costs."

"Of course he did a lot of Medicare. That's the age group that gets in trouble," Cornea said. "Don't pile on with wrong conclusions."

"But his is almost twice that of other practices reviewed," Tim said. There was a discussion and agreement among most in the room. "Tell us, Luke, about the details of Sandra Perez's dismissal," Tim said.

"I talked to her twice by phone recently. She's finishing her fellowship in Oregon. She confirmed and clarified what I've already told you."

"I hear he tried to block her appointment in California," Retina said.

"I don't know anything that would make me believe that," Luke said. "But he did dismiss her. He did it through human resources without a trail, but two of the staff readily admit he was the one to put the pressure on to dismiss her. I was told Modesto Sanchez wrote bad evaluations a few weeks before the dismissal. I talked to him at the time and he admitted it. A.J. had written the evaluations for him to sign. But I asked him recently and he refused to be involved. He won't confirm or deny A.J.'s activity."

"But A.J. was covering up," Pediatrics said, her face wrinkled with concern.

"There is no doubt," Retina said. "Wouldn't you agree, Luke? Even though he's your father-in-law."

Luke nodded. "I thought so at the time and I've never been comfortable about it. But it would be extremely hard to prove. Even if Modesto was forced to speak out, a skillful lawyer could make A.J.'s actions seem within the boundaries of his duties as chair. They'd defile Sandra, too. It's part of the technique to justify his action."

"She was a good fellow," Cornea said.

"I've always thought that," Luke said. "Me too," Pediatrics said.

"And all of her other evaluations were excellent."

More opinions were expressed. Updated data were reviewed. "What are we going to do?" Retina finally said.

"We're not a jury," Tim said. "Guilt or innocence was not our charge."

"But the facts speak for themselves," Pediatrics said.

Tim stood still at the head of the table and raised his hand for the attention of all. "My responsibility is to the chancellor at this point," he said. "I need accurate reports from each of you. Factual. Supported. Write them yourselves. None of this can be leaked, and it cannot be lying around on a secretary's desk. Hand-deliver it to me. I'll consolidate all reports in one and type it myself. I'll bring the original to each of you for signature as committee members. I will make one copy and secure it where only I and the chancellor can access it. We've done our job. It hasn't been easy. But I thank each of you."

They all stood to leave. "And I know you know it," Tim said, "but I must say it again from a legal standpoint—and this information will undoubtedly be sought when the legal battle becomes intense—do not discuss this with anyone, even among yourselves. Justice must not be hindered by the rumor mill inflating or ignoring key data."

The meeting adjourned.

Luke went straight to his garage apartment after the meeting. A.J. had left a message on his answering machine to call him. He said he was calling from a phone booth at a convenience store near the house.

"Meet me," A.J. commanded without greeting. He said he'd be parked in a school parking lot nearby.

Luke undressed and put on comfortable sweats. He drove to the school. A.J.'s was the only car in the lot, and he had parked in the shadows of the school building. He stood beside his car; he got into Luke's car without a word until the door was closed.

"Drive around," he said. "I can't tell if my car is bugged. Probably illegal stuff by private investigators. The lawyers say anything is possible for the prosecutors to build a case. They've already started."

Luke pulled out onto a residential street where there was little to no traffic after dark.

"I wouldn't think they'd bug your car. Not yet," A.J. said, mostly to himself. "What happened?" he asked.

Luke pretended he didn't know what A.J. was talking about. He said nothing.

"The committee!" A.J. said.

"It's confidential, A.J."

"I'm family, Luke."

"We've been instructed to say nothing, especially to family and each other."

"So it's bad. If it were good, you'd tell me."

Luke shrugged involuntarily.

"Don't tell me details, then. Just tell me what you think I should do."

"There is nothing I can advise. I don't know what's best."

"Are they going to make recommendations? To whom?"

A.J. seemed uncharacteristically threatened by this committee. Luke realized that for the first time ever, A.J. was feeling the hopelessness of being out of control in a crucial situation.

"I can't say, A.J."

"No one will ever know. I wouldn't say anything. Even if they guessed it was you, no one would care."

"I won't go against my word, A.J. I can't do it."

A.J. slammed his fist on the dashboard. Luke braked to a stop. "Don't you ever go against me, Luke," A.J. said. "I mean it. I need your support. Information has dried up for me. I've got to know what is going on."

Luke angered, ready to lash out at him, but he held back. There would be nothing gained by arguing with A.J.

"Goddamn it," A.J. said loudly. "Talk to me."

Luke reversed direction to take A.J. back to his car.

"You'll regret this, Luke. I still have friends in power. You'll regret this more than you can imagine."

Luke said no more in the few minutes it took to get to A.J.'s car, and A.J. left without a word.

CHAPTER 34

Lucy

Lucy's spirits lifted the first night she was back with Howie. She was too weak for sex, and he gave up after two brief tries, an hour apart.

She was awake, content in the pleasure of being near him. She felt safe and, for the first time in months, that the possibility of imminent death was not with her.

He was awake, too. The sliver of the new moon was visible in the window, and weak pewter light flowed into the room onto the floor. Her low-heeled shoes from before she got sick were still there. He had not moved them.

"How are the conversions?" she asked.

"Slow but steady."

"Are you still traveling to the villages?"

"Collette needs you back to help with the vaccinations, and directing referrals. I've been working on the water supply to three villages. We're digging wells. The river water is not reliable, and the sewage is not contained and drains near where they work and bathe. Most of it is education, but the natives are resistant to take on new ways, and sometimes the language barriers are too much to be effective."

"Do you miss Georgia?"

"I miss the States, sometimes."

"Has anyone come after you?"

"I had heard at one time there was an attempt at extradition. But we're too far into the interior to be found easily."

"But do you miss the rallies? The TV. The crowds."

He rolled over to face her. "You've always thought it was about the power, haven't you?"

"It was. You can't deny it. You loved the swell of crowd responses. The healing." She laughed. "Did you ever heal a serious disease?"

She sensed the pulse of anger in him. "I helped more than I didn't."

"You were curing homosexuality. I saw it the first night."

"I put ideas into minds that might or might not stay. But where's the harm?"

"You treat them as diseased inferiors. Crush their self-confidence."

"Maybe their self-confidence could improve if they thought they were more mainstream in their appetites. Really. It's about how you climax and who you do it with. So what's wrong with making a mental shift from man to woman?"

"You're impossible," she laughed. She turned with her head on her hand supported by her arm and touched the side of his face tenderly. "I don't doubt you anymore," she said.

"I'm not a fraud," he said.

"Many believe you are."

"Well, not the ones I help."

"Will you go back if you ever can?"

He thought for a moment. "I don't know. But I think I would."

"For the power? The glitter?"

"Life is easier in the States. That's what I think about."

She ws asleep when she heard the generator kick in. Howie was brewing coffee. She sat up and wrapped herself in a tattered afghan. Howie handed her an almost-full cup of hot black coffee. "I'll get the milk," he said. "I hope Manny remembered."

She took a sip of unaltered brew. It was the first coffee in weeks. It was strong and bitter; unused to it, she made a face involuntarily.

"Manny's out of the routine," he said from outside the door. "I'll be back in a moment."

She tried another sip but put the cup down. The taste was unpleasant without her milk to blunt the bitterness. And she thought of how bitter her daily coffee and milk had been. And then it was clear. It was the only source of food that had not been investigated by Collette. Only a little milk, but the coffee was so strong she might never know there had been poison.

Howie returned. He took her cup to pour milk from a glass.

"No!" she said.

But he had already started.

"That could be it. Poison in the milk. I would never detect it." He set the milk down in the sink.

"It's possible," he said.

"Could Manny want to do it?"

"Not Manny. I don't think so."

"Is there anyone else?"

"They milk the cows by hand. One of the milkers would probably have access to the milk before Manny brought it. Any of the cooks."

"Goodbye to coffee with milk for a while."

"Can you drink it black?" he said handing her cup back.

"I'll pass," she said.

Later in the day Collette brought her lunch. Lucy told her of Manny's milk delivery. Collette went to investigate. In a couple of hours she was back.

"It is possible. But I find no one who would want to. They are mystified."

"What about Manny?"

"I do not know."

"Does she have a reason to dislike me?"

Collette looked away and down and stayed silent.

"What is it, Collette? Tell me. You are my friend."

"It is long time now."

"Tell me what I did wrong. I've never hurt Manny."

"It is not that. No, no."

"What then?"

"Manny think Pearl's baby come from the Reverend. She want that. To have grandchild smart and strong. She think that it happen when Reverend teach Jesus to Pearl."

"He wouldn't do that."

"It not his child. It the boy who delivers things," Collette said.

"The suitcases?"

"He the one. He tell me." Collette thought for a moment. "Manny think you come and Pearl never get her grandchild she want."

"That's crazy."

"She simple woman. Worried about future."

"She should be stopped."

"I don't think she do it. She not mean. I just say she might have reason. But I don't think she the one."

"Will you ask her?"

Collette looked distressed. "I ask around," she said.

That night Hower got back from travel well after dinner. She blurted out the news to him. He was silent.

"Well? What do you think?" she asked.

"You're too suspicious," he said. His defensiveness surprised her.

"It's possible, Howie. Collette told me of Manny's devotion to you. She wanted a grandchild of yours. By Pearl."

He did not respond. It was as if he couldn't find the argument to refute it. She wondered if Pearl had carried his child. If the charges in Atlanta were true, he might very well have taken advantage of a girl here, in essence away from the public eye. That kind of man can't help himself.

"You didn't screw that girl," she said. "Did you?"

His eyes blazed. "Don't start with that shit."

"Did you?"

"Why would I take advantage of Pearl? She's not attractive," he said.

"She's a child. If you craved children."

"I've never 'craved' children."

"Well, you've craved women. Lots of them."

"Not children."

"But grown-ups."

"I'm not promiscuous, Lucy. Don't try to imply that."

"Bullshit. You were screwing anyone who was breathing in Georgia."

He turned away from her. "I won't listen to this," he said.

"Did you screw someone here when I was sick? I thought I heard you. Then I thought I imagined it."

"You were delirious."

"Did you?"

"Of course not."

But she didn't believe him now. Even if he were innocent, she knew he was capable and would have done it if the opportunity arose. She was sure. And maybe Pearl did abort his child. Maybe he was guilty. After all she'd done to prove his innocence in Georgia. Maybe she was blinded to his guilt, and doomed to failure in front of a jury. She probably looked like a lovesick defender arguing for the acquittal of the devil himself. And t was obvious to everyone but her.

When he spoke his voice was softer. "You're not well yet," he said. He took her hand and she pulled it away. "I want to take you to Collette."

"No," she said.

He picked her up, one arm behind her back and the other under her legs. She fought to get down.

"Stop it," he said with such vehemence she froze. Now she was afraid of him. How different she felt than the night she had first arrived and he had carried her in this position into this room. She did not protest as he carried her back to the infirmary and Collette. "Take care of her," he said to Collette. And he left.

She stayed with Collette. Howie did not speak to her for weeks. She asked Collette about Manny. She had not seen Manny since the night Howie had asked her to leave the mission.

"She afraid," Collette said of Manny.

"She's guilty."

"No, she just afraid."

"How do you know that?"

"I ask her. She do not lie to me."

"Then who did it?"

"It may be accident after all."

Lucy angered. "Don't lie to me, Collette. She's guilty and you know it."

"I do not lie," Collette said.

Suddenly she was suspicious of everyone. Collette wasn't really her friend. She had always been cold and distant.

She was determined to leave. She talked to Paul about driving her the five hours to the airport. She knew he checked with Howie, but he didn't refuse. Obviously Howie wanted her gone. The next morning, before dawn, she gathered as much money as she could from the various places she remembered Howie and Carla, the administrator, hiding it. She had $3,437 American in her satchel when she climbed into the jeep.

As Paul cranked the motor, Howie came out of his house and stood motionless on the steps. She turned away but glanced back. He did not move. She wondered if he knew about the theft. If not, he would eventually find out.

Paul engaged the gears; the jeep lurched forward to a steady speed, weaving around the ruts in the road. Collette was nowhere to be seen. There was no one to say goodbye.

CHAPTER 35

Elizabeth

Elizabeth adjusted the covers over Jennifer, who was curled up on her side on the sofa in the main-house rec room. She heard Agnes's hesitant stride down the hall to the door of A.J.'s study; the door opened and closed. A real estate agent had put a lock box on the house yesterday and would begin showing on Friday. A.J. had put it on the market without telling them. She heard her mother begin talking, her voice more piercing and strident than she ever remembered. She leaned against the door, her hands clenched, her jaw tight. She imagined her mother standing in front of the mahogany kneehole desk, her father sitting in his leather-upholstered wing chair, where he had read and worked alone every evening she could remember.

How could you do this? she thought. She imagined her father's impassive stare, the smoldering, angry look deep in his eyes that had been there, even in subdued times, for months.

"It's my home. You can't sell it." She heard her mother's voice clearly. He would not move a muscle, Elizabeth was sure. A.J. and her mother did not talk now. Her mother's lawyers urged her not to abandon the home.

There was silence.

Her mother spoke. "I won't let you do it."

"There is nothing you can do. The house is in my name."

"But it's our house."

"Don't be your usual infantile self, Agnes."

"Any fool knows what you've done," her mother said. "I have no other choice but to fight you."

Elizabeth had imagined her mother would back away. Her mother had never confronted her father since her hospitalization. She feared him.

"Where will we live? Where will we put the artwork?"

"I don't know and I don't care," he said.

"Why are you doing this?"

"I need the money."

"What about the investments? The savings? Retirement?"

He didn't answer. Elizabeth had never known the details of her father's finances. He had set up lifelong trusts for Lucy and her. He had dissolved Lucy's; she wondered if hers would be next.

"I'm moving to a condo next week," he said.

"What about us?"

"Work it out, Agnes. Take control of your life."

"And Elizabeth and Jennifer? And Luke?"

"Luke can no longer stay on the property. The lawyer has sent a letter."

"He'll take Jennifer, my grandchild."

"She's not your grandchild, Agnes. She's not from your real daughter."

"She is mine."

Elizabeth could hear her mother sob for an instant, then she could imagine her gaining control, standing tall.

"I hate you," her mother said.

A.J. would not respond. That was the way to hurt her.

"Mother told me marrying you was a mistake," Agnes said. "She never liked you."

"Your mother was retarded. I doubt she ever had an original thought. Like you, Agnes. I abhor your vapid ramblings. Just get out."

There was some sort of movement she thought was her mother.

"You are soulless, Abner. I will fight you. You will not take what is ours. I will bring you down into the gutter. I've hated you for years." Her mother's family still held fortunes that went back to slave-trade days.

"I will do just fine, Agnes. Now I must ask you to never bother me again. I do not want to see or hear you ever again. Are you capable of understanding that? I don't want you around."

"You're a sick human being."

"And you're an idiot."

Something slammed against the desk. She imagined her mother hacking at the expensive antique with a fire iron from the fireplace. But of course not. Agnes was not that person. It was a fist, or a book, or something like that.

"May you rot in hell," her mother sobbed. The door opened and she walked down the hall, climbed the stairs, and Elizabeth knew the sound of her second-floor bedroom door closing with a slam.

Elizabeth checked Jennifer, who was sleeping soundly on the sofa. She went upstairs and opened her mother's door without knocking. Her mother sat on her made bed, her legs dangling, her hands in her lap. She was dry-eyed, staring at the wall, and rarely blinking. She did not look at Elizabeth, who pulled up a straight-backed armless chair and sat down.

"I heard it all, mother. He's stressed. He didn't mean it."

"He's evil," her mother said.

Elizabeth leaned forward and placed her head in her hands. She knew her father was not going to change, and she did not expect her mother to ever speak to him again without strong purpose.

"I'll go with Luke, mother. We've been thinking about it—a place of our own."

"I'll manage," her mother said.

"We may look for a rental house in Roswell."

"I can stay with Gladys."

"You can stay with us, mother. We'll have room for you. We love you."

"No. I'll be in the way."

"Not at all. You'd never be in the way."

Her mother stood and began turning down the bed. "The divorce will go through, Elizabeth. I've had excellent legal counsel. From what we can tell, he'll be bankrupt soon. I've taken every precaution to protect my assets from my mother and daddy. I want to be sure you will never be affected after I die too. Nor Jennifer."

"Should Lucy know?"

"Not from me. That's for you to decide."

"She's family."

"Not really. She never liked your father. I think they were too much alike sometimes. But she turned her back on all of us. It was her choice. I don't feel anything for her anymore."

Elizabeth leaned back in the chair. The wooden splat was uncomfortable and she frowned.

"I'm going to take a warm bath, dear," her mother said. "You run along."

"I can stay here with you for a while."

"I'll be fine," her mother said, and Elizabeth heard rare determination in her voice. She sat for a moment as her mother closed the bathroom door and turned on the tub water. Then she stood. Things would never be the same again.

CHAPTER 36

Luke

The university chancellor received the committee's information about A.J.'s performance, but the committee members heard nothing from him. Not one member was contacted for clarification or additional information. And no action had been taken to restrict A.J.'s practice. The dean, in an emergency mandatory faculty meeting about the affair, didn't mention the committee's work; he fully supported A.J., and warned those in the department who were saying "unsubstantiated" things about A.J. to stop. Administration was backing A.J., no matter how loud the opposition. And they were covering up the truth. Most of the faculty did not feel good about it.

The next day, Luke discovered that Tim Roberts, chair of the review committee and CEO of the hospital, had been let go. He went to see him as soon as he heard.

"What's going on?" Luke asked.

"I'm fired. No word from anyone, other than this letter dismissing me. I go to the chancellor. He hints that my work on the committee was vindictive, and that he could not let a smear campaign against A.J. fester on his watch."

"You were more than fair."

"It's getting out of their control. Newspapers are calling for action. The ethics committee for the Academy will be in soon. Administration doesn't want committee reports to get out or committee members to be interviewed. The state board of licensing has started an investigation, too."

"Who do I speak to?" Luke asked. "You didn't even want to be on the committee."

"Stay out of it, Luke. I've got a solid offer in Seattle that I'm going to accept. I'm gone. And you don't want to go against them. They're ruthless."

"A.J. barely speaks to me. He was irate that I wouldn't tell him anything about the committee actions."

"We discovered wrongdoing. We were asked to specifically sort truth from rumor, and we did it well. But what we discovered threatened all of them—their reputations and their careers. And they've hunkered down into aggressive cover-up mode. Don't let it ruin your career. Tell the others, too. Don't sacrifice for me."

For weeks, investigations continued. There was never any indication that the committee report had ever been released. The day before Tim Roberts left the city, he brought Luke the only copy of the original report that he had been carefully protecting. He asked Luke to make copies for everyone on the committee and distribute them, which Luke did immediately. Now each committee member would have to make his or her decision about releasing information. Luke made his decision the same day and sent a copy to the chair of the National Academy of Visual Science ethics committee, which was scheduled to be in town conducting an ethics evaluation of A.J., who was expected to be the next president of the Academy. The next morning, A.J. called Luke. "There was no need for you to send that report to Clarence. I've seen it now. Much of it is wrong."

That A.J. found out so fast showed the power and connections he still had.

"Everyone worked without bias. What we presented was documented," Luke said.

"You think you've ruined me. After all I've done for you, for Christ's sake."

"You can't change what happened," Luke said, "Or cover it up. Step up. Admit what you think is true. Make a big deal about what you're going to do to change the future."

There was a long silence on the other end of the line. "You'll regret this, Luke," A.J. said. "You'll rue this day."

Luke hung up.

Luke didn't see A.J. often after that, and when he did see him, A.J. never greeted him. A.J.'s wrath relentlessly surfaced. But Luke was tenured, and to dismiss him was complicated and next to impossible, even for A.J.

First, the administrator called Luke to tell him there would be no bonus this year. It was the first time ever that a routine bonus, determined by A.J., was denied to Luke. Luke checked with other faculty members. All were getting bonuses. The same day Luke was told the position for his administrator had been terminated. She had been told without Luke's knowledge that Human Resources would help her look for another job. A week later Luke's office space was reassigned, and he was given temporary smaller space in a Quonset hut that had been set up a few years ago to house offices while the new clinic was being built. He had no room for a secretary or an assistant.

Luke was on the OR committee, and when he went to the routine monthly meeting, Terry Chapman from Luke's department was there as the new department representative to the committee. Terry had recently been appointed by A.J. without Luke knowing. As a final insult, Luke received an official letter from the head of the OR committee that he no longer had surgical block time on his traditional Wednesdays, a critical move that would not allow him to schedule patients with any certainty, and would make it impossible to do as many surgeries as he had become accustomed to over the years.

Luke spoke to the dean and the chancellor; both were cold and unsympathetic. The chair of faculty council was outraged and promised to support Luke whenever he needed, but he was pessimistic about having any impact with administration. Eileen Turner, the fellowship director who hated A.J., was supportive and wrote a letter to the editor of the Journal-Constitution about unfair labor practices. But it was not published. A.J. was calling in the chits he'd seeded over the years; Luke felt the turn of the screw.

CHAPTER 37

Lucy

In Atlanta, after two nights in a motel near I-75, Lucy found a furnished apartment in a complex that would rent by the month and required only a one-month returnable deposit. She paid cash. She had $236 left from the money she had taken before she left Africa, and she went directly to her father's office at the hospital.

A.J.'s secretary said he refused to see Lucy, and she demanded to know where he was. "I am his daughter," she said, and for an instant she wondered if the secretary knew she was the adopted one. But the secretary's face gave no clue.

The secretary had some clandestine way to notify security. Two uniformed guards appeared and escorted her out of the building.

She knew where her father parked; he'd had a choice reserved spot for years. She entered the multistory parking garage through the vehicular exit and walked to a shadowed spot close to where he would show up. A car was in his spot; she had to trust it was his.

For three hours she stood and crouched, kneeled and sat with her legs extended. Her mind roamed her predicament. She wanted to see Jennifer. Although she wouldn't hope, she kept close a mental image of once again being a happy family, being able to contribute to Jennifer's formative years, telling her how much she loved her even though she'd been gone so much.

But she had no money. Tomorrow she would go to Alan McCormick and Peter Townsend to find work as a legal assistant. One of them should need help. She'd been disbarred for ethical violations. The profession considered sex with a client unprofessional. She had accepted the decision from afar as just and without complaint. Consorting with a client actively on trial was wrong, and she never thought she'd need to practice law again.

Her father was a few feet away before she knew he was there. He stopped. Her legs ached from the wait as she got to her feet and faced him.

"I need money," she said.

His laugh pierced her. "Get out of my way," he said.

"I have nothing," she said.

"You deserve nothing."

She felt like crying in anger and frustration. "It's because I'm adopted. You wouldn't do this to Elizabeth."

He shoved her out of the way against a car. "You could never be an Elizabeth."

She cried now, not in anger but with hurt and frustration.

"Stop sniveling," he said. "It's repulsive." He opened the car door, the edge hitting her thigh, and got in. He slammed the door shut without looking at her. Before she could gather herself to stop his leaving, he had backed out. She lifted her skirt to look at the purplish bruise that was already forming.

The next morning she was at the office of Peter Townsend. A receptionist behind a glass framed window with a slide-up pane in the center told her to sit down. It was early, and only one other client was waiting. She thought Townsend's and her work together on the ups and downs of the vehicular-manslaughter case had formed a permanent friendship. The door opened to the corridor to the offices. Townsend saw her, surprised, obviously uninformed that she was waiting for him. He stopped some distance from where she was seated. She stood and held out her hand. He did not take it, and she quickly lowered it. He looked away briefly to hide his awkwardness.

"You seem to be doing well," she said to Townsend. He nodded.

"I'm just back from Africa. I need work, Peter."

"You've been disbarred."

"Work as an assistant. I could do research. Interview. Write drafts."

He shoved both hands in his pants pockets. "I don't have anything.

Full up with too many helpers," he said, his lips forming a straight line.

"Please. Just until I can find something else."

She saw the client was staring at them now. She was making a fool of herself.

"I wouldn't even if I had an opening," Townsend said. "Don't come back."

"Why? We worked well together."

"I was doing my job."

"You didn't care?"

"I didn't like anything about your case. I think you were guilty."

"We didn't hit that woman."

He shrugged.

"You suggested I neutralize the witness. That was your idea."

He grabbed her arm and took her out in the corridor that led to the outside. He closed the door and released her. "Don't ever say that in public or private. Never, you hear?"

"It's true."

"And you're a disgraced lawyer. I hope you starve."

She stood frozen with a wave of intense humiliation she'd never remembered experiencing before. Then he was gone and she was alone. She took deep breaths to clear her thoughts. She'd try Alan McCormick. At least he was a former colleague. But she'd have to approach him carefully. And she'd contact Carrie Malroy, her former assistant. She must still be a friend. Carrie could help with a reasonable strategy, maybe even ask Alan on her behalf.

She left the building and found a cab to take for the ten miles from downtown to Buckhead. She went directly to the offices of her former law firm. The receptionist was new, an attractive older woman with dyed brown hair.

"May I speak to Carrie Malroy?" she asked.

The woman looked down a list of names laminated in plastic and thumb tacked to the edge of her desk.

"I don't see a Carrie Malroy."

"She works here."

The woman smiled. "I'm new. Let me check." She went to the door that led to the corridor where offices were. The door closed. Lucy remained standing. The door opened. Alan McCormick came out.

"Alan," she said.

He stopped, his hand still on the doorknob. He stared, speechless.

"Could I talk to you?" she asked.

He was still staring at her. He shook his head no, reversed direction, and closed the door behind him.

How uncivil. And rude. The door opened and the receptionist reentered.

"I talked to the administrator," the receptionist said.

"Perry? Is he still here?"

"Yes. Carrie Malroy left more than a year ago for California."

"Can I get in touch with her?"

She offered a slip of paper. "Here's the last number Perry had for her."

Lucy took the number. She didn't recognize the area code. "Perry said to say 'hi,'" the receptionist said.

After a few seconds of indecision, Lucy thanked her and left to return to her apartment where she could use the neighbor's phone; she did not yet have enough money to have a phone installed.

Carrie was pleased to hear her voice. She was working for Lou Panetta in San Francisco.

"I need work," Lucy said. "I don't think I'll find anything here. I'm desperate."

"I'll ask Lou. He needs someone. And I know he's always respected you since law school days."

"Can I call you back? I don't have a phone yet."

"Tomorrow morning. I should have an answer."

The next morning Carrie said to Lucy that Lou would hire her as a paralegal—on a temporary basis at first, of course. He was looking forward to seeing her again.

"I'll be out as soon as I can. A couple days, maybe," Lucy said. She hoped to get her deposit on the apartment back.

"Terrific. Call me. I'll pick you up at the airport. I have a place in Sausalito. Plenty of room."

Lucy thanked her. She almost asked for money for the flight, but she didn't want to sour their relationship. She had to find money somewhere else.

She would figure out something, even if she had to walk.

CHAPTER 38

Lucy

The house where Lucy grew up with Elizabeth and her parents was the same gray with white trim, but now freshly painted. The red-shingled roof with two stone chimneys jutting up was the same as she remembered it. Standing high above the road, its cement drive curving twice as it crossed the property to the garage that sat to the left, it was impressive. Its display of American suburban architectural features—with roots stolen from Elizabethan, Victorian, and Edwardian styles—as well as its size and trimmings spoke to considerable wealth. Her time in Africa returned to her briefly—the poverty, the edge of survival—before she paid the taxi and walked up the drive.

She paused as she neared the portico over the front door. She hoped that Jennifer might be playing alone in the yard so that she might see her and talk to her without dealing with the family. But that was a dream, and she forced herself to ring the front door bell. Maybe no one was home. There was a "FOR SALE" sign stapled to a wooden stake on the front lawn. She heard no movement inside the house. She leaned forward to peer in one of the thin tall windows that flanked the door. The rooms were bare.

"What are you doing?" a voice said behind her. It was her mother walking toward her. She couldn't find words.

Her mother stopped a few feet from her. "We don't want you here," she said.

Lucy felt a surge of anger. "I've come to see Jennifer. I've come to see my daughter."

"Impossible," her mother said. "She's not here. We're all moving out."

"Where is she?"

"You have no right to know. You've ignored her for too many years."

Lucy wanted to tell her mother she couldn't have helped it. She'd been away in the Georgia mountains and in Africa. She'd always loved Jennifer.

"Where is she?" Lucy asked. "I brought her into this world."

"I will never let you see her."

"You can't stop me."

"I have. There is a restraining order in effect if you come back."

"On what grounds?"

"That you're capable of abducting her from her father, the parent who has raised her and has had custody over these years." Her mother sounded tired now, as if the strain of the family was too much for her.

"I've got to leave again in a few days. I want to see her," Lucy said.

"No, Lucy. She barely remembers you. It would be cruel to invade her happy world."

"I would not invade."

"You would demand emotions she can't give."

Lucy thought for a moment. That did not seem reasonable. She would not demand anything. She wanted to say, Hello. I'm your mommy. I love you.

"Don't come close to her. I'll have you arrested."

Lucy glared at her mother, but she could see no immediate action that would allow her to see Jennifer. Her mother could easily lie about Jennifer not being here. True, she'd heard no sounds from the house, but it was a big place. And Jennifer could be in the garage apartment, too. But from a distance, there were no signs of the garage apartment being used. Her mother would not lie about the restraining order. She was sure it was in effect.

Lucy walked by her mother without speaking, strode down to the street, and turned to walk the mile to the main road where she'd have to figure a way to get to her apartment. She did not look back, although she could feel her mother's glare.

Lucy knew, almost without doubt, that Jennifer would be going to the school she and Elizabeth had attended: the posh north-side private day school anyone who was anyone attended.

The taxi let her out before the school was in sight, and she walked a few hundred yards to the door and entered the office. A woman she did not know was busy at a desk flooded with papers. She was on the phone and hung up when Lucy walked in.

"Hello," Lucy said, "I'd like to see Jennifer Osborne. I'm Lucy MacMiel, her mother."

"Just a moment," the woman said, and left the room. Lucy waited.

The woman reentered. "I'm sorry. She's not available."

"That's outrageous. I'm her mother."

"We've been instructed not to permit you to see her."

"Let me speak to the owner."

The owner must have been listening outside. She stepped in—a well-dressed, middle-aged woman unfamiliar to Lucy.

"I attended this school," Lucy said.

"Before my time," the owner said.

"I'd like to see my daughter."

"That's not possible. We've been alerted you might come here. I've called the authorities." She brushed by Lucy to open the door, her glare insisting that Lucy leave.

Lucy paused outside the door. She would not be rejected. She looked to the only window at the front of the building and could see no one there. She turned right off the path, onto the grass. She kept close to the bushes that lined the wall. On the side of the building there was a window. Standing on tiptoe, she looked in but saw only a storage room. She went around the back. A young woman was wiping down equipment in a fenced-in play yard. Lucy reversed her progress, again going out front and crossing to the other side of the building. She found two windows. The first opened into reception and she avoided it. The second was higher and larger—the room for the children. She moved a rock close to the wall, and with one foot she boosted herself up so she could see comfortably. The attendant had her back to her. The children were in an irregular circle, sitting at individual desks with attached seats, writing on paper with pens. She saw Jennifer immediately. Tan skin, light brown hair. Much older than the image she held in her memory. She could imagine the rich umber of her eyes. Jennifer moved from her desk to take her paper to the teacher. Jennifer was limber, agile far beyond the other children. Tears welled in Lucy's eyes. She had to stop herself from calling out.

A hand gripped her arm and she stumbled off her rock. Another hand gripped her other arm and she dropped her shoulder bag. Two officers held her steady as one reached down and picked up her purse, handing it to her.

"Lucy MacMiel?" one asked, with a disturbing disinterest in his voice.

Lucy said nothing as they walked her to a squad car and placed her in the back behind a wire mesh screen, and started the engine. One officer radioed their arrest and their position.

She held back her tears. She knew it was useless to argue, and they did not talk to her or read her rights until they were at the station house. She was not charged, but warned of any future attempts to contact Jennifer.

The apartment manager refused to return her deposit or any of her rent. She wondered if Luke would help her. He was her husband, obligated to support. She deserved support for the past and the future. He had always seemed reasonable. He might see her argument. He certainly had enough money after years of practice. Yes, that was what she'd do. She'd not be able to go to the house; she didn't know where he lived. She'd have to go back to the hospital, avoid her father, talk to Luke alone. Yes, that is what she'd have to do. She called a taxi using the apartment manager's phone.

She slipped into the halls of the hospital and found Luke. He acted as if he had expected her.

"I'm not having an easy time right now," she said. "I'm still your wife and I've never demanded support. But I need that support now." She looked away from him, somehow feeling uncomfortable with the request although she had convinced herself it was justified.

He was impassive.

"Don't you still have some feeling for me?"

He did not speak. He took out his wallet from a jacket pocket. He slipped twenty one-hundred dollar bills from behind a credit card in one of the credit card slots. He had expected her. He found two fifties and three twenties in the bill slot. He left the smaller bills. He handed the larger bills to her.

"That's all?" She hoped he registered the indignation she felt.

"I wish you the best," he said.

"Then give me what I deserve."

"That's it, Lucy," he said, "and don't come back again. There will be no more." He walked away.

She remained immobile for many seconds.

Then her mind began to function again. She had enough to reach the West Coast. Then she'd work things out from there. "I can do this," she thought. "I can."

Two days later she was on the plane to California.

CHAPTER 39

Elizabeth

Jennifer was asleep. Elizabeth was reading in the living room of the rented house when Luke came in from work. She looked to him. "Need something to eat?"

"Thanks. Had something before surgery." He sat down in a chair. "Jennifer okay?"

"She's asleep. I didn't send her to school today. She didn't feel well. Her temperature was 100."

Luke stood and went alone to Jennifer's room. He returned in a few minutes. "No fever. But she's pale, don't you think?"

"She doesn't eat at all. All her favorites don't interest her. I think she's lost weight."

"Is she vomiting? Loose stools?"

"No. But she sleeps almost all the time she's home."

"Bring her in tomorrow morning. I'll arrange for Sandy Bruckner to see her."

The next morning Elizabeth took Jennifer to the hospital. Blood was drawn and tests were done. Luke left the clinic to hear Dr. Bruckner's findings.

Jennifer stayed with the nurse in an exam room while Elizabeth and Luke left to greet Bruckner.

"She's anemic. Her white count is low," Bruckner said.

"From what?" Luke asked.

"I looked at a slide. I'll have path look at it too. I think it's ALL."

"I don't understand," Elizabeth said.

Luke could not speak.

"Acute lymphoblastic leukemia," Bruckner said, a strain obvious in his voice. "I'll set up a bone marrow."

"Is it serious?" Elizabeth asked.

Bruckner paused. "Yes. It can be."

Elizabeth hesitated. "Will she die?"

"We have treatments. But the outcomes are erratic. This age group does better than infants."

"We need hematology," Luke said.

"And neurology. But I'll admit her on my service," Bruckner said.

Bruckner left to make arrangements for admission, and Luke used his office telephone to cancel patients and find coverage for patients who had already arrived. Elizabeth and Luke went together to walk Jennifer through the admission procedure and assure a private room where they could stay the night.

Jennifer was scheduled for a bone marrow aspiration the next day. She was taken to X-ray. Elizabeth and Luke followed and went with her during the procedure. Elizabeth felt emptiness. She wanted to remain cheery for Jennifer, but her heart felt fear and she imagined pain and suffering.

"It's going to be okay," Luke said. But he spoke with a hesitancy she'd never heard before.

"How can you know?" she asked, with more anger than despair.

"You have to believe," he said, "for Jennifer's sake."

But her mind could not erase a future without Jennifer. Luke took her hand.

"She's lucky to have you," he said. She heard the stress in his voice, heard his own doubts about the future.

Jennifer was a bright child with a pleasant disposition and irrepressible spirit. Why would she have this? What possible reason could there be to give her suffering?

She still held Luke's hand. "We should let Lucy know," she said. "She'd want to know."

He hesitated.

"She's her mother."

"But she hasn't been her mother," he said. "You've been her mother for years."

"Lucy loves her."

"Lucy doesn't know how to love. The only love she knows is about her, not someone else."

Elizabeth didn't know what to say. Lucy wasn't perfect, but she'd want to know about her daughter.

"What good would it do?" Luke said. "She'd worry. She wouldn't know whether to come or not come. Then she'd decide she'd have to. Then what would she do? What would she say? Would you want her making decisions about Jennifer? Would you want her forcing her emotions on her? Jennifer might not even recognize her. Would that be fair? Having to figure out how to feel about this strange woman who's trying to act like her mother?"

She let Luke's hand go. There was nothing more to say. But she knew Lucy cared, would always care in her own way. She did not feel good about being silent, especially since Lucy was back in the States, somewhere close enough to easily come to see Jennifer. She'd bring it up with Luke again when the time was right. Somehow, sometime, Lucy would have to be told.

PART THREE

CHAPTER 40

Lucy

On the flight to California, Lucy felt as if she had escaped the hostility of Atlanta. She felt strangers looked at her without judgment. And her tension was less; the vague, nondescript apprehensions about almost everything were nearly gone.

It became clear from her short time in Atlanta that she could never live with Luke again. Luke liked his honorable, self-important, boring persona. She had not been intimate with him for years, and she could not imagine succumbing to his passions ever again. And his talk, although more civil than she had expected, was laced with hidden incessant recriminations. Even if he had agreed to leave his rented house and move in with her, he would have demanded her loyalty. And to be around him, see his desire to be a husband, to take over her life, only made her think of how little Howie demanded. And Howie infused her life with intensity. Even his philandering perversely made her want him even more. She yearned for his physical presence, his unyielding quest for pleasure—yes, that was what it was, he was his own man and she wanted to surround him, make him need her. Maybe that was impossible now. Still, he was in her dreams, with what she believed was a loyal and focused need for her love. He had not answered her calls or letters since she left Africa. But she could not stop thinking about him.

Carrie Malroy, her former legal assistant, had arranged for her to work as an assistant to Lou Panetta, a lawyer well known to her since law school. The pay was insulting and barely sustaining, and Carrie suggested she move in with her in her apartment in Sausalito. Panetta had cancer, and although he was trying to maintain his usual schedule, he could barely manage. He needed help. His prime political client, Maria Sanchez, was running for reelection to a congressional seat and needed legal counsel. Panetta accepted Lucy under the condition that he would do any of the legal work from his office, but Lucy would act as the daily consultant during the campaign.

Maria Sanchez lived in her district in a commune on the coast. She was a twice-divorced activist for women's rights. Accused by opponents of lesbianism, she supported immigration reform, amnesty for illegals, legalized marijuana, and universal health insurance, and was pro-life on the abortion issue. This platform made her popular with almost everyone in the community except pro-choice activists and far-right conservative radicals—mostly older, successful men and anti-Hispanic whites, who had begun rallies and demonstrations to vilify Maria as an alien lesbian and anti-American.

Lucy liked Maria. She saw similarities between Maria's life and career and her own struggles.

They were in the official campaign headquarters in the medium-size town of Zodiac—farm country. The building was a hastily renovated old dairy with piping crisscrossing the ceiling and huge steel tanks still lining some of the walls.

Lucy sat at an oval oak table with Maria and her team: Fenly Cooper, a wealthy, non-practicing doctor eager to campaign for legalized marijuana; Paula Warez, in charge of finances and fundraising; and Henry Cid, the campaign manager.

"Don't make abortion an issue," Lucy said, "either way." She pointed out that in Pennsylvania, Rouget had gained votes by simply saying he would vote as the majority of his constituency wanted. Who could argue with that vague but supportive strategy? "Let the issue rest at least until we poll where the majority settles," she said.

"Avoid it all together," Fenly said. "Who could really determine what the majority wanted on any issue, much less abortion?"

Lucy glanced at him and held his gaze.

"It is what I believe," Maria said. "A fetus has rights. It's how I'm going to push for legislation and Supreme Court action. It is who I am, for Christ's sake."

"You can be who you are without losing votes," Fenly said.

"It's the violence," Lucy said. "Most voters don't approve of the violence over the issue no matter how they believe."

"I am not violent," Maria said.

"But you'll provoke violence if you make it a prime issue," Henry Cid said. "And you'll suggest your approval of violence."

Maria slammed her palm on the table. "No more discussion. I expect your support on this."

"You're making a mistake, Maria," Lucy said.

"No more, Lucy. I've heard what you have to say. That's the end."

"We all agree," Henry said.

"Don't argue with me. I will not change my mind on this issue."

"And you'll lose votes," Lucy said.

Maria glared at Lucy. "Enough!"

Later that evening in a diner booth, having a late meal with Fenly Cooper, Lucy shook her head.

"I like her spirit," she said. "I want her to win."

"You're a fucking feminist," he said.

"You're working for her."

"I like that she's supporting Prop 16."

Lucy ate part of her fruit salad. "I don't get it. The marijuana bit. What's the big deal?" Lucy said, "It should be legalized."

"For treatment?"

"I don't think it has any medical value, or if it does, there are better drugs."

"You like it!" she laughed. "You want to smoke ad lib."

"What's wrong with that?"

Lucy laughed again. "So much for citizens' rights for medicinal purposes. You're a hedonist."

"Proud of it."

"And you're a doctor."

He leaned forward slightly, wiping his mouth with a paper napkin. "Lost my license."

"For what?"

"Dispensing controlled substances."

"Illegally?"

He grinned. "Profit. I made a fortune."

"And you're still around?"

"Spent a little jail time."

"And she takes you on for the campaign?"

"For my money. Not my personality. Or my criminal record. And the constituency thought of me as a local hero."

"For selling drugs?"

He nodded. "For a while, I was a local celeb."

Lucy smiled. "You're unbelievable. What about your family?"

"Not so understanding."

"I can see why."

He signaled the waiter for another beer. "And what about you. Your family?" he asked.

Lucy hesitated. She usually never talked about her past, but she liked Fenly.

"A bust. My mother and father disowned me. I think my husband screws my sister. My daughter isn't allowed to speak to me, and I haven't really seen her for years."

"How do you feel about that?"

Lucy finished a glass of wine and signaled the waiter for another. "I don't feel good about it, Fenly," she said. "I'm not proud, if that's what you mean."

"Like me," he said.

"Not like you," she said.

"I'm not proud, deep down," he said, looking away. "I still love my wife, who has married another. I miss my kids, who are ashamed of me. They went to Colorado to college to get away. Both of them."

Thoughts of Jennifer had crowded Lucy's mind. She did love her, and she felt like a profound failure as a mother. It was neglect, she could not deny it, but she hadn't seen it at the time, and it was definitely not that she didn't care. She'd been distracted by her career and Hower Bain. That's what life had dealt her. That's what she had decided was right. And she now was thinking often about Jennifer and what she should have done, and what she should do now. She had no room for sympathizing with Fenly.

"C'est la vie," he said. Lucy signaled for the check.

"I'll pay," Fenly said, tapping her hand. She shrugged.

"Campaign expense," he said.

She stood.

"After-dinner drink?" he asked.

"I don't feel like it," Lucy said. She left before the check came, eager to get back to her hotel room and sit alone until she became sleepy.

CHAPTER 41

Lucy

Maria's campaign heated as weeks progressed. Maria was not a good speaker and had a weak presence on the stage and Lucy became an important opener at rallies. Lucy was a natural with a crowd, and she effectively preceded Maria outlining the issues, praising the Maria's record and character. As she became more experienced, Maria learned to stand tall after Lucy, to project more confidence and to benefit from the interest of the crowd that Lucy had ignited. Lucy let Maria take full credit for her improvement and let her bask in her success. But Maria never gave Lucy credit, never thanked her, and it was irritating enough that Lucy soon began to see Maria as ignorant, and soaked in hubris.

After a vibrant rally in the North, Lucy was driving as she and Fenly returned to their base closer to San Francisco. Fenly attended every rally, often mingling with the crowd to measure the results. His driver's license had been revoked for a series of DUIs and he had to be ferried to rallies by staff. This evening, it had been Lucy's turn.

"You're a beautiful woman, Lucy," Fenly said. He took a sip from a pocket-size silver flask.

She laughed. "You letch. I don't respond to comments about beauty. I want to be successful. Make an impact."

"You should be the one running for office," he said.

"Don't be disloyal to our leader. She has the talent for Congress."

"You've got the gift."

"I have no patience to compromise and accept less than what is right."

"That's what lawyers do," Fenly said.

"I was defense. It was usually all or nothing for me. I lost a big one on a celebrity preacher who was accused of underage sex."

"Was he guilty?"

"I don't know. Sometimes I think so, but most of the time not. It was complicated by his continuous sexual exploits with any adult woman who was near and willing."

Fenly's look seemed to ask if she was one of those women. She kept quiet. He took another sip and laid his head against the headrest. He closed his eyes.

"You drive like a Georgia moonshiner," he said. "Hard to believe you have a driver's license."

She looked at him. His eyes were still closed. "I've been suspended a few times. Speeding," she said.

"Never had an accident?"

Lucy's jaw tightened. "I'm an excellent driver."

"At your speeds, I bet the accidents were spectacular."

Lucy relaxed her grip on the wheel a little. "I've had only one bad one."

"Total?"

"A Porsche. Red. I loved that car."

"Speed of light."

"With no effort," she said. And her mind went to Luke, and that night, and how she learned to love him. And that was her mistake. Not knowing about love, she had convinced herself. And then, without reason, she'd fallen in love with Howie. She was too naive to know what tumultuous love could do to a human. She refused to blame Howie for that. He was a cad. A social misfit. A sex fiend. But below all that was a complex man she loved. She refused to be blamed. Especially by a loser like Fenly. So she did not talk about Howie or Luke.

"I've come to like you, Lucy," Fenly said, his deep-set eyes still closed.

She frowned with distress. Then she smiled ironically. "What's to like?"

"A lot," he said. "Anything like that stirring in you?" he asked. He was holding his flask flat on his narrow, concave chest with both his bony hands.

She had not thought about Fenly in that way. She didn't crave sex, from Fenly or any man now—except Howie. Only Howie had ever satisfied her. She slowed for a hairpin curve in the darkness of the coast road, the ocean sky overcast and gray. She liked Fenly enough; she found him frank and genuinely good. She also appreciated his funky lifestyle.

"You like me as a friend," he said. "It's okay. It's the story of my life."

She liked him more than that, than just a friend. But she did not love him, and she couldn't imagine what copulation with a little man like Fenly would ever be.

"I'm worn out on relationships," she said. "They've never worked out for me."

"Miss your husband?"

She hesitated and angered at the thought of Luke. "Not at all," she said.

"Is there a boyfriend?"

"Never."

"So why not a little fling? You and me. Doesn't have to be permanent."

"I don't think so," she said. But she was struck with loneliness. Her need for Howie had never waned, and against her will, her heart ached. They were close to Fenly's place.

"I got a good bottle of wine," Fenly said.

Wine! Since she arrived in California—for the first time in her life—she'd been drinking wine. It tasted okay, felt good, and was always available.

"Come on," he said. "You're always turning me down."

She didn't have anything pressing. She stopped in front of his place. She shut off the engine, and reached into the backseat for her shoulder bag.

"Great," he said, and unbuckled his seat belt.

Lucy held onto to a bottle of California red to replenish her glass. Fenly laboriously poured whisky straight from a bottle into the tiny flask opening and swigged from that. He followed up with sips of white wine. Why didn't he drink from the bottle? But she forgot the question before she could get it out.

On a sofa he groped her once, but she firmly took his hand off her and he did not try again. He passed out after midnight, and she sat with his head in her lap, replenishing her wineglass. God, she still felt alone, even when she was not. She would never be with Howie again, but she couldn't forget him. But she forgot lots of other things. Important things. And she'd often think of Jennifer, wonder how she was. She decided to send her a gift with a nice note. She'd use a catalog to find something— something feminine for Jennifer who would soon be a young lady. Then Lucy passed out.

She regained full consciousness the next morning after nine, before Fenly. She remembered little of what happened. He had taken her, but she was too numb to respond much, and she had no memory of feeling anything at all. She ached from her awkward positioning on the sofa. Fenly sucked in air through his open mouth. He did not move when she lifted his head, slipped off the couch, and settled his head back down.

At her hotel room her head hurt, she ached, and she had no appetite. She drank coffee and took an aspirin but was quickly consumed by fatigue. She lay on the bed, deciding not to go to campaign headquarters until afternoon. She slept as if escaping from the world, but did not awake rested and had to force herself to shower and go to work.

On and off during the weeks, Lucy spent many nights with Fenly. On some nights, she had been commuting back and forth to Carrie Malroy's place to save money, but now it was easier to stay with Fenly. He was usually fun to be with. They'd drink wine and he'd smoke marijuana, and they'd re-watch favorite videos of classic movies in bed. They'd laugh and cry together and drink a pot of coffee in the morning to take on the campaign duties. Lucy had taken on more of the mechanical campaign chores of setting up rallies and arranging speaking engagements—from retirement villages to union meetings. Maria had a bus refitted and painted with her image on both sides for campaigning, and she was demanding more time from her staff to accompany her on the road, where they slept in motels and in supporters' homes when they were too far away from home base to return at night.

On a Wednesday evening, after working the entire day on voter lists at headquarters, Lucy picked up her forwarded mail from her post office box. In the twilight she turned on the overhead internal car light to sort through her mail for anything important. There was a hand written letter marked personal from Elizabeth.

She almost ignored it, setting it aside. The thought of Elizabeth raised a cloud of disagreements that still angered her. When she finished with all the other mail she stared at Elizabeth's letter. That goody two- shoes, sucking up to people her entire life. Always the first to clear the table, wipe up the spills, fold the laundry. Why was it so irritating?

She opened the letter. Jennifer had been diagnosed with a childhood form of leukemia. She'd been under treatment for months, with some improvement, but had had a relapse. They were taking her to a specialist for treatment in a clinical trial. The outlook was not totally bleak . . . to date more than sixty per cent had responded to the drug. Jennifer's spirits were up, although she seemed afraid to leave home.

Does she ask for me? Lucy thought. I am her mother. But she knew that was unlikely, and she knew she didn't really want to know that Jennifer never asked for her. Sadness swept through her. She cried silently for a few minutes.

The next morning she drove to Fenly's place.

"What a pleasant surprise," he said. "Nothing to do at the office?"

"You're still in your underwear."

"I'm preparing slowly today to achieve stunning perfection."

"In jeans and a T-shirt?" she asked.

"I grace any outfit." He grinned.

She sat down on a straight-back wooden chair and put her head in her hands. "My daughter has leukemia."

Fenly frowned with concern and sat down facing her. "The treatments have gotten better recently."

"They're going to give her experimental drugs. That can't be good." She took Fenly's silence as agreement. "I don't know what to do," she said.

"I could call doctor friends," Fenly offered. "Find out about the treatments available."

She thought for a moment. "Her father's a surgeon. He'll have sought out the best of everything. That's what he's good at. Searching out the best."

"He married you," Fenly said.

"Stop it."

Fenly went to the kitchen and brought back two cups of coffee. He sat back down.

"I should go to be with her," she said.

"I'll make the arrangements," he said. "How soon do you want to leave?"

She stood and went to the sofa, sitting with her legs stretched out and her head back. "I don't want to go."

"She's your daughter."

"I've seen her only a few times in years. She won't remember me. She thinks my sister's her mother. That's what Elizabeth would do. Tell my daughter to call her 'Mommy.' I couldn't stand that."

"You're making up excuses."

"There's nothing I can do. I can't comfort her. Elizabeth and Luke will do that. I can't be involved in the treatment decisions. They'll do that. My mother will use every opportunity to recount my failures. My father's disowned me, and I can't afford the trip. And the last time I tried to see her, they had a restraining order on me."

"I'll pay."

She brought her knees up and leaned forward. "I don't know what to do."

"Call your sister. Ask her what's best."

"I hate her. Besides, she's not my sister. I'm adopted. And nothing like her."

"There must be some connection." He handed her the walk-around phone. "It's about noon there."

She took the phone and held it without moving for more than a minute. Then she dialed. Elizabeth answered. She sounded pleased to hear Lucy's voice. But that was the way she always sounded, as if she'd been waiting for your call.

"I'm worried about Jennifer," Lucy said.

"She's having a good day today. She's right here. Say hello to your Mommy," Elizabeth said.

What did Jennifer call Elizabeth, then? Auntie? Really?

There was some clatter as the phone was passed. Then a silence. "Jennifer?" Lucy said. "It's me."

"Say hello to Mommy," Elizabeth said in the background.

Lucy felt the silence, thought of the indecision it suggested. "I love you," she said.

Almost immediately Jennifer said, "I love you too." "It's Mommy," Lucy said again.

Lucy felt a modicum of tension leave her. There was the sound of Elizabeth taking back the phone. "Mommy's calling you from California," Lucy heard Elizabeth say to Jennifer. Jennifer gave a lyrical laugh of joy. "Mommy!" she said.

"You doing okay?" Elizabeth asked.

Lucy said she was doing great and asked about Luke and Agnes. She talked about the campaign. Then she asked if there was anything she could do.

"I don't think so," Elizabeth said. "She's going into the hospital this afternoon. We should be there about two weeks."

Lucy asked Elizabeth to let her know how the treatment went and said her goodbyes. She disconnected.

She looked at Fenly. "I can't go. I can't do it."

"Why not?" he asked.

"I can't stand how they'll treat me."

"She sounded friendly to me. Your daughter sounded excited to hear from you."

"She didn't mean it."

"Of course she did. Let me make the arrangements. It will do you good. Meet them at the hospital. Maybe your mother won't go."

"Oh, she'll be there. Believe me."

"I'll pay for a round trip, and you can come back when you're ready."

"I can't."

"I'll tell Maria this morning. You get details from your sister. And pack. I'll have tickets for you on the red-eye tonight."

Lucy couldn't find the energy to resist. But she wouldn't call Elizabeth. She slumped back on the sofa holding back her need to cry.

CHAPTER 42

Lucy

Lucy took a cab from the Atlanta airport to the children's hospital where Jennifer was being treated. She checked into an adjacent hotel for families. A sign at reception said members of a family were encouraged to stay with their child. The receptionist did not question Jennifer Osborne's mother might not be Lucy MacMiel. She had not told anyone she was coming. She had dialed her mother's number twice from Fenly's place but hung up before it could be answered. If there was to be unpleasantness about her seeing Jennifer, she'd rather deal with it when she was able to see Jennifer, and not try to convince Agnes or Elizabeth on the phone of her sincerity. She'd never backed away from confrontation that she could remember. But she dreaded seeing them

all again . . . except Jennifer.

Her plan was to see Jennifer, talk to her, spend some time. If she were lucky, she could make it happen before anyone knew. She had brought a gift. A book purchased in an airport bookshop during a stopover.

She reached the ward and approached a nurses' station. She introduced herself and asked to see Jennifer Osborne. The floor nurse looked puzzled for a second. She hesitated.

"Is something wrong?" Lucy asked.

"I thought Jennifer's mother went to the room more than an hour ago."

Shit, Lucy thought. Should I leave? Come back at another time? Most likely someone would be with Jennifer now all the time.

"I'll call the attendant." The nurse clicked on the intercom.

Lucy considered leaving. She had wanted to make it simple, but this was escalating against her. She could feel it, like when things go wrong in final summaries before a jury. Only here, she couldn't make any effective adjustments. She either had to wait or leave.

The attendant was male and burly.

"This woman claims to be the Osborne child's mother," the nurse said, moving her head toward Lucy but not looking at her.

"May I see your identification?" he asked Lucy. Lucy showed him a driver's license. "MacMiel?"

"Maiden name. I'm a lawyer. I kept it after I married Luke Osborne."

"Divorced?"

"No. What difference does it make?"

He frowned. "We've had abductions. As a lawyer you must see the need for precautions."

"I'd like to see my daughter."

"Of course. Wait here." He left and Lucy sat in a chair along the wall. She thumbed through Time magazine.

The attendant returned. "I'll show you the room. Your sister is eager to see you."

Jennifer lay on her back in a hospital bed with metal side rails. Her eyes were closed and her head was turned to the side; her long, reddish-brown hair fell onto the pillow and over her shoulder. Elizabeth sat in an upholstered armchair. She did not move when Lucy came in. The attendant left.

"Is she all right?" Lucy asked.

"She's sedated now," Elizabeth said, still not moving.

Lucy did not react to Elizabeth's tepid reception. She expected no more and maybe less. She walked to the bedside and reached out to take Jennifer's hand but thought better of it and placed both hands on the side rail. "She's beautiful," she said.

Elizabeth didn't respond for a while. She had readjusted and brought her left leg under her right, her skirt above her knee. Always fit and flexible, Lucy thought. She'd lost her chubbiness of a few years ago. She was quite attractive. Lucy closed her eyes. I've let myself go. I'm getting fat.

"Where are you staying?" Elizabeth asked.

Lucy kept her gaze on Jennifer. How much she had missed in her daughter's life. "In the hotel for families next door," she said.

"Mother's at her friend's house. Luke has a case. They'll be by later. Jennifer's having a treatment today."

"Does it hurt?"

"She's sedated the whole time." "After. Does she suffer?"

"She cries. It seems to hurt to move."

Lucy felt the guilt of her neglect. She teared up, and wiped away moisture from her lower lid with her finger.

Elizabeth stood. "Sit here. I've got some phone calls to make. I'll bring you back a coffee."

"I don't drink coffee anymore."

Elizabeth frowned as if questioning the accuracy of her memory. "They have soda."

"Nothing," Lucy said.

After Elizabeth left, Lucy sat in the chair. But it was low and she couldn't see Jennifer well. Lucy stood to see if she was all right. Jennifer turned her head without waking. Lucy stood by the bedside until Elizabeth returned almost an hour later.

Lucy did not ask why Agnes and Luke had not arrived when Jennifer was taken for her procedure. She did not want to know the reason, although she was sure they did not want to see her. When Jennifer returned, she was awake; she looked at Elizabeth, who was close by the bedside.

"Say 'hi' to your mother," Elizabeth said. Jennifer looked to Lucy and smiled weakly.

"Do you feel okay?" Lucy asked.

Jennifer nodded.

The attendants moved Jennifer to the bed, tucked her in, and rolled the gurney out of the room.

"I'm so happy to see you," Lucy said to Jennifer.

Jennifer had already closed her eyes, seemingly drifting into sleep.

"Can you stay here with her?" Elizabeth asked.

"Of course," Lucy said, offended by Elizabeth's tone.

"No one requires it, but we like to stay awake when we're with her. Just in case. She'll sleep most of the time."

Lucy didn't respond to what she thought was the obvious.

"Agnes can't come. I'll go get six hours' sleep. Relieve you after midnight. Then you can get a little rest."

She couldn't detect Elizabeth's motive. She couldn't believe Elizabeth wanted to give her some time alone with her daughter. All the get-some-rest shit was probably made up. There had never been that kind of caring between them. True, Elizabeth probably was tired, but she wouldn't worry—the staff was excellent, and Jennifer was groggy but not in danger of dying, for God's sake, and why wouldn't she stay here? Well, it was a chance to be with Jennifer, and she'd take advantage of what had been given to her.

An hour later, the staff made rounds and explained that Jennifer was doing well and should soon be more alert. Lucy sat in the chair, standing often to watch her daughter. She was satisfied that she had come to visit. Jennifer was real to her now, not just memories. But she realized how proximity to family increased her stress now that she could sit quietly with her daughter.

Her mind wandered to the campaign. She was relieved to be away from Maria's increasingly vociferous attacks on staff, and Fenly's constant need to control her every need and thought.

"Auntie?" Jennifer said, her eyes open and looking around the room. Lucy stood up and went to the bed. "It's Mommy," she said. "Auntie will be back in a little while." She reached for Jennifer's hand but

Jennifer reached for the call button that was next to the pillow. "Juice," Jennifer said.

"I'll get it for you, baby," she said, taking the call button away and draping it over the side of the bed railing.

She could have called for the nurse, but she suddenly had a fear that Jennifer in some way would reject her. She'd called out for Auntie. That couldn't be surprising. Yet she hadn't seemed surprised when Mommy was there. She seemed to take it as a matter of course. She was only a child. Maybe she hadn't built up the hatred for her that Lucy dreaded from the rest of the family.

She brought back juice to Jennifer and tried to help her drink, but Jennifer sat up and took the carton in both hands, sucking on the straw.

Lucy took the carton when Jennifer had finished, threw it away, and returned to the bedside.

"You're such a big girl now. And so pretty."

Jennifer smiled and lay back.

"Are you going to school?"

"I drew a picture."

"A picture. What did you draw a picture of?"

"Of Mommy."

"Of me?"

"It was big."

She took Jennifer's hand. "Do you like school?"

Jennifer nodded vigorously. "I know all the dinosaurs."

"Really! Do you sing songs too?"

Jennifer nodded again.

"Can you sing me a song?"

Jennifer smiled shyly, lowered her chin.

"Please. For me?"

Slowly and softly Jennifer sang: "In a cavern, in a canyon / Excavating for a mine / Lived a miner forty-niner / And his daughter, Clementine." Lucy smiled and clapped in rhythm. Jennifer laughed without losing a beat.

When Jennifer had finished, Lucy said, "That was excellent. You are a very good singer."

"I know 'Frère Jacques' too."

"Would you sing that for me too?"

Jennifer nodded again, and sang. "Frère Jacques, Frère Jacques / Dormez vous? Dormez vous? / Sonnez les matines, sonnez les matines / Ding ding dong." She leaned back when she had finished.

Lucy couldn't help leaning over and kissing her again. "That was wonderful. Would you like me to read you a story?"

Jennifer looked at her as if deciding, a blank stare without emotion, more like she was thinking about something else, something about Mommy, maybe thinking this was Mommy but she wasn't sure how to feel. But it could be the book, too, Lucy worried. Was it too young for her? Was she humiliated?

"You choose?" Lucy said, determined to give her a gift.

Jennifer still stared at her. Lucy went to her shoulder bag and unwrapped the book she had bought at the airport. She opened the book, standing by the bedside, so Jennifer could see the pages. Cinderella. Lucy was increasingly apprehensive, but she began to read.

"Once there was a widower who married a proud and haughty woman as his second wife. She had two daughters who were equally vain. By his first wife, he'd had a beautiful young daughter who was a girl of unparalleled goodness and sweet temper . . ."

Jennifer followed the story, watching Lucy. Of course she already has this book, Lucy thought. She's bored stiff.

Toward the end, Jennifer's eyes closed. Lucy knew she was still listening. Lucy believed Jennifer wanted to hear the prince had come. Lucy finished, " . . . ever after." And then Jennifer was asleep.

Lucy leaned over the rail and kissed her forehead. She pulled up the sheet to her chin. She went to the window to put her book with the two stacks of other books and saw the same book, well used, near the top of one stack. She put her book on top anyway and went back to sit in the chair. She felt a full sense of contentment, even though she was crying.

Elizabeth returned just after one in the morning. "She okay?"

"Fine. Can I stay?"

"Get some sleep," Elizabeth said. "Come back in the morning. She'll be up running around."

Lucy gathered her shoulder bag, gave Jennifer another kiss, and went to the elevator. She exited the elevator on the ground floor and walked the corridor to the lobby where a covered walkway led to the hotel. As she crossed the lobby, she heard her name. She turned. A uniformed sheriff's deputy stepped up to her. "Lucy MacMiel?"

She didn't answer. He held out a large white envelope. She didn't take it.

He shoved it in her open bag and left.

She stood there, shaken, as she opened the envelope. She knew what it was. She was a lawyer. Still, it was a surprise. A subpoena. She was to appear in court two weeks from today. Luke Osborne versus Lucy MacMiel. Divorce.

"Shit," she said. She imagined them waiting for an opportunity to serve her, Luke getting the lawyer to wake the process server to get to her before she left the state. "You bastard," she said aloud, seeing Luke in her mind.

She couldn't sleep well knowing she might see some of the family again, and left for the airport before five the next morning to catch the earliest flight possible back to California.

CHAPTER 43

Lucy

Lucy held daily sessions with Maria for more than two weeks preparing her for the debate. Lucy drilled her daily on the majority of important issues, outlining the controversies, laying down facts, and how to explain her position. This had been effective in allowing Maria to speak from the heart, with guidelines of course that had already been laid down. But the first of three nationally televised debates—because of the crucial positioning of the district in the state—would bring heavy emphasis on her position on international affairs. Maria cared nothing about international affairs. She had never been out of the country and couldn't find Russia, much less Great Britain, on the world globe a decorator had placed in her Washington office. She voted the party line on every international issue, and never spoke to any question ever posed about the world, instead slipping in answers to her favorite, and usually unrelated, themes that were mostly local and of interest to her constituency.

A few days before the debate, staff gathered to conduct mock interviews with questions. Maria turned blank on many of the international questions, forgetting the sides of an issue, and sometimes mispronouncing a country's name so erroneously that is was obvious she couldn't spell it and had rarely seen it written out.

In the staff meeting three days before debates began, the only topic was the discussion about debate preparation.

"How am I doing?" Maria asked her staff. She was leaning her backside against a metal desk, her legs straight out, her hands back for support. She was wearing a tracksuit of light green polyester and had her hair in a ponytail held with a rubber band. Henry Cid slouched in an overstuffed chair, his leg draped over the arm. Paula Warez was stretched out belly down on the floor, her head supported by her hands, her elbows on the floor. Fenly sat in a folding chair backward, his folded arms on the top of the curved metal back. Lucy stood near him, leaning against a bookcase. The atmosphere was dense and dulled with fatigue and weariness from no sleep. Maria smoked a cigarette, the ashtray on the desk overflowing with butts. Fenly held a can of Diet Coke that Lucy knew had been fortified with bourbon from his ever-present flask.

After a silence, Maria said, "I'm paying you fuckers to speak up. How am I doing?"

"Great," Henry said, unenthusiastically.

"Don't bullshit me. I'll never be great. I want to beat Waring's ass into the fucking ground."

"You're doing good," Henry said.

Maria dragged on her cigarette. "Paula?"

Paula gained some time by twisting into a sitting position with her arms around her knees. "It's coming along," she said.

"How do I bury the fucker?"

Paula didn't respond.

Fenly spoke: "Keep working to build confidence in the issues. You can't let any insecurity leak out. And you've got to be decisive. If you're on the fence about anything, Waring can destroy you."

"How will he do that?"

Fenly raised his hand. "I'll be Waring. Lucy, you be the moderator. Ask a tough question."

"Jesus Christ. We do this thirty times a day," Maria said.

"Put out the cigarette," Fenly said. "Stand up straight. Both feet solid on the floor. Keep your hands still and use them only when you want to emphasize a point."

"Don't patronize me."

"You'll be standing during the debate."

Maria stood and put out her cigarette.

Lucy began. "Congresswoman Sanchez. The unprovoked Iraqi attack on the USS Stark cost thirty-seven American lives. Are you satisfied with the administration's response?"

Lucy was pleased that Maria took a deep breath, remembering her instructions. "No, I'm not. This administration has repeatedly been slow to react to threats on our troops—troops who serve their country without concern for their personal safety. Troops who are underpaid. And they spend years away from their families. That's wrong."

Lucy turned her head to Fenly. "Mr. Waring."

"I share the congresswoman's concern for our troops. They are brave and dedicated soldiers. But the administration gave careful consideration to our interests in the Gulf. And given our dedication to protection of the oil lanes, I agree that our troops need support, but I am sure that withdrawal was not an option at that time. In considering the Iraqi provocation, it was appropriate to consult the Saudis, who seemed to find the issue complex from the Arab point of view. No military response was right, and the concept of carefully considered action on diplomatic and undercover fronts seemed prudent and pragmatic."

"Congresswoman?" Lucy said. "Rebuttal?"

"That is so typical of Mr. Waring. He ignores that America will be seen as weak. What's happened to our leadership in the world? No one fears us anymore. Any crazed dictator can kill our citizens, and Mr. Waring prefers that we don't support our men and women who are fighting on the line." She paused. There was a silence in the room.

"Well? Speak out," Maria said.

"Not bad," Henry said.

"He'll bury you," Fenly said.

Maria leaned back against the desk, her face creased with concern. She lit a cigarette.

"Look," Paula said, "you sounded sincere and forceful. That was good."

"It's what I said, isn't it?" Maria asked.

"You didn't address the question," Lucy said.

"I don't give a fuck about the question," Maria responded.

"You've got to give a fuck," Henry said. "You're a congresswoman. You voted the Democratic line. Give them the reasoning for your vote. That's what Fenly did."

"No one cares about the Gulf. They care about our troops."

"You've got to appear competent and in control. It's not good to talk about loosely related ideas. It erodes confidence in your leadership,"

Henry said.

"Is that what you think, Lucy?" Maria asked.

"We'll add 'the Gulf' to our agenda," Lucy said.

Fenly spoke up. "If you don't have a considered answer, or if you don't think you're going to come across strong with the answer you've got, don't answer the question."

"I've got to say something," Maria said.

"Gracefully decline to comment. Make the grounds legitimate," Lucy said.

"You could say," Fenly said, "you're carefully considering all aspects of the issue and will need more historical perspective to judge the administration's response."

"That seems a little insincere," Paula said.

Fenly shrugged. "It's the right idea, believe me."

"Give me another question," Maria said.

Lucy gave many more, for more than an hour. Maria tired and said she didn't want to do any more.

Lucy spoke as they were about to break up. "Wait," she said. "I think we've got to consider an option we've not talked about. We might need to make up a believable excuse to cancel at least the first debate."

"Political suicide," Henry said.

"I'm not sure we can be ready in time," Lucy said.

"I agree," said Fenly.

Maria flushed with anger. "Don't you go against me, you bitch," she said to Lucy.

Lucy paused, her muscles tensed. "Deep down I don't care what happens to you and your asshole campaign," she retorted.

Maria shook her head. "God. I don't deserve this."

"Stop bickering," Henry said.

"It's an option you have to consider," Fenly said. "Look at Nixon's debate. It buried him. You're a fool to let it happen."

"Shut up," Maria said. "I'll do this debate in spite of you. I'm the better candidate. And I'll show them." Maria picked up her shoulder bag to leave, stubbing out her cigarette.

"Do you still want to do the afternoon practice?" Lucy asked as Maria was leaving.

"Of course I want to do the afternoon session!" Maria shouted. She looked back at Lucy. "Bitch."

The door slammed.

"She didn't mean it," Paula said to Lucy.

Fenly laughed without humor. "Well, she convinced me."

CHAPTER 44

Lucy

The debate was staged at a regional TV station and fed to most of the country on cable, although coverage was not close to national.

The party seemed satisfied with less coverage than anticipated and openly expressed serious concern over Maria's capabilities in front of an audience, much less in a one-on-one debate. The male moderator—more local look-good celebrity than newscaster—perched on a stool next to a female political analyst who was seated behind a desk with the station's logo on it. Maria and the challenger Mr. Waring were positioned side by side, each behind a podium. The fifty auditorium seats were half filled. Lucy and the staff sat in front-row seats away from cameras so Maria could have a direct view of their silent but animated assessments of how she was doing.

The format was a question directed at one debater with time for the opponent to also comment, and then rebuttals of less than two minutes possible for each candidate. The moderator made the introductions, and the analyst Miss Rarity began her questions, her eggshell-white teeth shining, her flowing long hair glittering on her shoulders, her plain, no-power lenses in dark-rimmed glasses accenting the sincere dark brown of her eyes in an attempt to intellectualize her obvious craving for a memorable-star image.

The first question, by toss of a coin, went to Waring. It was about his weak record of legislative experience. The next question went to Maria, about the Gulf War. Lucy cringed without sound or movement. But Maria handed back what she'd been coached, although she confused Iraq with Iran until the moderator corrected her. When Maria finished with the Gulf War, Fenly gave Lucy a shrug and a smile to let her know it wasn't as bad as he expected.

With the next few questions, Maria responded with increasing hesitancy. Lucy could see her confidence seeping away, fear taking hold. Lucy held up a fist and raised it high when Waring was talking. Maria saw her but didn't look any more confident. In the rebuttals she was losing focus, and her voice was becoming strident and irritable. Fenly poked Lucy in the ribs with his elbow. There was nothing they could do.

On the last question of the debate, Waring was asked his view of abortion.

"Yes, Miss Rarity. I'm glad you asked that question. I wish to be very clear that my personal feelings about abortion will not be used to influence voters in this election. It is a complex issue that generates high emotions on both sides. The courts now are repeatedly addressing the question, and legislation that stands continues to be tested. I personally will not let my views affect what I perceive to be the will of the majority of my constituency. If called to act while I am in office, I will be guided by the will of the majority of the people."

"It's a bull's-eye," Fenly whispered to Lucy. She dreaded the next few seconds.

"Congresswoman Sanchez," the moderator said. "Your response."

"I will not allow evasion on the part of my opponent." Maria looked away from the camera lens and addressed Waring directly. "What is your position on abortion? Mine is pro-life. It always has been. It always will be. Voters deserve to know your feelings."

Waring continued to face the camera. "Again, I will be objective when and if legislative action is presented to me. I will work for the will of my American constituency."

"What do you believe?" asked Maria. She spoke forcefully, as if she had him now in the grip of her claws.

Fenly had his hand on Lucy's forearm.

Waring continued. "My personal opinion is that the government should remain out of the issue. That each woman should have the choice. That they should be given the benefit of as much information as possible to help them with the decision. And when appropriate, health care—and only when appropriate—should be provided, no matter what her choice might be. But I emphasize, I will not force this will on the people. I will serve, not command."

"You want to kill the unborn," Maria said loudly. "You have no respect for human life."

"Not true," Waring said. "I have the greatest respect for human life. And I have respect for the rights of a mother regarding what she feels might be best for her offspring. But I will not let my feelings change my service to the majority of our community. I will act in accordance with the will of the people as it is expressed at the time. In my view, that is what an elected official should do."

"Elected officials should not contribute to the murder of innocents. Living organisms that cannot defend themselves," Maria said.

Fenly's grip on Lucy's arm tightened. She shared his apprehension. "A complicated issue to end our discussion . . ." the analyst started her close-out.

"Make him commit. One way or the other," Maria interrupted.

"I would like to thank both of you . . ."

"It's immoral," Maria said.

Fenly groaned.

The camera zoomed in on the moderator, removing images of the candidates from the screen. Maria tried to say something but they had turned her microphone off. There was hesitant audience applause. A commercial came on the monitor after the moderator said goodnight. The audience started talking all at once.

"She's an idiot," Fenly said.

Paula leaned over. "It wasn't too bad, was it?"

"A disaster," Fenly said.

"We've got to script every public appearance, even the debates," Lucy said. "She can't say anything that hasn't been written for her, and memorized."

"She'll never do it," Henry said, hunkering down in front of them.

"She will when she reads the commentary."

"The commentators, seated behind a semicircular desk and visible on the station's monitors, were already discussing Maria's performance. But there was no sound.

"It's the only way I'll continue," said Fenly.

Maria came to them from behind the podium, down two steps and across the few feet to where they were sitting.

"I nailed the son of a bitch," she said.

There was a brief silence.

"You did great," Paula said. But everyone else was quiet. Lucy forced a smile and reached out and shook Maria's hand.

"Well, what did you think?" Maria asked.

"We've got some work to do," Lucy said.

Fenly did not offer his hand. "Never again. No more spontaneous responses," he said.

"Fuck you," Maria said.

"My point exactly." Fenly backed away.

CHAPTER 45

Lucy

A few days later Lucy spent the night with Fenly. It was after seven. They were sharing a pepperoni pizza with extra cheese. There was a bottle of wine for Lucy and beer with whisky chasers for Fenly.

"I was at the bank today, filling out a deposit form. My divorce settlement check came in."

"No alimony?"

"None."

"No custody agreement? I thought they always favored the mother."

"The judge probably wasn't impressed that I didn't show up. I was tired of fighting."

"I thought the lawyers were good," Fenly said. "I sent them enough money for the best."

"They thought I'd lose at trial. And the cost would have been over $200,000. They suggested settlement for as much cash as I could get."

"How much?"

"$55,000."

"That's peanuts."

"They thought I was lucky. And it at least covered what I owed."

"We'll, at least you're free." He smiled.

She remained serious. "I was at the counter at the bank window. I saw you come out of Kioto's restaurant. You got in a sedan."

"I keep trying to get my license reinstated."

"It was Tom Blanchard driving, wasn't it?"

Fenly had a quizzical look on his face.

"You're thinking about lying to me?"

"Never," he said.

"But it's a little inappropriate to be riding around with Waring's campaign manager in pubic before the election. Are you going to deny that?" Lucy said without rancor. But she threw him a glance of interest.

"I'd never lie to you."

"What was it about?"

"I've known him for years."

"But during a campaign?"

He pulled off another triangle of pizza. He wasn't fat, really. But he was beginning to look worse, like he didn't care for himself. Weak and skinny-flabby. And she wondered why he was hesitant about Tom Blanchard. Why would Blanchard pick him up? Then it dawned on her. Why didn't I suspect before?

A slice of pepperoni slipped off his pizza as he took a bite. He left it on the floor where it landed.

"Are you working for Blanchard?" she asked.

He laughed.

"You are!"

"Not exactly."

"What does that mean?"

He was still smiling. "You don't like her any more than I do."

"But I'm not selling her out," Lucy said. "Is that what you're doing?"

"Of course not. I've given the campaign all that I have," Fenly said.

"What are you doing then with Blanchard?"

"It's not what you think."

"You're incorrigible," Lucy said, but she was smiling at him.

"Just perceptions. Observations."

"And he pays you?"

He laughed again. "Not much."

"Did you set up that abortion shit?"

"Not at all. I let him know she felt strongly about it. That was all."

"I don't like her. But I don't think I can let you go on, Fenly. It's sleazy."

"We don't have anyone embedded in her campaign staff. I learn stuff from Blanchard."

"That's duplicitous."

"Pragmatic."

"And profitable."

"I'll share it with you. Always."

"Cancel that. I don't like her," she said. "She's a lousy representative . . ."

"And she's stupid."

"But I can't go against her. Panetta sent me to help her get elected."

"You're doing your best. No one could think otherwise."

"Not if I know you're a spy."

"I'm not a spy. I'm involved in the political game. I enjoy it. And it's not all for money. It's like playing Monopoly. It's fun to have control of the board."

"It's unethical."

"Not at all. It's sharing information."

"For money."

"Being paid for information is not unethical."

She finished off her glass of wine and stood to clear the coffee table of pizza debris. "I don't like it," she said.

"I'll stop," he said. "To make you happy. It's not the money. And I really don't care." He frowned.

She wasn't sure if she could believe him.

"Really," he said. "Never again."

Two weeks later, after a four-day bus excursion through the district with Maria, staff met in the dairy headquarters. Three members had been added to supervise phone solicitations and to expand mailings. Henry Cid reviewed progress and then nodded for Maria to speak. She thanked her staff. Commended them for their work.

"I'd like to announce that we've signed for a pre–election day debate with Waring. We'll be starting preparation immediately."

Lucy asked about the format, the moderator. If topics could be submitted ahead of time—and restricted.

"We can submit topics," Maria said. "Of course."

"No freewheeling discussions?" Fenly asked.

"Would it be a debate, then, Mr. Cooper?"

"You need written-out responses for every contingency," Fenly said.

"Oh, I'll be prepared. I can guarantee you that."

The last debate had been almost uniformly criticized from many aspects. Yet Maria continued to think her performance was a success.

Maria glanced around at the members of the staff. "I want each of you to feed Lucy ideas. We were short on originality at the last debate."

Lucy bristled. "If you don't like my work, find someone else."

"Don't be sensitive. I'm asking for help."

"You're no Ronald Reagan," Lucy said.

"Don't get uppity," Maria said.

Lucy's hands were tight fists but she said no more.

That night she went back to Sausalito to Carrie Malroy's place. Carrie was gone and Lucy needed to be alone. She would never forgive Maria for talking down to her in front of the other staff. Never.

CHAPTER 46

Elizabeth

In the last months of her life, Jennifer suffered the last few months her life beyond what any human deserved. Services were held at Agnes's church. Elizabeth sat with Luke and Agnes in the front row. Luke spoke, and Elizabeth, too. As Elizabeth said words for her niece, she saw Lucy seated alone near the back. Lucy gave no recognition that she knew Elizabeth had seen her. When Elizabeth sat back down and the minister had begun his sermon, Elizabeth leaned to Luke and whispered, "Lucy."

Luke nodded.

"I'll invite her," she said. Luke flashed a questioning look and then shrugged almost imperceptibly. When the service ended, Elizabeth circled the crowd of sympathizers that surrounded Luke and Agnes and sought out Lucy.

"Ride with us," Elizabeth said, without greeting. "Please." After a few seconds' consideration, Lucy nodded acceptance.

Elizabeth did not expect Lucy to thank her for telling her about Jennifer. And Lucy, as the day progressed, had said nothing more.

The stretch limousine was hot. The thermostat was broken, the driver said. The air conditioner wasn't functioning. Elizabeth felt sweat under her arms and worried that her dress might stain. Lucy sat next to Agnes, across from Luke and Elizabeth. Agnes's two sisters sat in the rear.

"Where's father?" Lucy asked.

Agnes was the first to answer after a long silence. "Strange you should ask that," she said.

Elizabeth wasn't sure what Agnes meant. She thought Lucy deserved an answer. "Father has had a difficult time at the hospital," Elizabeth said.

"He's ignored us," Agnes said.

His own granddaughter, Elizabeth thought. He's the only one in the family who knew, besides Luke and me, that Jennifer truly was his granddaughter.

"Thanks for coming," said Luke to Lucy.

"I didn't come for your thanks," Lucy said harshly.

"Of course not," he said.

"She was my daughter," Lucy said defensively.

And Luke's, thought Elizabeth. And my niece, by blood, not just legal adoption. But she said nothing.

"You don't deserve to be here," Agnes said to Lucy.

"Mother!" Elizabeth exclaimed.

"I'm saying what everyone thinks. What must be said."

I shouldn't have asked Lucy to ride with us, Elizabeth thought. Lucy remained silent and stared ahead.

"Jennifer always had your picture by her bed this last year," Luke said to Lucy. "And she slept without fail with a Cinderella book she said was your gift."

Lucy's face didn't change. "I carry her picture in my wallet, the one you sent me in Africa," she said.

"That means nothing," Agnes said.

They rode silently for many minutes. Finally one of Agnes's sisters commented, "We're almost there."

Lucy stood away from the family at the graveside ceremony.

Elizabeth didn't notice when Lucy left, just knew she was no longer there. At the reception, even when she got involved in the flood of sympathy from relatives and friends, she still noticed that Lucy had not come.

CHAPTER 47

Lucy

The next Saturday night back in California, alone at Carrie's apartment, Lucy had cheese and rice crackers with a bottle of wine for dinner. She sat with her head back in an overstuffed chair, her eyes closed. The doorbell rang. She decided it was probably not for her. The bell rang again. "Lucy," a man's voice said, "Open up." Probably Fenly. He was getting possessive recently. She opened the door a crack.

"Let me in," Hower Bain said.

She hesitated, and he pushed the door open with enough force to make her stumble backward.

"You can't just force . . ."

"I want you to come back," he said. "I love you. I've been acquitted."

"I didn't know."

"The ministry is growing again. I'm back on international TV. I want you back."

Her heart was beating fast for the need of him. He was never indefinite. Never indifferent. Always exciting. She resisted throwing herself against him, putting her arms around his neck, kissing that husky-smelling mouth. Let him do what he would.

"That's crazy," she said.

"I've filed for divorce from my wife. I want to take you back."

"I can't, Hower. I've got a job. I'm working for a campaign."

"After the campaign, then. I was crazy in Africa. I should never have let you go."

"I was poisoned."

"It was Manny. I know of no other explanation."

"Did she confess?"

"No. She disappeared. And I've come to believe it was her. I think Collette thought so, too."

"Why have you come here?"

"To be sure you wouldn't say no." He started toward her but she backed away. "It's a new life," he said.

"Sit down," she said. "I'll get you a drink. Tell me about it. And about all your friends."

She brought him a ginger ale with ice and had wine for herself. He told her Collette was well, still working at the African mission, now headed by a native minister. Carla and more than a hundred and ten of the converts had returned with him to Georgia.

She was glad for him. He seemed a new man. And she felt comfortable now that her initial faith in his innocence was not folly. "How did you get the conviction overturned?"

"The girl recanted her testimony. It was the mother who pushed her to lie."

She replenished his glass and then sat and leaned toward him. "You're a powerful man, Hower. I care for you. But we're in different stages of our lives now. I can't go with you. I don't like Georgia."

"It's our life, Lucy. Our life to nurture, to let grow."

"I just can't." Although she wanted to be with him again, she couldn't imagine returning to Georgia and all the memories lurking there. She said no again.

He made love to her. She let him. Wanted him. And he didn't leave until the next morning. Even when she told him no again, he was determined to convince her. Finally, he left. Even though it was late morning, she finished a bottle of wine so she could quell the turmoil in her, and she finally fell into a troubled, light sleep that lasted until mid-Sunday afternoon.

CHAPTER 48

Lucy

Lucy and Fenly were alone in the mail room, sitting across from each other at a long, rectangular drop-leaf table. On the table between them were stacks of letter-size envelopes, all addressed, stamped, and presorted. Each of them also had a stack of single-sheet flyers. They took flyers one by one, folded them in half, removed the flyer that had been printed with libelous errors from the envelope, and inserted the correct flyer. Lucy could do three to Fenly's one, even more when he paused for a sip from his flask. "I'm getting shitfaced," he said.

Lucy threw a removed, useless flyer on the floor. It landed on top of hundreds of others.

"Doesn't this piss you off?" he asked.

Of course it pisses me off, she thought. Everything done with or for Maria pissed her off now.

"The printer made the mistake?" he asked.

"Or that jerk of a marketer. No one admits a mistake, and no one agreed to pick up the bill for reprinting."

He leaned back, added a little whiskey from his flask to a can of Diet Coke, and took a swig. "This campaign stinks," he said. "She's a fucking idiot, capable of single-handedly sinking the American dream."

"Like an enemy torpedo heading toward a Carnival cruise ship," Lucy said.

He sipped again without starting back on his task. "You're good at this," he said, holding up an envelope.

"I don't want to be good at this."

"Why do it?"

She stopped and looked at him; she said nothing.

"You don't like her any more, do you?" he said.

She started back on the envelopes. "Not one little bit."

"Her philosophies—or lack thereof. She's stupid. It's the only thing that qualifies her to be a political candidate."

Lucy smiled. "I don't like her mouth. I don't like her screaming at me for things I have no control over. She doesn't have a whiff of courtesy."

"Or good sense. She's turning everyone off."

"She's been calling me 'bitch' a lot."

"Quit."

"It's a job. Panetta supports her."

He finished his Coke and started folding. "She had the gall to tell me to make the back lease payments on the bus. 'You can afford it,' she said. I told her to fuck off. I was through supporting her. This wasn't fun anymore."

"And you weren't accepting checks from the opposition?" Lucy laughed.

He laughed and took her hand. "You want to know the truth?"

"You never stopped accepting checks?"

He let go of her hand. "You frosted?" he asked.

"I hope she flops."

They worked for a while.

"You're writing out all the responses for the debates," Fenly said. "She's memorizing them. Why not write them like she'd say them. Misinformation. Fuzzy thinking. Spontaneous misunderstandings."

"The opposition must have doubled your pay."

He stopped his work. "It's not that. I don't think she should be elected. She shouldn't be in any public office with any power."

Lucy stopped working. "I hate her enough."

"You should fight back. She's out of control now."

"I'd have to stop practice sessions with staff. They'd make corrections."

"How many more do you have?"

"Three."

"Claim urgency. Get her into self-destruction in private."

"She wouldn't know," Lucy mused. "She never credits any of us for helping her with the public persona. It might work."

"Of course it will work," he said.

"Screw this," she said. She picked up the remaining stack of uncorrected envelopes and fed them into a shredder at the end of the table. "We'll work on it tonight. I have a session with her in the morning."

"We'll focus on abortion, drug legalization, foreign policy."

"The economy. I could feed her false facts and she wouldn't know the difference."

"Yippee!"

She shook her head in disbelief with what Fenly could come up with. Sometimes she thought he was psychotic. "That sounds like they tripled your pay."

"You wouldn't believe me even if I told you the truth."

The election eve debate was better attended and more widely viewed on TV than any other event, even local sports. Maria and Waring were seated facing each other with the moderator in the middle. The format was answer with unlimited-time rebuttals, except at the moderator's discretion. Maria had worked hard with her responses. When she started, her delivery had definitely improved, and she answered questions with less birdlike twitter than usual. The indoctrination of strange ideas and false data had an immediate effect on Waring's responses, as well as the follow-up questions by the moderator. Waring seemed to progressively get clearer in etching out the differences between Maria and him. The moderator corrected Maria's misstatements and couldn't keep a tone of incredulity out of his voice. Toward the end of the half hour, Maria had moments of doubt, and then she began to see Waring and the moderator as picking on her. She became the feminine alien victim of the prejudices she perceived. "You wouldn't say that to a man," she said after one rebuttal. And at the end, "Don't think because I am Hispanic, that you can belittle me . . ."

"No one could belittle her," Lucy whispered to Fenly.

"Except you," he whispered back, smiling.

On election eve at party headquarters Maria, staff, and supporters milled around, drinking and talking. After the first hour of early results, there was no laughter and the mood turned somber and sour. Maria's face showed a flush of crushing humiliation and she retreated into a private room where only close staff were allowed. She sat in a chair, rarely talking, staring at a TV with election coverage from San Francisco, interrupted only by Paula, who gave her updates. Maria made no attempt to appear upbeat. She knew the worst.

A short time later, Henry Cid clanked two glasses together for attention. There were fewer than twenty people in the room and silence quickly descended.

"We've got to consider a concession speech. The sooner the better," Cid said.

"No," said Maria.

No one spoke. Finally, Henry moved closer to her and sat in a folding chair. "You owe it to your supporters. The party needs you to keep the faithful."

Maria looked up, her face flushed, her eyes angry. "Get out. All of you."

"The concession speech," Henry pleaded.

"You want it so bad? You give it."

"It's traditional . . ."

"Give the speech, Henry. And get the fuck away from me."

Lucy felt a touch of pity for Maria. She had tried to climb beyond her capabilities. She'd learned to ride a balloon-tired bike with training wheels attached, and then she tried to ride in a long distance race on a racing bike; she'd lost her balance and crashed. And she would have crashed on her own without Fenly and Lucy's help. The thought made Lucy feel a little more justified in her sabotage.

"Stay here, Lucy," Maria said, as Lucy started to follow the others out of the room.

Maria stood and came to her. "I'm not stupid, Lucy. I know what you did. It was inhuman."

Lucy saw Maria's pain, saw that under the tough exterior Maria had created for her protection during the campaign, there was more of a person than had been evident.

Lucy resisted her first instinct to defend herself, to point out the unnecessary and crude criticism she had been subjected to for the past few months, the lack of appreciation for what she and all the staff had sacrificed. Any guilt Lucy had for Maria's failure disappeared. "Pull yourself together, Maria," Lucy said. "You're acting like a child."

"Fuck it."

"Go out there. Give that speech. Be as gracious as you can be."

"Nobody wanted me to win," Maria whined.

"Always the victim," Lucy said. "Take some responsibility. You were a shitty candidate."

Maria looked like she might strike her. Then she groped for control, and after a few seconds she relaxed a little. She turned and went toward the room with the cameras.

Henry Cid had already ascended to the podium and started speaking. Maria entered the glare of the spotlights. "Get off," she said, loud enough that the microphones picked it up. Henry stopped mid-thought and moved aside.

Maria demeaned the opponent's tactics. She railed against the district's lack of support. When she finally thanked those who had worked for her, it was meaningless.

I still hate her, Lucy thought.

CHAPTER 49

Lucy

After the campaign loss, Lucy worked for Panetta in San Francisco. She moved what little she had at Fenly's house to Carrie Malroy's place in Sausalito. She worked as assistant to the medical malpractice division, collecting evidence and directing investigators, tracking down records, filing freedom-of-information documents. She didn't want to go to Fenly's. She liked him, although she didn't trust him. She never longed to be with him, and he had never captured her heart with his premature and unsatisfying lovemaking. And much of her time with him was spent trying to fathom his often bizarre thoughts that came through his alcoholic and drug-infested haze until he passed out.

Fenly came to her at Carrie's place two to three times a week, and often on weekends. He'd let himself in during the day and wait. He always left if Carrie would be there for the night; Carrie had made it clear she didn't want Lucy to have Fenly or any man in the apartment when she was home.

On a Monday morning Lou Panetta called Lucy into his office as soon as she arrived at work. He was alone. He offered a cup of coffee that she accepted; she was now drinking coffee regularly again after she was able to forget the suspicion of poison in the coffee in Africa.

"What's up, Lou?" she asked.

"Maria was here last week, twice."

"How is she?"

"Strange you should ask. She seems suicidal to me."

"I doubt she's the type."

"She was destroyed."

"She was an inept candidate."

"But not stupid."

"She wasn't bright, Lou. And her emotions were out of control most of the time."

Lou fingered the pages of a book with a purpose. "She didn't deserve it."

Lucy pretended she didn't know what he meant.

"You know what I mean. Maria brought the tapes of her speech. She told me how you coached her in private for the last few sessions. She blames you."

"She said what she wanted to say."

"She was insecure. She depended on you. She trusted me in recommending you."

"She cursed and swore at all of our efforts to help her."

"That's what I mean. She's insecure. She climbed in a white-male-dominated world. It was not easy for her."

Panetta's lack of perception of Maria's tired, unimaginative, always defensive ways of working with staff irritated Lucy. "She was impossible," she said. "I came to dislike her."

"She was a client. You were working for her at my discretion. I expected you to treat her with respect."

"I worked day and night. I carried her through rally after rally."

"I gave you work when you'd been disbarred in Georgia. I respected your intelligence and liked you personally. You took advantage of my generosity."

"I don't accept that, Lou. I did more than most."

"You destroyed a woman who didn't deserve to be destroyed."

"She would have lost no matter who you sent to help her. Christ, the quality of her staff was miserable. Paula Warez, Henry Cid, Fenly Cooper. She couldn't find anyone of quality."

"It was cruel. She wouldn't have humiliated herself on her own, for Christ's sake."

"You're an idiot."

Panetta paused. "You're fired."

Lucy didn't hesitate. "I quit."

"Eight weeks' separation pay, but don't come back to the office."

"Thanks for nothing." Lucy said.

She left, her jaw clenched, without looking at Panetta.

Lucy borrowed Carrie Malroy's car and drove north to spend the weekend with Fenly. He was with a group organizing illegal farmworkers to strike for benefits. She failed to see the logic in his involvement and thought he endangered their staying in the States, but Fenly was passionate about his cause and was busy enough to not be drinking as much. His marijuana stockpile was twice what it had been a few months ago. With free time after the campaign, he'd returned to selling to dealers. Fenly felt as safe from the law as he ever had in his life, which was important, since he was still on probation from his last incarceration. Illegal sales were ignored by local authorities but the Feds' every movement was scrutinized and tracked by the populace, eager to protect their sources. They effectively let Fenly know of any danger of discovery. Lucy scolded him for the risks he was taking. He laughed and kissed her affectionately.

A few weeks later Fenly came to San Francisco for a concert, and afterward Lucy went with him to an Italian restaurant in Cow Hollow. It wasn't crowded, and they chose a booth in the corner. Fenly wanted to talk about Panetta. He must have been thinking about Lucy's firing.

"Isn't there some legal action? Can't you sue his ass?" he asked.

Lucy had put it in the past. She had thought about some action, but couldn't find anything reasonable. And being disbarred did not lend to the easy acquisition of the expensive and experienced help in labor law that she'd need.

"You have rights," Fenly said.

"I've thought of everything."

"I'll give you what you need, if money's a problem. Hire an investigator to find where Panetta's screwed up."

Lucy laughed. "The man is going to die of cancer in a year or less."

"He shouldn't have fired you."

"Maria was your idea," Lucy said. "The miscues. You thought it up. And it crippled her."

Fenly turned silent.

"I didn't mean that," Lucy said. "We may have thought it up together, but you didn't do it. I did it."

"He still shouldn't get off with firing you."

Lucy picked at her salad. She wasn't hungry now. "He had his own reasons. Let's forget it."

Fenly concentrated on twirling spaghetti Bolognese on his fork. Lucy thought it was time to tell him. She had no income. She wasn't getting along well with Carrie Malroy. And she was lonely.

"I'm going back to Georgia," she said.

Fenly looked up and set his utensils on the plate. "Why?"

"There is nothing here for me."

"There's me."

She smiled. The felon with a heart of fake gold. "I'm restless. I need to find work," she said.

"I've got some friends who might help."

"It's more than that."

"It's the preacher, isn't it? You've got to get back to him."

The truth of his words made her pause.

"He's a charlatan," he continued. "A celebrity faith healer without conscience."

"You don't know him."

"I've looked him up many times. Watched his shows. He's a crook."

Lucy laughed derisively. Fenly had little justification to question the morality of Hower Bain. She wanted to go back to Hower. It was true. That was the main reason. But instead she said, "I want to be back with family."

"You can't stand them. You're adopted. I'm more family than they are."

She didn't respond. After Jennifer's funeral, she had determined never to contact family again. Only Elizabeth had a wisp of kindness in her.

"You need money for the trip, don't you?"

She needed money for everything. She didn't answer.

"I'll do it," Fenly said. "But you won't be happy. And I want you to promise you'll come back here."

She looked away.

"Give me your word," he said.

"You'll find someone else."

"You must promise!"

She looked back at him and stared for a few seconds, then nodded.

But she knew she would never return.

Lucy deplaned and went to the baggage claim carousels at Atlanta's Hartsfield International Airport. She was searching her shoulder bag for the $100 bill Fenly had given her as emergency funds, after he'd bought her ticket and new clothes. She was sure she couldn't find a taxi to take her to north Georgia for that amount. She was hoping to find a kid with a car who could use the extra cash, when Howie stepped up to her.

Seeing him confused her. She never thought he'd come to pick her up. Intense and mixed emotions robbed her of a response for a few seconds. "Oh, my bag," she said, pointing. Then she was laughing.

He took her in his arms. "Relax. Bags go in a circle, you goose."

And she held him as to never let him go again. Hower Bain. Where did the anger go when she was in his arms?

CHAPTER 50

Lucy

Jason Campbell had come back to work for Hower at the Georgia compound. In a few weeks he had hired and organized a staff. The television ministry had been rejuvenated by Hower's return and had again turned extremely profitable, and Hower needed Campbell's investment skills.

Lucy liked Jason better now. That was a surprise. He seemed happy to have her back and frequently had lunch with her at the dining hall, asking her about Africa and detailing his plans for the church expansion.

Lucy's days were filled now with exercise and reading. Hower suggested she join the singing groups, but she had no talent and didn't like the drone of church hymns. She visited the small towns of Cashiers, Boone, and Highlands, usually alone, but she did not like the arts and crafts that were hawked relentlessly in shops and on the streets. There was little entertainment in the towns, and she stopped her excursions after her first few weeks back.

Jason Campbell mentioned the restlessness he saw in her. "Why not help us in the office?" he asked. At first she declined, but Howie thought it was a good idea. She could write brochures. Help with correspondence.

After only a few days, Jason saw her capabilities at finance and began including her in meetings and strategic planning sessions. The church had investments of more than $260 million, accumulated over the years. Hower's operating funds were from pledges and donations, mostly via TV. The church had continued to make a profit even while Hower was in Africa. New churches had been established in seven cities. A large portion of the income was invested in real estate and commercial properties.

Since his return from Africa, Hower was flying in his private airplane, a twin-engine prop plane with a full-time pilot, who connected him to Atlanta, Memphis, Nashville, Little Rock, and any place with a landing strip within an eight-hundred-mile range. Hower had also built himself a four-bedroom house on the compound. He had hired a cook and a housekeeper. His appointment secretary had an office at the back of the ground floor, near the kitchen. He had a private office near the bedroom on the second floor, which he used for reading and writing in the evenings. Most of his daytime administration took place in a new building with four floors, each six thousand square feet.

Jason soon gave Lucy her own office and a part-time secretary in the administrative building. He had assigned her to work with the Atlanta lawyer as the on-compound contact for legal issues. The obvious wealth of the organization had spawned numerous lawsuits over a variety of issues. The threat of legal action against the church had made Jason review all important correspondence for accuracy and libelous material, and he undertook periodic reviews of the grounds and buildings for potential liability issues. With time, he trusted Lucy, and she became the prime assistant in all the legal issues. Although she didn't practice law, her experience became invaluable.

Her life with Hower turned from serene to hectic within months. He was with her only two or three nights a week. During the day she rarely saw him. He was building satellite churches and frequently spent days in other locations. He was expanding the weekly television ministry to other sites to draw crowds and increase membership. All this activity kept him away from the compound. But she was not unhappy. Their time together fulfilled her, and she loved him as much as always. And since she had returned, in his times with her, he had become supportive and attentive in ways that pleased her to no end.

Lucy picked up the phone at Jason's intercom request. It was Abe Singerman from Atlanta, whom she had met a few times over the years. "I'm going over the Sienna Jones case," he said. "Do you know about it?"

"The name isn't familiar," Lucy said.

"It's this crippled girl accusing Bain of assault. They've filed in federal court."

"What were the circumstances?"

"She was in a healing session. She claims she was lifted from her wheelchair and Bain told her to walk. She fell and fractured two vertebrae. She had some bone problem to begin with, and her bones were soft from treatment, and she claims all this aggravated the condition she inherited."

"They've got to stretch to make assault stand."

"It's not a common argument that I know. But I think they'll make the pitch that Bain saw her as a profitable medical commodity. That he used her to garnish sympathy for the church and its causes."

"The church gives back to the sick."

"Not this girl. That they didn't do. There was not much enthusiasm to pleas for help. And the girl's insurance ran out years ago. She had no regular doctor, and most of her care was in emergency room visits where by law they couldn't turn her away. The mother's angry as shit. She wants Bain in jail. For pain and suffering."

"I don't think there was wrongdoing. I attend many of the Sunday-night ministries. Some people are helped by the sessions."

"I know it well," he said. "I find it useless tomfoolery. Those people go for the experience of being there. Being seen. Being talked to. Most of them live alone, watch TV all waking hours. Nothing happens in their lives. They come to Sunday-night sessions and experience being a part of something. That's not seeking medical science. That's just trying to belong, checking to be sure they're not alone, that they're alive."

"You sound like the enemy."

"I'm telling you what I'm up against."

"Well, Hower Bain understands all that. And he tries to use his position to encourage and help," Lucy said.

"I don't care about his status with God. Many sane human beings see him as assuming the adoration and excitement generated in his emotionally hyped sessions, this new sense of belonging to something, as adoration for him. He loves the power it brings. He feels greater than life."

Lucy sighed to herself. There was a lot of truth to that. "What can I do?" she asked.

"Get as much evidence as you can to prove there was no intent."

"I'm sure of it," she said. "I know Howie. He had no intent to hurt that girl for any reason, much less for profit."

"You being sure won't help in court. Get anything you can find. I need it soon. This needs resolution before the papers get wind of it, which the prosecution guys will do soon. Believe me, a lot of people don't approve of Bain."

"He's a complex man."

"I don't judge his motives or his results. I'm paid to keep him out of jail. Depending on the charge, he might get five to ten."

"I'll do what I can. Have you talked to Hower?"

"Not for a while."

"I'll let him know what you've asked."

"Tell him to start praying."

"Don't be a cynic."

"Don't be callow."

Lucy waited until Abe could send her the charges and the supposed date for trial depositions. The girl had been thoroughly investigated. Her father was unknown. Her mother, who made a living as a hairdresser, brought her up with no other children. The girl attended school but never graduated. Her illness, which involved lung and heart complications from some genetic disorder, had made her deformed.

It was the third Sunday in July. Lucy went to the archives and retrieved the tape of the session with Sienna Jones. A technician set up a screening on a fourteen-inch TV and explained pause, forward, and reverse.

She fast-forwarded through the setup, Little Margo, the choir, the save-me-Jesus converts. She paused. During Hower's sermon she could see a girl in a wheelchair, old enough to be Sienna Jones. She was lined up among other sufferers. From two different views she could see at least two staff circulating among them. Then the televised view went back to Howie, until the end of the sermon.

She watched as sufferers were held back by the extended arm of a staff member until their turn came. When the laying of hands, the trembling, and healing was over, another staff member stepped forward to lead the sufferers off. The flow was constant, and once each sufferer was released by a lowering of the arm, if the sufferer could walk alone, he or she started forward. Staff always assisted those who needed help.

She watched as each one progressed. Sienna Jones was the eleventh. Someone, not her mother, wheeled her out. Hower Bain took one of the wheelchair handles and turned the chair so Sienna faced the audience. She had a small body and a large head. Her thin arms gripped the side rails and her bony legs were twisted so one foot splayed out, the other turned in. The crowd noise was intense, but Lucy could hear Hower say, reading from a card, "Sienna Jones, sick and infirm, confined to this chair for half her life." He knelt beside the chair and looked into her face. "Do you believe, Sienna? Do you take Jesus Christ as your savior? Will you forever do the will of the Lord?" Sienna said something indistinguishable as a response. "Speak out, Sienna! Shout it to the world. 'I love Jesus. I believe.'" Sienna seemed to shrink with fear but she yelled in a high, parchment-like voice, "I love Jesus!" The crowd roared. "I believe," Hower urged her. "I believe!" Sienna shouted, animated now by the crowd's energy, her face fearless for an instant.

Hower Bain stood and slipped his hands under her arms, lifting her high into the air, like a father with a child, and then he lowered her slowly, glanced to his right as if to see where the attendant was, and held her out as to let her walk while he supported her weight. "Walk to Jesus, my little lady. Take your first steps." And he moved forward slightly, catching his foot on the chair. He stumbled, dropping her, going down on one knee. She hit the stage in a heap. The audience gasped. Then, in silence, as Howie was getting up and reaching out to her, she pushed herself up, pulled her legs up under her and, with concerted effort, partially stood.

Seeing the amazement of the crowd, Hower stopped. "Praise God," he said into the microphone. An attendant was within a few feet of her now. And she screamed in pain and toppled forward, landing on her shoulder and sliding to the edge of the stage before Howie or the attendant could get to her. She slipped over the edge, dropping five feet to the auditorium floor. The camera was off her now. The audience held its collective breath until a woman screamed. Hower stood. "Praise God for this miracle. Sienna Jones has made her first steps for a full recovery." But even on the small screen, she could see Howie was shaken. He recovered quickly and signaled for the next sufferer, who was with him in seconds. He reached into his pocket for his cards. "Palmer Espy. Suffers from recurrent headaches that make him vomit, pain so bad he must go to bed for hours, weak and exhausted. Has anything helped you?" The boy seemed to be explaining and Hower leaned over for a few seconds and then turned to the audience while the boy was still talking. "Nothing. Nothing any doctor has ever given him has helped the young man. Nothing!" Howie laid hands on the boy's temples and turned his face to the heavens. "Jesus. Dear Jesus. Relieve this believer of his suffering. Take the pain from his skull. Never let it return." He gave the boy's head a severe jolt. The boy looked around, dazed. The crowd was with Hower now. Sienna was not to be seen, apparently carried out of the arena.

"Is the pain gone, my friend? Do you feel the change? Is the pain floating from your being while we speak?"

The boy threw up his hands. "Yes!" he yelled.

The crowd roared again, completely reengaged. Sienna was mostly forgotten.

"It's gone. Totally out?" Howie asked.

"Yes!" the boy yelled.

"Praise God."

Two more healings were completed and the show ended with Howie and the speaker singing in a line in front of the choir, cameras sweeping the audience.

Lucy ran the Sienna Jones segment four more times. The audience must have thought Sienna was all right. They recovered quickly. She wondered if the stumble could have been prevented. Was there liability? She wondered what the procedure was with a wheelchair-bound sufferer. She needed to talk to the staff.

She called in the technician and showed him the tape segment. "Who is that girl attendant? The one with her arm out to hold them back."

"Pam Sessions. She's been doing that as long as I've been here."

"Thanks."

Lucy introduced herself to Pam outside the dining hall. "Everyone knows you, Miss MacMiel," Pam said.

Lucy suggested they have dinner together.

"Why?" Pam asked.

"There's nothing wrong. I want to know what the routines are during the show."

"There's nothing special."

"Could we talk about it anyway?" Lucy decided to be straight about her purpose. "I'm trying to find out what happened with Sienna Jones. Do you remember her?"

"Everyone remembers."

They went through the cafeteria line, flashing their meal cards to the cashier. Lucy waited until they were seated across from each other at a table for two before asking questions. Pam seemed withdrawn. Lucy wondered what she had to hide.

"I've done nothing wrong," Pam said.

"I don't believe anyone did anything wrong. I just want to walk through what the routines were. There's a lawsuit and I'm trying to aid in Reverend Bain's defense. Sometime we're going to have to prove that everything was normal. I just have to understand what happened, and that it wasn't something that could have been prevented."

"I won't go to court," Pam said.

"You won't have to go to court," Lucy said.

"How can you be sure? Can't they subpoena me?"

"I'm as sure as I can possibly be. In fact, I doubt any of us will go to court. The church has hired excellent legal counsel."

They ate in silence for a moment.

"How do you choose the order of the sufferers. Do you do that?" Lucy asked.

Pam didn't hesitate. "Not me. Annie Pearson does that. She's the director. She varies the conditions. That night Sienna was the second wheelchair sufferer. I think there was headache, infertility, and homosexuality before her. I can't remember the order."

"Are there instructions to them? Do they know if they'll walk alone?"

"Each sufferer is given instructions and introduced to the attendant responsible. If they can walk alone, they're encouraged to use the wheelchair for safety until they are told to walk. Most of them need some guidance and a staff member is assigned to take them out. An attendant waits to take them offstage on the other side."

"I've never seen The Reverend lift someone out of the chair like that."

"He's done it many times. And he supports them in other ways, too. He'll encourage them to do what they think they can't. We all find it amazing. Some people are cured. No one is like him."

"But Sienna Jones looked incapacitated."

"Last year eighty-three percent of the ambulatory physical deformities were thought to have total or partial mental components," Pam said. "We've all agreed that Reverend Bain helps them over the mental barriers of their particular illness. He takes away their fears. He makes them feel they can do it. And with the energy from the parishioners, every soul willing for success, the sufferers seem transformed sometimes."

"Did anyone know Sienna was injured? The crowd seemed to move on to the next sufferer almost as if they forgot about her."

"We were all worried. I saw her behind the stage curtains. She seemed not to have much pain unless she tried to move."

"Did she go to the hospital?"

"We have a nurse. I believe she looked at her and advised her to go to the emergency room at the hospital. But I don't know. I was back at stage left getting the last sufferers ready."

"So nothing unexpected happened that night. Nothing abnormal?"

"The Reverend Bain tripped. I've never seen that happen. A big man. A small wheelchair. He must have caught his foot, and it threw him off balance given the weight of her."

"Did you ever see Sienna Jones again? After that night?"

"No."

"Someone must have."

"I don't know. But it was common practice for the nurse or Annie Pearson, the director, to contact believers who had been healed. There was always interest in how they improved."

"And they get better?"

"Many do. A few don't. A small number claim to be worse. But I believe miracles happen. If I didn't, I wouldn't be doing this."

"Of course," Lucy said, and asked her about her schooling and her plans for the future.

CHAPTER 51

Lucy

Lucy surveyed mountains below as the church's twin-engine turboprop leveled off. It was a clear day. Two staff sat near the galley in the rear, and Hower sat next to her, working on redrafting an editorial opinion on a recent call to take away tax exemption for the church, a perennial threat posed by various dissenters. The engines reduced to cruising power. They could speak comfortably in the front of the plane without being overheard.

"Have you ever thought about just settling with Sienna Jones?" Lucy asked.

He let his pencil fall to the tray table and placed his hand on it to keep it from rolling off. "Why would we do that?"

"It might be the right thing to do," she said.

"It was an accident. To settle would be to admit we were at fault. Open the floodgates for hundreds of suits."

She reached to touch his arm, her eyes intent, a faint few wrinkle lines on her brow. A touch of a smile raised the corners of his mouth.

"I'm serious," she said, offended that he might be laughing at her. His face hardened with controlled sobriety. "She suffered," she added. "She couldn't afford care, she didn't heal well. It was terrible."

"We gave her money for treatment."

"It wasn't for long, Hower."

He looked ahead as he spoke and not at her. "The mother wants millions. It was an accident. She fell off the stage."

"That's all lawyer talk. The mother really wants to have the best care for the girl. She'll never get better. I've checked with experts."

He smiled. "You've taken on her case."

She looked out the window.

"Hey. It's okay," he said.

"Don't diminish me . . ."

He turned over a sheet of paper and drew a happy-smile face. He showed it to her.

"I'm not a child," she said, but she wasn't as angry now.

"I'll tell Jason to settle it, if that's what you want," he said.

"It's more than that. It's what people are insinuating about the whole incident. Your reputation. They say you use health to promote your cause. That your entire mission is a sham. You set it up to draw attention to the suffering and then you pretend it's successful when it often is not. And for some illnesses, what you do can delay effective treatment by competent physicians, sometimes even lifesaving treatment. That seems the most damaging."

"Look to the reality," he said. "Every one of those sufferers has been to doctors without cures, often giving their life savings and without receiving one word of support. And don't doctors fail? Yes! They do. And often. And don't patients get worse? What we do for these poor souls, shunned by the system, often rejected by family and loved ones, is let them become part of the spirit of what we do. You've seen it. You've seen the hope, the joy, the belief that it might get better. It turns their hearts from stone to life-pumping muscle."

"I saw that boy with the epilepsy years ago."

"It happens two or three times a year. For some, it brings their condition out in public, making them less afraid to leave the house, letting them know that experiencing life doesn't mean sure death or even rejection."

"The bit I saw didn't seem to make him better."

"I don't remember him specifically, but I'm sure he felt a part of the audience."

"If he did feel a part, he felt he was part of you. You're the one holding him, helping him breathe. He will think you saved him."

"And what's wrong with that?"

She knew his logic, knew there was some truth in what he was saying. "You believe," she said. "Yes, there may be benefit from the experience of the healing sessions. But you believe you are the one with a special gift."

"Few can do what I do," he said.

Why was she in this discussion? She loved him. It wasn't just for this girl or for some morally superior dedication. She wanted him to love her with the same intensity as she loved him. And she wanted him to need her. He cared for her, wanted her—she believed that—more than any woman, she was sure. But he couldn't really love her the way she craved. And they would never be equal in love. He was too involved with his image—an image mixed with divinity healing and the promise of eternal life. So why keep trying? Well. She couldn't do without him. That was all she could think of as an explanation, such as it was.

"You believe you have a divine gift to heal, don't you," she said.

"Ridiculous."

"No. You think you're more than human."

"You're a little off course," he replied, and his voice had turned cool and distant.

"You dropped this girl . . ."

"I stumbled . . ."

"And you've ignored her plight. How callous can you be? And all because you think of yourself as God's chosen disciple."

He paused and then laughed. "I see your point. And you're right. I do have the sin of false pride on my conscience. But what I do does help. And I can't save these infidels without confidence in what I can do."

She couldn't erase her thought that the reason he delayed marrying her, not just officially, but in his mind and heart, was his ever-present need to be God. It was what energized him and made him content, contentment that was his alone, never shared, and always above the contentment that most of the human race could ever know.

"Make sure Jason gives what Sienna deserves," she said.

"You have my word."

CHAPTER 52

Lucy

Lucy stayed busy at the compound. She now edited promotional materials and searched for ideas for Howie's sermons. She knew she'd upgraded his allegories, inserted some logic into his emotional rants, and encouraged him to correct his grammar, which he mostly ignored since he felt he needed to use grammatical errors that made his audience comfortable. She didn't argue since that made some sense to her too.

She exercised daily. Enjoyed cooking meals and they ate together when he was available. She contacted the office of the local congressional representative and had done volunteer work that she expected to grow into a paid campaign position as midterm elections neared.

For the last few weeks she'd felt a progressive fatigue. She barely left the house, afraid that when a wave of drowsiness hit her, she wouldn't have a place to lie down.

She'd been to town to buy makeup. She was concerned that her face looked drawn and her skin sallow. For the first time she used more makeup than simple blush and eyeliner, covering her skin and highlighting her cheeks with rouge. Her mouth was dry, and she was vomiting frequently now, sometimes after eating but also without obvious reason. She'd been to the compound nurse, who'd given her Compazine for nausea, Tylenol with codeine for joint pain, and multivitamins with an additional dose of vitamin C.

"You feeling okay?" Howie asked one night at dinner when she was eating nothing that she had prepared.

"Don't I look okay?"

"You look wonderful. But you're not eating."

She took his inquisition as a probing of what she wanted to deny. "I'm not hungry."

"What have you had today?"

She didn't answer.

"You didn't eat anything, did you?"

She'd had only juice that morning.

Nausea struck her. She got up quickly but the weakness in her legs left her with no support and she sprawled to the floor facedown, her arms out to protect her. Her face still hit the floor, and she rolled over into a fetal position. She dry heaved twice, and moaned.

Hower had her in his arms. He rushed her to the bathroom. The heaving made her feel a little better.

He helped her drink water. She did feel better with that.

He picked her up again and laid her on the bed, adjusting the covers over her. He went immediately to get the nurse, who came to administer a shot and more fluids.

After the nurse left, she felt him beside her in bed with the light off. He remained sleepless. "Are you okay?" he asked repeatedly. She touched him to be quiet. She didn't know if she was okay. She certainly didn't feel good.

"I'm taking you to the doctor in the morning," he said.

Early the next morning Hower took her to a doctor, who was also a church member, in Clayton, Georgia. The doctor drew tests, suspected kidney failure, and arranged an appointment with a nephrologist in Atlanta. Lucy was uremic, in chronic kidney failure. The nephrologist strongly suspected the poisoning in Africa as the cause.

Lucy's thinking had been dulled and her emotions blunted so much that she took the news calmly. She heard the need for immediate treatment of the unemia and acidosis, attention to a strict diet and no alcoholic beverages. Hower carefully took down instructions and managed the prescriptions. The treatments hardly fazed Lucy. She had little energy to fear consequences or face an unknown future. She might need dialysis or a kidney transplant. Repeated creatinine levels were needed to further make a recommendation, the doctor said.

"But transplant is almost inevitable, isn't it doctor?" Hower asked.

Lucy barely followed the conversation, her mind clouded with fluid retention and electrolyte imbalance.

"I'm afraid so," the doctor said.

CHAPTER 53

Luke

Luke, and most full professors, were scheduled on a Wednesday or Thursday to meet with five members of the academy ethics committee who had flown in from various parts of the country to investigate A.J. MacMiel's complicity in the allegations. A.J. was president elect this year, and would soon take the presidency of one of the leading clinical organizations in the field. Because rumors were rampant, the committee had to come up with some action to prevent scandal at the top levels of management and fundraising.

Luke knew each of the members in different ways, from training together to serving on national committees: Clarence, the chair, Nick, Esteban, Jose, and Paul. And they all knew A.J.; some were his good friends. Luke had no idea how the meeting would go. Each of the professors was to be interviewed individually by the committee in a downtown motel conference room. No transcripts would be taken. Luke was told there would be no recording, although he doubted that was true.

Clarence began. "Thanks, Luke, for agreeing to meet with us. As you know the academy is concerned with the allegations against a member. We at first thought no action was appropriate. But it's just been learned that the State Board of Medical Examiners thought enough had occurred to consider revoking Dr. MacMiel's license in the State of Georgia. There were intense negotiations from a number of organizations to modify the board's proposed action before it became public. The state board agreed to drop the action against the licensee, if A.J. would agree never to practice surgery in the state again. Given that it was necessary to divert their action, the academy felt the need to erase the accusations and restore A.J.'s reputation. Part of that was through the purview of the ethics committee making objective determination of A.J.'s not being guilty."

It was appalling. The state board making deals where justice was not served, and that could endanger patients in other states. All politics where politics shouldn't be.

Clarence continued. "We are not a jury, and we are not here to serve justice with sanctions and penalties."

You're here to dodge and weave so A.J.'s mistakes will not hurt the specialty or the organization.

"However, we do have the mandate from the president and the board to determine as truthfully as we can the validity of the charges and suits and then recommend an action A.J.'s membership to the board: dismissal, censure, reprimand, or no action on. Any questions?"

"A couple of you might know that A.J. is my father-in-law," Luke said. "I will speak candidly but I want you to know of that potential conflict of interest."

"Thank you," Clarence said. They were sitting at a rectangular table, Luke at one end, Clarence at the other. Each member of the committee had a stack of folders and papers.

They started off by asking about the dismissal of Sandra Perez. Luke repeated the details, which he was sure they already had in their papers.

"And you felt it was unjust."

"Without cause."

"Couldn't it have been done without A.J.'s insistence or even knowledge?"

"It was handled through Human Resources, so I don't know what exactly happened there. But I was told directly by the one faculty member, who wrote the only seriously negative evaluation ever recorded on Sandra a few weeks before dismissal and out of the regular cycle of evaluations, that A.J. wrote—at least dictated—the evaluation and A.J. had strongly urged him to sign."

"Are you implying intimidation?"

Luke thought for a few seconds. "Yes," he said. "The faculty member feared that he would not be promoted."

"That faculty member should talk with us."

"I think he'd deny what he said. And I don't think he'll talk to you."

"Under oath, if it came to that?"

"I don't know," Luke said.

Nick spoke. "Do you have any opinion of the validity of the wrong eye surgery?"

"A.J. admitted it at one time, then later reversed . . ."

"Or clarified?"

"I believe an error was made, and covered up. I have listened to evidence gathered by the internal quality assurance committee . . ."

"Full professors committee. That the one?"

"Yes. No one thinks the wrong eye charge is an error. The eye operated first had evidence of minimal visual potential."

"Couldn't it have been within the purview of the individual surgeon which eye to do first? They were both affected."

"What was done was not within common clinical practice here or nationally."

"You're a retina surgeon?" Jose asked.

"I'm an ophthalmic surgeon. I have full knowledge of what is common practice."

"Do you have reason to dislike your father-in-law, Luke?" Esteban asked.

Luke clenched his teeth but made sure no other movement could allow them speculation against his testimony's validity. "A.J. was my mentor and colleague. He always treated me fairly. I do not have reason to dislike him."

There was a pause.

"Why speak out against him, then?" Paul asked.

Luke's heart was pounding. "I believe excessive surgery was done for financial gain. Poor patient care follow-up on the transplant resulted in uniocular and binocular blindness, and I believe inappropriate action was taken by administration against those involved. All actions that were wrong and hurt the faculty, the school, and the profession. There are those who have suffered and deserve compensation. Some penalties must be applied."

"You don't think he'll ever operate again, do you?" Clarence asked.

"I don't know. But I already believe he's arranged a position in another state."

"And you continue to be willing to ruin a surgeon's, and a chairman's, career over what might have been an honest mistake that could happen to any of us and that has been blown out of proportion through vindictive slander?" Jose asked.

"Jose," Luke said, "I resent your accusation. Many wrongs have been done. I, and many others, believe they were not simple mistakes without reason. You may not want to believe that. I accept your right to do that. But do not call my appearance before this committee, or any of the faculty, vindictive. Or slander."

"I didn't mean to single you . . ."

"What you said was inappropriate and . . ."

Clarence interrupted. "I think we've had enough," he said. He thanked Luke profusely for his time. Luke stood to leave and there was no movement of any one but Clarence to rise. Luke made no attempt to shake the hands of the men who had once been friends and colleagues.

Three weeks later, a mild reprimand was issued from the Academy as a public letter to A.J. It was nothing, really, although it would eventually prohibit A.J. from ascending to the presidency of the Academy.

The school continued to support A.J. as chair and the insurance companies were ready to litigate, fearful that a settlement would flush out more than the five suits already filed against A.J. At about the same time, Luke found out that all direct referrals to him from his colleagues were being shunted to a junior faculty member—without his knowledge, or the knowledge of the referring physicians.

Luke's practice was now less than half what it had been just last year. He knew he would have to resign and work elsewhere, and sent out feelers to determine what was available. He interviewed at four places. The best seemed to be a private solo practice opportunity with a surgical group in Savannah. And it was Elizabeth's favorite of all the places he looked. He took the job.

Luke married Elizabeth in a quiet but elegant ceremony in the church on Peachtree that she had attended off and on since childhood. A few days later they made a permanent move to Savannah to a nineteenth-century historic house surrounded by live oaks, facing the water.

CHAPTER 54

Elizabeth

A few days before Elizabeth and Luke left for Savannah, they took Agnes to Sunday brunch at a restaurant in Lenox Square. It was a buffet; they were seated at a reserved table.

"Is A.J. going down to work with the McDonald guy?" Agnes asked Luke.

"I hear he's going to San Antonio," he said. "I don't know about McDonald. I guess he's the logical one to take him on. They've been friends since Harvard days."

Elizabeth saw the stress crease his face.

"What will he do?" Agnes asked.

"He can do anything, from what I understand. He's been licensed in Texas for years. And there has been no action against him by the Georgia board," Luke said.

"They were afraid, weren't they?" Agnes said. "They think that action by the board will affect the court case, especially if it comes to trial."

"The word is that there will never be any action by the board, or the academy," Luke said.

"But they investigated?"

"No one will ever know exactly what went down, but I understand no action is a fait accompli."

"You've got to stop worrying about it," Elizabeth said to Luke.

"I think it's criminal to take no action," he said.

"I can't forgive him," Agnes said.

The time had come to fill plates from the buffet. Once they were settled again, Agnes spoke up. "Did you see the article in the Sunday news section about that Hower Bain?"

Neither Elizabeth nor Luke knew what she was talking about. "He's been indicted on tax evasion or fraud or something like that. An investigative reporter has questioned his use of church funds. Flying around in that airplane. Building a mansion."

"Is it really a mansion?" Elizabeth asked.

"Well, from the pictures, it is a mansion for a preacher."

"Did it say anything about Lucy?"

"No, thank God. But it did say he's suspected of shady real estate deals using church money."

"I hope Lucy's all right."

"She always seems to survive," her mother said. "I wonder how her health is sometimes."

"It's the renal failure," Elizabeth said.

"It's a debilitating condition," Luke said, "and the dialysis is exhausting."

"Poor Lucy," Elizabeth said. "She doesn't deserve this."

She looked at her mother, who didn't look up or say anything. Elizabeth knew that Agnes thought Lucy deserved anything she got, mostly for her treatment of Jennifer, who now would be a young lady. They all still mourned her passing.

CHAPTER 55

Luke

Hower Bain went to Luke and Elizabeth in Savannah. Luke's first impulse at the sight of Bain was to refuse to see him, but Elizabeth, out of habit, invited him in and offered him a drink. "Coffee? Iced tea? We don't have much. We're still in the process of moving in." He accepted a Diet Coke.

Luke and Bain took chairs in the living room. Luke had never met him—this large man, over six feet and more than 250 pounds with rugged features, heavy scowling eyebrows, thick lips on an asymmetrical mouth, and slightly uneven teeth.

Luke waited for him to speak, to explain why he had come all this way, but he remained silent until Elizabeth returned with Diet Coke over ice in a glass. She sat next to Luke on the sofa.

"Lucy needs a transplant," Hower said. "Did you know that?"

Luke had told Elizabeth the probable inevitability of it. Luke put his hand briefly on Elizabeth's arm to warn her to be silent.

But she frowned and said, "Why are you here, Mr. Bain?"

Luke expected some hesitation from Bain, but Bain said, "You ignore her. She's family. I find that reprehensible."

Elizabeth tensed.

"Lucy needs a donor," Hower said. "A living donor."

It was a terrible thing to ask. It brought so much of the past to the surface. And although Bain didn't know, Elizabeth being the half-sister of Lucy might make her the best match available.

"I don't believe you're aware of the family's difficulties over the years," Luke said. "Difficulties precipitated often by Lucy. Difficulties that make such a request awkward."

"Lucy wouldn't ask you. She couldn't bring herself to do that," Hower said.

Elizabeth still couldn't find words. Luke was sure Elizabeth's humanity, her responsibility to her half-sister, wouldn't let her say no.

"I'm afraid that's not possible," Luke said, before Elizabeth could speak. "And it's not your business, reverend."

Luke had, of course, thought of this possibility ever since he knew Lucy was in renal failure. Chronic renal failure almost always led to the need for a transplant. But he knew his blood type and hers were not compatible. Elizabeth was the only obvious best donor. But she didn't deserve this guilt-laden pressure, nor should she ignore the risks of surgery. Luke saw no reason to share his knowledge of her possible compatibility with this jerk.

"Do you feel the same?" Bain asked Elizabeth. Luke spoke. "She does."

"Let her speak," Bain said. "I want to know what she thinks."

"No," Luke said. "It's time for you to go."

Bain hesitated, trying to find words. "May God forgive you," he said, standing up. "You are family. You have responsibilities. I can't ever forgive you."

Bain let himself out. Elizabeth cried silently.

"Don't do it. There are significant risks," Luke said. She wiped her eyes with the sleeve of her dress.

"I know I'm not compatible," Luke said. "But I wouldn't do it even if I were."

"She'll die without it?"

"She's going to die with or without it. With it she probably will live longer, but she has no guarantee of a normal life ahead of her."

"I don't know what to do."

"Think about it, then. We'll get advice. But we don't owe Lucy anything because a doctor advises her that a living donor is best. She's been placed on a cadaver donor list, I'm sure."

"But that's not as good?"

"Not as living, no. A living donor might increase her life by years, but it could also be only a few months. I don't think it's worth the risks of your undergoing surgery, or of your possibly losing function in the remaining kidney, and needing a transplant yourself."

She was trembling.

"Come to bed," Luke said. "See if you can sleep. We'll have lots to talk about."

CHAPTER 56

Lucy

Lucy traveled from the compound to Atlanta for her dialysis three times a week. Twice Hower had used the plane to fly her down, and he once accompanied her himself. The other times, Jason Campbell, who had a daughter in Atlanta whom he would visit, usually drove her.

She had continued to work more and more frequently with Jason at the compound. She found her times with him civil, and at times even enjoyable. He had a sense of humor she liked. He was a strong family man and told lively and caring stories about his four children and two grandchildren. He had long ago abandoned hope of converting her, and he rarely mentioned religion or his job. He was fascinated by politics and she enjoyed his opinions and prejudices, which at times might have been her own if she'd wanted to dwell on the subjects.

To drive, they had to start early, and this morning Lucy dressed and crossed from Hower's house to the administrative building where Jason would be waiting for her. But he wasn't waiting for her this morning.

She set her small suitcase by the door and entered the building. The corridor was dark, but there was light seeping around the edge of the door to his office. She went to the door and knocked. There was no response. She pushed down on the door handle that yielded and she opened the door slowly. Jason was behind his desk with his head on his folded arms on top of the desk. She thought he was dead.

"Jason!" She started to run to him.

His body jerked. He lifted his head and slowly opened his eyes. "Are you all right?"

He put his head back down on the desk, refolding his arms.

She ran to him and shook his shoulder. "Talk to me!"

He sat up again and looked at her, still disoriented. "Why are you here?"

"We're going to Atlanta. My dialysis is at one thirty."

He leaned back in his chair, resting his head on the headrest, his eyes closed. After a few seconds he sat up and looked at her, stood, and went to a sink. He splashed water on his face and dried with a paper towel from a metal dispenser on the wall.

"It's Thursday," he said, almost as a question.

"Have you been drinking?"

He said nothing and sat down in an armchair. She stayed standing. "I can't miss my appointment," she said.

He concentrated. "I'm not going," he said.

"How will I get there in time?"

"I don't know, Lucy. I don't know. You'll just have to figure it out yourself."

"Why are you doing this?" she asked.

He shook his head. "Why am I doing this?" he asked no one.

"This is ridiculous," she said, and started for the door.

"Sit," he said.

"I've got to find a car. I'll drive myself."

"Just for a minute. I want to explain."

She hesitated before pulling up a chair across from him. "I've quit," he said. "Everything. I'm moving out this morning."

"You're leaving Howie?"

"And the church."

There were tears of anger and frustration in Jason's eyes. It was the last thing she would have expected. A wave of fatigue swept over her, and she wasn't sure if it was her disease or because she was suddenly tired of Jason and his always subservient nature.

"You can't leave Hower."

"It's not going to be pleasant for you, Lucy. There will be no one to pay for your treatments any more. No one to support you."

"Hower does that . . ."

"Hower's going down. The church is going down, too, although they're trying to cover the worst and stay in business."

"You're crazy."

"He'll be indicted for tax fraud within days. There is an article coming out in the Sunday paper about his misuse of church money. Airplanes. The house. Property investments. I believe they'll include supporting you."

"That's illegal?"

"It's improper, from church operating funds. But it's worse. They'll expose a trail of professional prostitutes he's paid in different cities with church funds. They'll hype the hypocrisy of it, and the amounts. More than $200,000 over the years."

She felt sick.

"And he used two lump sums to buy off that girl," he said. "The one you defended him against."

She was confused. She didn't understand. "How could he buy her off?"

"She recanted her testimony. It was the basis of his appeal."

"That's illegal."

"He did it to never be traced."

"He was guilty?"

"Of course he was guilty."

"You lie," she said angrily.

"You're a fool. There were a least two others underage."

"You're jealous of him."

"Not at all. But I hate him. He's put blame on me. I'll be indicted, too. He's ruined me."

She could not sort out the charges, or if they were true. Guilty of underage sex? A trail of prostitutes? She knew of women, but not prostitutes. Payoffs to accusers—not settlements? How could the press defy the court's process of determining guilt and justice? Was it possible? Not with the Hower Bain she loved. But suspicion made her pause. She knew he might be capable of these charges, and more. She had always been willing to ignore the obvious. She loved him. But could she ever ignore these accusations again?

"You know I've never done anything wrong," he said. "Will you tell them?"

"Speak against Hower?"

"Will you support me? You know he's capable of these charges. You never let yourself see who he really is."

"I cannot go against him. He's been kind to me."

"You're an idiot," he said.

"Sticks and stones," she said.

"You won't be getting any more checks. No more bills paid."

"Hower won't abandon me no matter what you think," Lucy said.

"He has nothing. No matter what he has left, he won't support you."

"You don't know him."

"You're the one who doesn't know him. You deserve what's coming, Lucy. It's justice. And I thank God for His wisdom."

She'd had enough. She stood, weak from her illness and the growing belief that some of what Jason had said might have truth. She'd never make her appointment now. She'd have to try to reschedule for tomorrow. Maybe get Howie to take her.

CHAPTER 57

Lucy

Lucy went immediately to see Howie. He was still in his robe. The morning maid had prepared his breakfast.

He looked at her, still sleepy. Then he smiled. "Back so soon?"

"I'm not going," she replied angrily. "Jason's quit."

He snorted. "I fired him."

"He said some terrible things."

He took an extendedly long sip of coffee. "Which of the many things I can imagine upset you the most?" he said sarcastically.

"To start, that you would be indicted on fraud."

"I think it's going to be tax evasion."

"Did you evade taxes?"

"Not that I know of."

She was still holding her suitcase. She set it down on the floor. "He said the Journal-Constitution was about to expose you for scandalous sex. And that there was evidence of prostitutes being paid with church funds. Can you deny that?" she asked, suddenly fatigued. She closed her eyes tightly for a few seconds.

He didn't respond.

She looked at him. "Jason says you are putting your fraudulent use of funds on him. That's why he's quitting."

"I fired him."

His detachment frightened her.

"He managed the books," he said. "He made the decisions to purchase this and that and knew where the money came from."

"He didn't make the decision to purchase an airplane."

"He saw it as a legitimate expense, or he shouldn't have paid for it."

She sat in a chair. She was very tired. "I don't know . . ."

"I'll take you down for your appointment. We can still make it, can't we?"

She was so tired. "Would you?"

"Of course. I'll get dressed. Call the unit, let them know we might be a few minutes late." He started to dress. She put her head on her arms on the table and slept.

He shook her shoulder to waken her. He helped her to the car. The plane was in Memphis.

He didn't speak for more than an hour and she dozed on and off. Then she began to think a little more clearly.

"Feeling okay?" he asked.

"Better," she said.

"This will all be cleared up, Lucy. I'm not a bad man."

She'd almost forgotten about the accusations. At least they didn't seem important now. The nausea had started again.

"I love you, baby. This will all blow over. And I promise, we'll get you well. I promise."

She dozed off again, vaguely thinking about payments to recant the girl's testimony. But she had no energy to ask.

For the next few weeks, Lucy spent almost all her time between her dialysis appointments in Hower's house alone. Hower had increased his TV appearances and lengthened the duration of his weekly show. The indictment had shaken him, and the growing public knowledge of the scandal angered him with a smoldering resentment against his enemies. He did not deny the tax allegations as much as speak of his private life as private. She had not heard him specifically address the payments for sexual favors—with her or the public.

CHAPTER 58

Lucy

Lucy had tried to do dialysis at the compound a few times with a nurse helping. But the nurse quit as the scandal evolved. She was suddenly incensed to be required to treat the Jezebel of the reverend. So Lucy returned to Atlanta for dialysis, being taken down in the morning but needing to stay the night before the return trip to the mountains. She had no money now for a hotel. She asked Elizabeth, who said the garage apartment in the main house was vacant, the house not yet sold. Elizabeth asked Agnes, who said she would never return to that house and did not care who used it. Agnes said Lucy would have to turn on the utilities. Elizabeth said she would take care of the utilities and asked Agnes if they could use the car still parked in the far bay of the three-car garage under the apartment. Agnes didn't care.

Hower was indicted on a Tuesday, and by Thursday the Journal-Constitution had an article and an editorial exposing what they thought was his downfall. They photographed and described his extravagances. They made estimates of the gross income from one TV broadcast and then from a years' worth of broadcasts before and after his African hiatus. The church and Hower were hard to separate, and it appeared he controlled church finances, although there was loose board-of- elders oversight of finances in general. They readdressed the accusation of molestation of an underage girl but found no new charges. Four prostitutes were discovered to have been paid through church funds under false names. More women were identified and expected to reveal additional misuse of tax-exempt church income.

CHAPTER 59

Lucy

Lucy continued to have muscle and joint pain, and prolonged fatigue that caused her to sleep most of the day and night. During her waking hours she still had surges of nausea. Television did not hold her interest, and reading gave her discomfort. She mostly listened to music, and often sat for long hours in a comfortable upholstered chair enjoying recordings of master musicians.

Staying now full-time in Atlanta, she couldn't help but miss Howie—the companionship, the arguments, the laughter, the shared opinions on a diverse number of ideas and observations. Late one Thursday afternoon her loneliness became intense and she decided to return to the compound for a few days. Her next dialysis was Saturday. She had not seen Hower for over a month. He did call her every few days, and the sound of his voice made her want to be near him.

She put a few essentials in two paper grocery sacks and began her drive to the mountains. She left just before five. On the road she tired about seven and pulled onto a secondary road and napped for thirty minutes or so. She awoke in darkness and quickly got back on the road. She arrived sometime after nine-thirty.

Geoffrey, the night gate attendant, did not recognize her until she explained who she was. Who could blame him? She'd lost weight. Her sallow skin wrinkled over her bones. Was she ugly now?

She parked and walked to the house with her bags in hand. The back door was open. All the lights were out. She flipped switches as she walked to the stairs. She flipped the switch to illuminate the upstairs hallway. She heard Hower call her name. She looked up. He stood at the landing railing, bare-chested and wearing only boxer undershorts, a shotgun in his hands. He lowered it, swinging the barrel over the railing. "I'll be right down," he said.

She began to climb the stairs slowly, fatigued after her drive. "Stay there," he said loudly.

She looked up. Carla had come down the hall. "Go back," he said to Carla. But Carla came up to him. She was nude except for an afghan she had wrapped around her shoulders. She saw Lucy, turned, and ran down the hall. Lucy stopped on the stairs, setting her bags on a step, and grasped the railing for support. Her fatigue was worse; she couldn't think clearly.

Hower came down and helped her to a chair in the dining room. "I'm too tired to drive back tonight," she said.

"You've got to rest," he said.

She wanted to tell him she couldn't think of where she would rest. She didn't want their bed, the bed they'd shared for years now. Even in the haze of her sickness, she just couldn't see sharing that bed with him again. She was too sick for anger, although she knew it would erupt when she felt better.

He knelt by her. "What can I bring you?" he asked.

"Why?" she asked softly.

She imagined his explanation. Carla was a longtime friend. He had missed her, and Carla had been able to console him during his loneliness, as Carla probably had, she thought now, in Africa, and who knew how many times in how many places. Lucy imagined Hower lying to Carla, as she now knew he had often lied to her about so many things. Her humiliation was eternal. She would never be the same.

He got up and brought her a glass of water. He knelt beside the chair again.

"It's hard to explain," he said. "We'll talk about it in the morning."

CHAPTER 60

Elizabeth

Elizabeth carried a cloud of guilt about not donating a kidney to Lucy. "I still don't know what to do," she said to Luke one night when she couldn't sleep.

"All surgery has risks," he had said.

"I know that," she said dismissively.

"Infection, hemorrhage, prolonged recovery. Organ rejection, too." He paused. "You could die."

She loved him, and he loved her, and she knew he didn't want to lose her for any reason.

"Cadaver organs are one thing," he said as he had before, "but these guys who seek living donors are ghouls."

"They must do good."

"While harming others. Ophthalmic surgeons do corneal transplants, but thank God we don't burden patients who have two normal eyes to give up one and risk partial or total blindness in the future."

She listened intently to his passion. Her love for him filled her heart.

"These are supposed healers," he continued, "who swear they do no harm. And because they can't find any other cure, they present a treatment that does physical and psychological harm to normal humans. It's criminal."

She held him, her head on his shoulder. After many minutes, she said, "She's my half sister. Family."

"Are you sure about that? Do you know any more than what A.J. told you in a fit of anger, obviously to hurt you? He'd have no hesitancy in lying."

"I don't know," she said. "But even if Lucy is not my blood relative, I've come to know her as a sister and family."

"She wouldn't do it for you," he said.

"I believe that. But it doesn't take away the guilt that I might be condemning her to a shorter life."

They talked for another half hour. "Talk to your minister," he said.

"I did. He advised prayer. 'Let God speak to you. Trust your faith. Put the decision in the hands of God,' he said."

Luke suggested a psychiatrist he had seen for months after Samantha's suicide, a compassionate doctor who had helped with his guilt over the belief that he had in some way been responsible for her death. "I'll arrange an appointment," he said.

The psychiatrist was a small, middle-aged man with gross features on a thin face, scraggly hair, and an unkempt black beard. He wore glasses with thin gold rims that made his eyes look small, the left smaller than the right. It was disturbing enough that Elizabeth needed to look away and was thankful when he directed her to the couch and sat up and to the left of her, where she couldn't see him.

Other than Luke, she had never told anyone about she and Lucy having the same father. She told the psychiatrist.

"How do you feel about that?" he asked.

She'd had all sorts of feelings at the time she was told. But she didn't think any of them had persisted. "I don't know," she said. "Is it important? Is it any more important than my feeling for my mother, or my father, or the clerk at the grocery store?"

The doctor laughed softly and stayed silent for many seconds. "You're right, Elizabeth. It doesn't make a difference. But I was trying to get a feel for the depth of your guilt if you refused."

She closed her eyes as she responded. She told him about Jennifer. About loving her and caring for her as an aunt, and knowing the child always thought about her real mother. That she had never forgiven Lucy for the selfishness in not taking on the mother's role that Jennifer seemed to think about, if not need.

"I don't like Lucy and I've never met her," the doctor said.

"But if I refuse the kidney, I'll always wonder if it was to punish Lucy.

And I don't think I could ever rid myself of that question."

He asked about her mother and her father. He explored her feelings for children, her passion for teaching the gifted children, her process of writing books that children could take meaning from and enjoy for many childhood nights.

At the end of the session he pulled his chair closer to her and looked directly into her eyes. "You are a good person, Elizabeth. Among the best. You are kind and selfless in ways few humans experience. I agree with Luke. You have no obligation to be a living donor. Be an organ donor after death, but not a living donor. I think it's a crime for a transplant surgeon to put this on you, or anyone. No one should have to make this decision. It's not fair. So if you need to, use me as your excuse. 'My psychiatrist says I cannot reasonably deal with the physiological stresses of being a donor, and he advises me strongly against agreeing to the surgery.'"

The advice helped a little, but for many weeks she continued to consider the possibilities.

She read more about the complications and the surgery. She sought guidance in the Bible, but found nothing that gave her any direction or comfort. She read philosophies, and she considered the conceptualization of Eastern religions of attaining immersion into the whole of humanity and losing the self. She read descriptions of the peace and acceptance of existence as a part of the whole and the joy that it allowed. It's like an extended moment of selflessness, one article said, those instances where a human acts entirely without concern for self, as when a child is in imminent danger of being killed by a car and an adult sacrifices his or her life to save a stranger. Those are the states of being we seek in our lives.

She could see how that thinking could justify her becoming a donor. The concept of seeking selflessness, sacrificing to the whole. It seemed the essence of her Christian teaching. It was surely what many donors must come to believe, what gave them satisfaction. And she began to think she should reconsider. It was maybe what her purpose here on earth was, to donate without personal gain to the whole. She talked to Luke about it, and the psychiatrist, too. But neither of them saw any change in her responsibilities.

Lucy's doctor's office contacted Elizabeth many months after Hower

Bain had visited. They suggested that Lucy was getting worse and that Elizabeth might come for an examination just to see if she might be a compatible donor. There was no obligation. If she was not compatible, then she would not have to think about it.

"Don't go," Luke said. But she went without telling him, and found out she was an excellent candidate. Healthy, and a good match.

Three weeks later she missed her second period. A drugstore pregnancy test was equivocal. She went to an obstetrician, who confirmed her pregnancy. He did not hesitate to advise against donation. The transplant surgeon would not operate on a pregnant woman, and would not reconsider Elizabeth as a donor until six months after delivery.

CHAPTER 61

Lucy
New Year's Eve, 1998

Lucy drove to Roswell to her favorite tavern. There were no parties here, and few patrons. She did not greet the bartender, who was only partially visible in the back room behind the bar, and she silently sat alone in a booth. In the dark, and with the high backs on the benches that formed the booths, she was barely visible. She brought out three magazines and a paperback book and laid them on the table in a stack. She adjusted the small shaded table lamp so she could read. The bartender brought her usual glass of wine and a basket of trail mix. "Weather getting bad?" the bartender asked.

"Raining," she replied.

"Weather Channel predicts ice."

"None yet, at least."

"Happy New Year."

"And you."

She thumbed through a magazine and finished her glass of wine. She signaled for another.

She started to read her book, but it did not grab her interest, and she leaned against the upholstered red back of the bench. She was swamped with a sudden sadness. She thought of Hower, and she felt anger and resentment at the memory of him with Carla. How could she love such a man for so long? Oddly, she still felt attraction for him. She had always been in love with what she had wanted him to be. How could she have denied the obvious about him time and time again? She would never let that attraction rule her life again, and the real Hower would never dominate her again.

She thought of Elizabeth. How difficult it had been for her. She must have been afraid of surgery; she was always squeamish. And how could she have wanted to give a kidney to her adopted sister after all the years they had fought? But Elizabeth had made the decision to donate before her pregnancy was known—Elizabeth had called to tell her. Lucy could not fathom that devotion and felt guilty that she would never have done that for Elizabeth, or anybody, except Jennifer. The thought of Jennifer triggered painful sadness. She called to the bartender. Her head was clear. She asked for a vodka martini. She moved to sit at the bar.

"Plans for the evening?" the bartender asked.

It was the New Year. She was on the cadaver list for a kidney, and everyone she asked thought she would find a donor before . . . well, at least soon. Luke was even asking friends, mostly former medical colleagues, to find a donor. He'd put considerable money toward the effort. Inexplicable. Why should he do such a thing? She had never treated him well. Why couldn't she have loved him? Why wouldn't the Howie-like passion come to her for Luke? But it never did. And she wasn't to blame. It was not her fault. And now Luke and Elizabeth were helping her. She was grateful but suspicious at the same time. What was the motivation in them that she would never understand? She just didn't believe selflessness existed in the human spirit. Oh, there was some, but mostly it was faked. Every human was about self. Still she hoped for a living kidney donor. Her remaining time might be more than doubled from that of the cadaver transplant, she'd been told repeatedly.

"This is my quiet night at home," she said, smiling to the bartender, raising her glass. The first sips of the martini had dimmed her feelings. "This is my New Year's," she said, raising her glass. "The first martini ever. A celebration. I've been sick."

"Well, I hope the New Year will bring you the best of everything," the bartender said.

She thoughtfully swirled the remaining vodka in the martini glass. Alcohol was bad for her, it made uremia and acidosis and everything worse, but she'd come to rely on wine to relieve the pain and apprehensions she'd felt since coming back from Africa. And Fenly had made it a fun drink, a lubricant for an easy laugh and a forgotten memory. And she never drank more than a couple glasses of wine. Tonight was a celebration with a martini.

"One more," she said to the bartender.

This was the New Year. She'd get a kidney. Get off dialysis. She'd find work when she felt better. She'd treat Luke and Elizabeth better. She'd be kind to Agnes. She felt genuine warmth for her mother now, which she was sure was love. It would be a good year. A year with a future.

"TV says it's going to ice soon," the bartender said to the customers now seated at the bar.

She stood and slipped into her coat. She gathered her books. She put cash on the bar with plenty of excess for a New Year's Eve tip. "All the best for a great year." She waved to the bartender.

He thanked her for coming by. Many of the customers wished her a happy New Year.

She went outside. Heavy clouds overhead filled the night with impenetrable darkness. She stayed close to the building, where lights under the eaves showed her the path. Then she was on a stone walkway that led across a vacant lot. She could faintly see the gray pebbles that lined the path—enough to make her way. She followed the path for fifty or so yards until she came to a wooden bridge without a rail that arched a few feet over a small creek. It was another thirty yards to the lot where she had parked her car. Ice was already forming. She stepped on the bridge. Her toe slipped. She shifted to the right side of the bridge where there seemed to be an un-iced patch of bare board. Gingerly, she started up the slight incline. Taking tiny steps, she started down; her feet went out from under her. She fell to the right, dropping her books as her arms flayed to keep her balance. She fell seven feet, landing on her side in the cold water, her head hitting a pointed rock. Pain shot through her skull. There was a lesser pain in her right leg. The water numbed her back and the lower side of her body. The head pain persisted. She passed out.

CHAPTER 62

Elizabeth

Elizabeth and Luke arrived from Savannah to the house Agnes shared with her friend to spend New Year's Eve, in preparation for the New Year's Day dinner with seventeen attendees from various branches of Agnes's family. All would assemble at a perimeter hotel for a catered celebration.

Elizabeth and Luke arrived at seven o'clock. Agnes's friend said that Agnes had gone to her old home to get Lucy. She had been contacted by the hospital because they could not reach Lucy, and a cadaver transplant was available.

Luke and Elizabeth drove to the old house. Agnes's car was in the drive; they found her with a flashlight searching the grounds, in the dark of a light rain.

"She's not here. Nowhere inside or out."

Luke found two more lights, and the three of them searched the property. Finding no clues, they then went up and down each side of the road.

"Where would she go?" Elizabeth asked.

"She went occasionally to the movies."

"Did she visit friends?"

Agnes didn't know.

"Is the car in the garage?"

"I don't have a key and it's too dark inside to see."

Luke broke the panel in the side door to gain entry. The car was gone.

They went to neighbors to ask about places Lucy might go. At the third house, an elderly woman said she occasionally spoke with Lucy.

She did not know Lucy's friends, but she knew Lucy enjoyed the theater, and she knew that Lucy had been excited about going to that tavern in Roswell. She was not sure of the name.

The rain had turned freezing. Already the trees were coated with glimmering, magical ice.

They went to the theater first but could not find her. Agnes decided to go home to call the hospital and anyone who might know about Lucy. Elizabeth and Luke went to Roswell to find a tavern that Lucy might frequent.

The bartender listened to Luke's description of Lucy. "You mean the sick woman, always bent over a little . . . like real thin."

"Yes," said Luke. "Is she here?"

"You can see she ain't here. But she was. Left maybe an hour and a half ago."

"Do you know where she went?"

"Never know a client's destination 'less I put 'em in a taxi."

"Did she appear despondent?" Elizabeth asked.

"She appeared happy enough when she left. More upbeat than usual."

"Was she drunk?" Luke asked.

"Two glasses of wine and two vodka martinis. Walked okay. Sounded okay, too."

They asked where she might have parked, and he described the most likely place.

The wind had picked up now, and the rain had turned to sleet. The ice on the road glinted in vehicle headlights. A car lost control at the intersection and slid sideways into the bumper of a truck, but the damage was not severe and Luke and Elizabeth did not delay to see if the car could move on.

They walked beside the building, hands pressed against the wall for support. Ice covered everything, and there was almost no traction. They found the path, visible under the ice. Elizabeth slipped, falling backward. Her head hit the ground. Luke helped her sit. Her vision was blurred and her head pounded.

"I don't think I can stand," she said, feeling blood at the back of her head and looking at her hand, the blood black in the night on the tips of her fingers.

"I'll take you inside," Luke said.

"Go look for her car. I'll go inside as soon as I can stand."

He braced and tried to help her stand. "No," she said. "A few more minutes. Go."

He moved off along the path, crouched to adjust to the constant slips and slides.

Minutes later Elizabeth got to her hands and knees, then slowly stood. With both hands on the wall of the building she side-stepped to the entrance. The bartender brought her a towel for her head, and she sat at a table waiting for Luke. After many minutes she felt better and went outside to find him. As she closed the door, Luke stumbled around the corner. He had Lucy in his arms.

"She's alive," he said. "I'll call an ambulance."

"They'll be hours to get here, if at all. Look."

The intersection was blocked now, the crossing filled with tangled cars and trucks.

They got Lucy in the back seat of Luke's car. They covered her with their coats. Elizabeth got in to cradle Lucy's head and shoulders and try to warm her.

Luke drove. He eased down side roads where there were fewer disabled cars. He called instructions to Elizabeth to keep Lucy warm, keep her airway open, check her pulse. He came to Peachtree Road. Stationary emergency vehicles blocked by snarled traffic flashed strobes as sirens wailed. Finally there was some traffic movement. The nearest hospital was Piedmont.

With flashers activated and blowing his horn, Luke tried to move through traffic, but the going was at a creep. Few cars had much control of their progress. He made it through one intersection. Then another. People could not adhere to stoplights. For a short stretch he moved fast enough to see the speedometer move up to between five and ten. Then he lost control. The car slid at a ninety-degree angle to the side of the road. He gained some traction and straightened the progress, inching back into the center of the lane. The car rocked. The grill of a delivery truck smashed into the front. Locked in twisted metal, the truck and car slid off the road, stopping when they hit a telephone pole. The impact rocked the car.

"You all right?" Luke asked.

Elizabeth wasn't hurt. Lucy's shallow breathing was unchanged.

Luke kicked open the passenger side door. Elizabeth unlocked the back door for him. "She's still breathing," she said.

He felt Lucy's pulse. "Lucy," he said loudly. "Wake up."

Lucy's eyes opened slowly. She tried to focus. "Luke," she said.

The driver of the truck looked in over the open door. "Any one hurt?" he asked. Elizabeth held up her hand to keep him quiet.

"Lucy," Luke said again. "Stay with us. We've only got a few blocks to go. Don't slip away. You've got to want to stay awake. Do you understand?" He shook her.

She smiled weakly.

"We're on our way," he said.

Elizabeth got out of the car and helped Luke ease Lucy out. Luke cradled Lucy in his arms. "We'll walk—try to find help," he said to Lucy.

"Walk in the street," the driver said. "I'll keep traffic away,"

"See if someone will stop," Luke said to Elizabeth.

Luke carried Lucy. The driver waved his arms to warn approaching cars. Even in the road, sheets of ice were forming. Elizabeth ran ahead, trying to stop a vehicle at the crossroad.

After two blocks, a pickup truck stopped. The owner dropped the tailgate; Luke put Lucy on his coat. Elizabeth held her head.

"Stay with us," Luke yelled to Lucy as the truck started up. He pushed two sacks of rock salt aside to lie beside Lucy and keep her warm.

Ice had stopped all movement of cars and ambulances at the hospital entrance. Luke carried Lucy, Elizabeth followed. "Lucy," he said. But she did not respond.

The emergency room staff took Lucy from his arms and placed her on a gurney.

A nurse tried to find a pulse. "Code red," she said to a tech, who moved to a wall phone.

A nurse lowered the gurney. A doctor began chest compression. A technician tried to find an arm vein. An anesthetist soon placed a mask on Lucy's face; her outer three fingers pulled up Lucy's chin while thumb and forefinger held the mask firmly, and her other hand squeezed a bag of oxygen. Luke steadied the foot of the gurney. Paddles were placed on Lucy's chest, a shock stimulus applied; the body jerked. An EKG monitor was in place. An irregular spike shot up on a flat line, then there was nothing. Work continued for many minutes until the nurse touched the doctor's shoulder and he stopped resuscitation.

Personnel began removing equipment, and a sheet was placed over the body. Elizabeth was rigid. Luke took her hand as the gurney was pushed into a holding room and the swinging double doors shut.

Books by William H. Coles

McDowell
Creating Literary Stories: A Guide for Fiction Writers
Illustrated Short Fiction of William H. Coles 2000-2016
Short Fiction of William H. Coles 2000-2016
The Surgeon's Wife
The Spirit of Want
Sister Carrie
Facing Grace with Gloria and Other Stories
The Necklace and Other Stories
Story in Literary Fiction: A Manual for Writers
Literary Fiction as an Art Form: A Text for Writers
The Short Fiction of William H. Coles 2001-2011
The Illustrated Fiction of William H. Coles 2000-2012
storyinliteraryfiction.com